Beautiful Sacrifice

Thin Ren Lines Book Two

GEN RYAN

Beautiful Sacrifice © 2016 by Gen Ryan

For information, contact the publisher, Hot Tree Publishing.

www.hottreepublishing.com

Editing: Hot Tree Editing

Cover Designer: Claire Smith

Formatter: RMGraphX

ISBN-10: 1-925448-20-7

ISBN-13: 978-1-925448-20-7

10 9 8 7 6 5 4 3 2 1

Dedication

To anyone, who has ever been dealt the shitty cards in life. Don't lose your faith, hold tight, you're stronger than you think.

DETERMINED TO FIGHT...
HESITANT TO LOVE.

Guided us toward the power we needed to harness.

Our followers stared excitedly at the fire. Their satanic cries filled the woods that enclosed us. Everywhere I turned, there were trees, endless rows of trees. I watched as they swayed whenever the howling wind whipped through. Nature was our connection to the lower realm of hell—our tether between this world and the next. Mother Nature knew what we were doing, and she opened her arms to us, embraced the need to worship the almighty Lucifer.

We had found our followers over the years and every day I saw beauty in their eager eyes, their open arms. But at that moment, the beauty I saw were the flames stroking their delighted faces. They had devoted themselves fully to our cause, to our mission. We had gathered to show the world that their prior religion was a farce. To show the world that those religions were a mask pulled over our faces to shield us from reality. The reality being that the world we lived in was godless, cruel, and unforgiving.

Jameson took a step forward, placing himself closest to the fire. He removed his hood. I was struck again by his power, his command of action. I stared at him, my heart beating wildly in my chest. His eyes had turned obsidian, and the light of the fire accentuated his chiseled features. Looking back at the faces of our followers, I knew they would follow him wherever he took us.

"My people." His voice roared over the growl of the fire. "Tonight, we will offer our first human sacrifice to the Angel of Darkness."

Cheers erupted from the crowd as I moved to the table,

Prologue

LORELEI

The fire blazed hot. Flames danced orange and red as they kissed the faces of all who stood before it. I glanced around at those waiting in anticipation for what was to come. The brightness in their eyes appeared blissful: calm and waiting. I placed my hands to my heated cheeks. My skin burned and throbbed painfully as though it might melt right off. Hot flames embraced melted flesh, piercing my body. I welcomed the pain.

Pain made me strong. Pain was a sacrifice for living a free life; a life I lived with Jameson. We were free from an overbearing church previously shoved down our throats since before we could walk. Free from the idiotic rituals of a social culture that worshipped a god who deserted them.

Freedom was bliss.

Our black cloaks hung low to the ground as Jameson and I walked through the darkness. The quarter moon hung in the sky like a beacon to our souls. It tugged at us. Surrounded us.

which sat near the fire. Three black candles were atop the table. I lit each, their blaze joining in with the flames from the large fire. Jameson had stepped away from the blaze in order to drag our sacrifice from the corner where she crouched. Silent tears fell down the sacrifice's face, but I had no sympathy for her.

Raw emotion streamed from her body, emphasizing her beauty in the sacrificial moment. The world needed to know the power of Lucifer and the destructive nature of all other religions. We had found the sacrifice at the local college practicing dark magic. It had been easy to coerce the girl. She'd been completely ignorant of the craft she had been practicing, and without much convincing, she had joined our cult.

As Jameson dragged her across the grass, she kicked and screamed, the ropes tearing her already raw skin. She was doing a great service to our community and to the life we had built in the outskirts of Virginia. We needed to do this. We *needed* to sacrifice her. It would make Lucifer happy, and in turn, he would bless us. In seven short days, we would be ready to give our Lord the ultimate sacrifice, one that would merge our fate with our Lord's forever.

I watched my love as a smile spread across his face. With so much control, he was magnificent, his presence captivating. His strong jaw and deep-set hazel eyes were highlighted by the fire. Even under the cloak, his muscular body made me want him, and I was so thankful he had chosen me to be on this journey with him. I would follow him all the way to the depths of hell. I smiled slowly, secretly, because that was exactly what I intended.

Jameson threw her body in front of the fire. She screamed, convulsing as her lungs gave voice to her frustration. Her screams fueled me; the need to be close to her and experience her pain tingled throughout my body. I knelt beside her and studied her face.

"Help me, please," she begged. Her eyes were wide. Panic overcame her and she looked around for help. No one would save her. Especially not me. I smiled at her, caressing her cheek. I was used to this. The women looked to me for comfort and hoped that I would save them. They saw my slight frame, my long golden hair and kind eyes. I looked like an angel, but I had been fallen for quite some time.

"We are helping you. We are setting you free. Soon you will be with Lucifer. He will take care of you now." The sacrifice's cries became more violent, but it didn't matter how hard the girl cried, no one would hear her. Not out here in the woods. Not anywhere. I stood when I heard Jameson chanting. It was time. The moment we would become one with our Angel of Darkness.

"Spirits of the underworld, hear my call. Lucifer, accept the blood of this innocent one as my gift for you. Bless me and my people." He looked briefly at me, his smile a secret between the two of us and our Angel of Darkness. "Our people. Allow us to be your disciples, your loyal followers until death. We will provide you with one sacrifice in each of the elements. Death is life. Death is something we welcome and embrace. Take thine enemy, those who worship the light. Take them, smite and break him. Make their bones crush, crumble and turn to ash. From the mighty depths of hell, cast your darkness on all those who have deserted you. Lucifer, oh great beacon of darkness who guides me through the days, embrace us as yours."

Jameson lifted the flailing girl as she kicked her feet at him. Effortlessly, my Jameson raised her and without any hesitation, he threw her into the fire. Greedy flames wrapped themselves around her, no stranger to innocent flesh. As the fire slowly peeled away the sacrifice's skin, layer by layer, the girl screamed, yet she didn't fight her fate. Despite her fear and hesitation earlier, she lay there, her eyes staring at me as she was burned alive. I respected her for that. A tear escaped at the beauty of the moment. Her death that was an all precious gift.

"Lucifer, my Angel of Darkness, this is for you," Jameson declared.

I looked into the eyes of my husband, watching them change and shivered in anticipation. Darkness glistened there even with the flames of the fire reflected in his pupils. He lifted his arms, closed his eyes, and screamed into the darkened sky.

Chapter One

AVERY

"Damn it!" I fumbled with my hair, smoothing back the red tendrils that had broken free from the bun. My hair had to be perfect, not a piece out of place.

"You look great, Avery," Madison commented. I looked at her, marveling at how healthy and beautiful she looked. She had healed well over the past month and her bruises and scars had faded. She was still struggling, still trying to cope with Liam's death, but just like her scars, those struggles were slowly dissipating.

"I'm wrinkled." I scrunched up my nose and sighed. My shirt wasn't nearly as pressed as I liked. Hopefully, no one would notice.

"You're not." Madison's eyes found mine and they softened and looked at me with friendship, not seeing the lack of perfection I saw. She didn't know what it was like to have a father who scrutinized her every move, who criticized everything she did. A question formed in her eyes, furrowing her brow, and I knew she wouldn't understand.

I inwardly sighed. "You just don't know what my father's like, Madison. He's—"

"You don't have to explain, Avery. I know what it's like to have an asshole for a father." She smiled at me. It wasn't filled with humor but with a sad understanding. Her father was a serial killer. *Was* being the key word in her situation. My father, however, ran the FBI and made sure I knew the high expectations he had for me as often as he could. And wrinkles did not fall into his plans for having a perfect daughter.

I offered Madison a small smile back, a simple gesture in an unspoken understanding between us. That was what I loved about our friendship. So often we could just be. No words had to be spoken. No long hash out of feelings. We just knew what the other needed. And in that moment, I needed to not be having this conversation.

"Let's go. We can't be late for our own graduation," Madison said as she grabbed my hand. Her change in subject was exactly as I intended. I didn't want to talk anymore. Not now, possibly not ever. Although I didn't like to admit to needing anyone, having Madison in my life was refreshing. When you needed someone it brought about this dependency, this expectancy that they would be there for you. But what happened when they weren't there anymore? What happened then? I didn't want to be left picking up the pieces of loss. So to avoid it, I dodged attachments. It was easier that way. It didn't matter whether I admitted needing Madison; she was the sister I always wanted.

Gathering my emotions, I nodded, letting her guide the way. "Right." We headed down the hall and lined up behind the other graduates. As we filed into the auditorium, the crowd had already filled the room. Reporters lined the sides, waiting to get a glimpse of Madison and the women who had helped end the reign of The Beautiful Masterpiece Killer. That was the sensationalist title. It was screwed up. They were criminals who needed to be caught and giving them this extra attention was just perpetuating their glory. They didn't deserve any other attention than rotting in jail.

I tried not to look at all of the people. I hated the pomp and circumstance of a graduation. I wanted the day to be over. I never liked being fussed over and gawked at. Heat crept into my cheeks as my self-conscious tendencies crept in, and I tried to remember if I had pressed my pants enough. I looked straight ahead and stared at the jumbled faces of the crowd, willing myself to remain calm and unaffected. Bright lights flooding the ceremony distorted each person allowing me to calm my self-conscious nerves. I let my mind wander, blocking out the monotonous voice of the speaker. Graduating from the FBI was all I had ever wanted for myself. Since before I could walk, I had mirrored my father, choosing to play cops and robbers over dress up. But waiting to be handed the badge I had wanted my entire life, I still couldn't help but feel like something was missing.

"Avery Grant."

The deep vibrato of the voice jolted me out of my thoughts.

"It is with great pleasure that I offer Cadet Grant not only her badge, but this plaque signifying her achievement as top recruit in her graduating class. She will be given her badge by her father, Deputy Director Ethan Grant of the FBI."

Everyone rose as they clapped and cheered for me. I took the badge from my father, and he hugged me awkwardly while whispering in my ear, "Good Job. Your mother would be proud of you."

Emotion tugged at my chest when he released me. I straightened my shoulders and stared straight ahead again, focusing on the illuminated EXIT sign. I willed myself not to succumb to the sadness that loomed over me. This was everything I ever wanted: to get my badge and live a life of fighting crime with no baggage to hold me back from achieving my dreams. No matter how many times I reminded myself of this, that sadness still found me.

Sadness was fickle. It wasn't loneliness. I was far too busy for that. I never tried to figure out what could be the cause. I just pushed it aside like every other emotion. The sadness left me as Desiree Garcia and Eden Marshall's names were called and I burst with pride. Each of us had struggled in our own way to get where we were. We deserved this. We deserved our badges.

When the master of ceremonies called Madison's name, the reporters snapped their cameras ferociously. Scott Reynolds issued her badge and they embraced. Scott was a special agent with the FBI and helped catch The Beautiful Masterpiece Killer. He was also Madison's fiancé. The reporters ate that up. A love story amongst the madness. There was no doubt in my mind that they had that real kind of love. The kind that women bought those romance books with the big strapping men on the covers for. It wasn't all flowers and candy; it was built in blood. A foundation grounded so deep in heartache and struggle that I knew no matter what happened to them, Scott and Madison would persevere and continue to grow together.

I couldn't help but frown at the thought of love. I believed it existed when I looked at my best friend and her fiancé and replayed their story in my head. I needed to apprehend the criminals. That was my life, my chosen path. There was no time for love, and I was content with that.

After the ceremony, families and friends greeted the new FBI agents. Everyone beamed with pride and words of congratulations flowed. Of course, my dad was whisked off to some crime scene, and I was left alone as I often was. I headed down the hallway to the bathroom, stopping at the work assignments on the bulletin board.

I smiled, discovering that Madison and I were assigned as partners to the Quantico Counterintelligence unit. I chuckled when I found Garcia and Marshall's name as they were assigned as partners but in Washington, D.C. on the Joint Terrorism Taskforce. We each had our areas of expertise: Garcia focused on religion and terrorism in her undergrad and Marshall terrorism and human trafficking. Madison was a forensic psychologist, but I had the criminal justice degree and prior experience working as a liaison for the police department. We were all new agents, but our experience and education were sound. This gave us the leg up to be set apart from the rest, given higher positions within the FBI. Not to mention, my father. He liked to control every aspect of my career. So I wouldn't be surprised if he had a hand in where I was assigned.

I was grateful that we were all still close. We could have our weekend get-togethers at the Down Under Pub. Since the night reporter Christopher Singleton was murdered, after talking with Madison there, the bar had become our local hangout spot, and we loved the laid-back atmosphere that catered to the local law enforcement.

"Ahem." The clearing of a throat brought me from my thoughts. I turned around. Madison's deep brown eyes stared at me, her hand intertwined with Scott's.

"Guess it's you and me."

"Guess it is," I said as I watched the families pass by together. Feelings of loneliness surrounded me, but like I did with every other emotion, I pushed it aside.

"Don't sound too happy about it. Sheesh." Madison smiled at my contrite expression and then frowned. "It just kind of stinks. I'll be staying here in Virginia, and Scott has to go back to New York. They need him at the field office, especially after what happened with Liam." As sadness filled her eyes, Madison looked at Scott. We had talked about the likelihood that she and Scott would be separated. I knew she would be upset, but I also knew they'd be okay because if their love could grow in blood and death, it could overcome anything.

"I have to go chat with Torres. I'll be right back." Scott kissed Madison on her forehead and left. He was now partnered with Agent Emmanuel Torres, a new guy who had just joined the force a few months ago. He'd helped Madison the night her father was killed and seemed like a decent enough guy. Madison liked him, and for Scott, that was all that mattered.

"What?" I asked as Madison stared at me. Emotion filled her eyes as she moved closer to me.

"I'm just thinking about that night Liam died—"

"Madison, don't," I growled.

"No. It's good. It wasn't all bad. It made me realize what a great friend I had in you. You hiding the journal for me. Giving me the closure has allowed me to be ten times stronger than I would've been." She closed her eyes, taking a minute to compose herself.

"So what I'm trying to say is thanks for everything. For having my back through all of this," Madison said, putting her arm around my shoulder. My body went rigid at her touch, but I softened as she smiled down at me.

"Anytime, Harper." I pulled her in and hugged her tightly. "Now, let's go catch these sons of bitches."

The ceremony dispersed, and we all headed out to the cemetery. Liam taking his own life was the ultimate sacrifice. Being an agent partnered with Scott, he struggled with his own demons and desires to kill. Madison was his escape, his tether to reality, but her love for Scott was unparalleled. She couldn't be there for Liam in the capacity that he needed. His death had impacted everyone, but it was Madison who felt it the most. I watched as she and Scott walked hand in hand and weaved in and out of the gravestones that lined the grass-laden rows. Garcia and Marshall walked behind them, huddled close together, silence permeating around them. Dead flowers and half-melted candles sat at the bases of many of the plots. I briefly glanced at the names as we walked by in silence. So many taken so young. So many who were never able to live their lives to the fullest.

We stopped in front of a small plaque that was embedded in the grass. No one moved, but I couldn't resist gently running my fingers over his name, Liam James O'Leary, and the years in which he was on this earth, 1983-2015. That was the only etching on the gravestone. It was too simplistic and didn't give a true indication of the magnitude with which Liam had touched our lives.

I looked around at our group, Garcia, Marshall, Scott, and Madison. They all shifted, trying to find a comfortable stance in such an uncomfortable situation. How did you stand when facing the resting place of a man who'd taken his own life? A man who had struggled so deeply with his demons he'd felt he had no other choice? It was then that Madison fell to the ground and wept. Deep sobs pierced through the darkening sky and Scott knelt down beside her and brought her close to his chest. Where she was weak, he was strong. They were perfect for each other. A perfect balance.

Tears glistened in Garcia and Marshall's eyes as they watched the scene unfold. I felt it all. Everyone's emotions barreled into my chest. I wanted to kneel down next to Madison and cry with her. I wanted to cry for Madison, for her life that had been irrevocably changed the day her father had killed her mother. I wanted to cry for Liam and the abuse he had witnessed and endured during his childhood. The abuse he wasn't able to leave behind. The abuse that had eaten away at him. But I also wanted to cry for myself. For my mother who was buried not too far away from where I stood. I couldn't bring myself to visit her, not even after twenty-two years. Tears stung my eyes and I fought them back. I had to be strong and push all my emotions aside. Opening myself up and allowing myself to be vulnerable left room for pain. I looked at my friend, who had gained so much love, so much hope over the past few weeks.

Everything fell silent, the wind, the noise of trees swaying behind us. The world seemed to stop and wait, opening its ears and heart to what was about to happen. Madison stood and her legs wobbled beneath her. Scott braced himself against her and helped her stand.

"Liam was a good man." Madison's voice broke. For the first time she was owning her feelings about Liam. She had shared these with me many times but voicing them so intimately with all her friends, it meant so much more. It was the truth. Her body shuddered with the cold as the wind crept in. It brushed at her hair, a live force entangling her curls in the stream of tears drying on her skin. "He took the life of Walsh, of my father." A single tear fell down her face. "He took that life so I could live. Free from pain. Free from the torment that had been his life." She bent over, placing her hand on the gravestone.

"Many would say taking his own life was the coward's way out, but Liam was anything but a coward. He sacrificed himself so others could live." Sobs came from Garcia,

Marshall, and Madison.

Scott turned his head to look at me. His eyes held the gentle love and care that seemed to seep from him all the time. He nodded at me, a simple motion that held so much. It was his permission, his acknowledgement of my struggle that allowed me to show what I felt going on around us. Each emotion. Each memory. One single tear broke free and I left it there before the wind whisked it away.

Chapter Two

EVAN

"Bradley. Wake up." I felt my ribs being poked. "Evan, Dammit!" Adams yelled, violently shaking the small cot I lay on. "God damn it, Bradley. Wake up!"

"Jeez, man. Can't you see I'm trying to sleep here?" I rolled on my back, putting the musty pillow over my face as I turned my back to Adams. I breathed in, and the mothballs and mildew stung my nostrils. *Bad idea*. I coughed.

Luke Adams needed to learn how to wake people up. I was partial to dumping water on him. I smiled. He was still new to the police force and had been assigned to me ten months earlier as my partner. He was good at what he did, but turnover in this job was high. Usually a newbie lasted a year, tops. I was cruising along, though. My seven years were coming up in a few months while Adams was dangerously close to his year. I was waiting for him to crack like the rest, go mental under the pressure of rape victims and hard crime, but he was unwavering and had a cast-iron stomach. Maggot-filled bodies? No problem. Stab wounds the size of the state of Texas? Show him more. He might just hack it. I was sure his brief stint in the army and working for the CIA helped with that.

He was tough, built like a brick shithouse, and he reminded me of a heavyweight fighter. Coupled with his dark brown complexion and his body full of tattoos, he certainly fit the bill. His body was a canvas for any tattoo artist who wanted to have a go. A few inches over six feet, he stood inches above me and I was five eleven. But Adams was pure muscle. Not an ounce of fat on the guy. When he was assigned to be my partner, I almost shit my pants. His tight military cut—a reminder of his days in the CIA—and his forever serious face let me know he could kick my ass any day. But seeing him with his family melted away that hardness. His wife, Airi, was about half his size, and they had a cute three-year-old little girl, Hana. He turned into a big teddy bear around them, and in the past ten months, they'd become like family to me. I had dinner with them as often as possible, Airi never hesitating to have a place for me at their table. Hana called me Uncle Evan and Jesus, did my heart not squeeze every time I heard those words.

"Yes, I see you're trying to sleep, but we've got bigger problems. A body just popped up," Adams said as he threw my suit jacket on top of me. "Duty calls, man."

I groaned, swinging my feet over the cot. There was a loud squeak as the cot tried to adjust to the shift in weight.

Goddamn budgets cuts. Couldn't even get the precinct decent beds anymore. The fact that I pretty much lived at the precinct made my body ache for a more comfortable bed. My shoebox of an apartment was infested with roaches and well, my cell phone never stopped ringing. It seemed the popularity of rape and murder was on the rise.

I put on my jacket, my shoes already on my feet for convenience.

"You drive, man. I'm still half asleep," I said as I yawned and threw the keys to Adams. He caught them without even looking. I glanced at my cell. 12:03 a.m. I groaned, flippantly wondering why people don't get murdered at a normal time of day.

"Nice!" He walked ahead, twirling the keys in his hand. I grinned. He loved driving, especially my car. Now that he was a family man, he'd traded in his Mustang for a minivan. I laughed inwardly. That would never be me.

"Hey, Detective Bradley?" The sound of the boss's voice pierced through my good mood. Shit. *What's he doing here at midnight?*

"Yes, sir?" I walked toward his office and stopped at his door. I looked at the new shiny nameplate that hung there: Lieutenant James Moyer. Budget cuts my ass. I massaged my lower back, the kinks already forming due to the hardness of the cot I had just slept on.

"This case, look, it's a shit show." He sighed and sat down in his chair. "Twelve a.m. and I should be at home sleeping next to my wife, but I'm trying to catch up on paperwork." He rubbed his sleep-filled eyes. "But cases like these always take precedence." He motioned to the chair across from him. I sat down and I waited to hear what mess to expect. I took out my cell phone and shot Adams a text, letting him know to bring the car around and join us.

"Some girl was found splattered on the ground below the Gateway Plaza building." He pulled out the file, flipping to the first page. He handed it to me and her smiling face stared back at me. It was a school photo, and her St. Michael's uniform was barely visible in the small frame of the picture. Her brunette hair hung loose around her face, just touching her shoulders. Her olive skin and bright green eyes reminded me of my sister, Mia, and I cringed thinking about what it would be like to lose her. She was all I had.

I hated this part, seeing them before they became victims. They all looked so normal. Alive. That was what made my job hard. I flipped to the next page, not wanting to look at the youthfulness of her face, the happiness fixed in her eyes. That happiness was gone, taken from her far too early. I glanced at the report. There wasn't much to it. Just information on when she went missing, her age, and a brief description of the man who was seen luring her in. The information was scarce but enough for us to get started when we headed to the crime scene. I glanced down at the chart again. Francine Dewitt. Our victim was only 16. My heart twisted in my chest.

"Not a lot to go on, sir," I said as I closed the folder and placed it on Lt. Moyer's desk.

Adams stepped into the office and Lt. Moyer handed him the folder of information. He sat next to me as he scanned through the file placing it back down on his desk.

"I agree there isn't a lot to go on," Adams said. "Seems we knew she was missing but did nothing." Adams leaned forward in his chair, making himself look even bigger and more intimidating than he already did. "Why?"

"I know, Adams, but we did do something. We called in the FBI and have been consulting with them." Adams sat back and seemed content with the answer. "And we have a lead," Lt. Moyer added.

"Her friend, Jocelyn Mathers, saw the victim being apprehended and described the perp to a sketch artist." He paused. "We think it's related to the Satanic cult. The description matches that of Jameson Cruz. Jocelyn mentioned seeing an inverted pentagram tattoo on his right forearm."

"Shit," Adams and I blurted out. Jameson's father had been the minister of the First Baptist Church in Burke, Virginia. He'd raised his son, Jameson, in the church, on strict religious principles. Apparently, they'd been a little too strict and the church's views incredibly fundamental. His parents' beliefs were on the radical side of Christianity. Founded in the ideals where women belonged in the kitchen and should serve the man of the house whenever needed and that children were to be seen, not heard, and obedient, whatever the cost.

Jameson had been beaten often. He'd never been allowed to question the practices of the church, and he definitely hadn't been allowed to act out against his father or his father's strict system. When he was twenty-one, his parents were murdered. Their throats were slashed, an inverted pentagram carved onto his father's forehead. We knew it was Jameson. He didn't even bother hiding evidence, but he had gone missing, taking his wife Lorelei with him. Since that day, inverted pentagrams had been showing up on churches in the Burke area.

"Like I said"—Lt. Moyer eyeballed Adams—"the FBI has been following this case closely. You may remember Scott Reynolds from the Beautiful Masterpiece case?"

"Yeah," I commented and Adams nodded.

"Well, he's been the consultant and now that Francine's body has surfaced, we will be working with the FBI directly."

"We can handle it, sir. Bradley and I are known for closing cases quickly," Adams interjected. I grinned at Adams. We were pretty good. We'd closed three cold cases and ended a major drug ring in less than a year.

"I need you to work with the FBI on this one. They're bringing in two new agents. Also part of the Beautiful Masterpiece case. One of them is a forensic psychologist and will be a great asset. Getting a profile together and getting into this man's head is essential." I sighed. "Be grateful. Agreed, gentlemen?"

"Yes, sir," Adams and I said in unison.

The FBI agents I'd worked with in the past could be pains in the ass, but I knew we needed to wrap this case up. Plus, Adams and I were stretched pretty thin. The fact that an agent was already consulting on this case showed the severity. We needed to end this case, and fast.

"I'll reach out to Agent Reynolds as well and collect the information he's gathered already."

"All right, then," Lt. Moyer said with a pat on our backs. "Good luck." His eyes barely looked at ours as we exited the room. The lieutenant was a straightforward guy, no nonsense, which I appreciated. Despite this case just landing on his desk, there was something about it that put everyone on edge.

I just hoped no one fell over.

Chapter Three

"Why are you so excited?" Madison moaned as she rolled out of the bed, her wild hair flowing free from her ponytail. The room was still dark, the clock blaring 12:00 a.m. with its blue fluorescent lights. We didn't have an apartment yet, so our home was the Extended Stay Hotel. After we'd graduated two weeks earlier, the FBI had directed everyone to settle in at their new agencies. It was compelling to be a part of something, to have a purpose.

"I'm excited because it's our first real case." I turned on the light.

"Jesus, Avery." Madison put her hand over her eyes.

"What are you? Some kind of vampire?" I asked as I pulled on my black dress pants.

"Not a vampire. I just love sleeping at 12:00 a.m." She jumped out of bed, stomped her feet, grabbed a heaped pile of clothes off the floor, and headed off to the bathroom.

"Hurry up! We have to leave as soon as possible." I shifted through my suitcase choosing a pale-blue button-up shirt. It was slightly wrinkled. Damn. I hated wrinkles. With not enough time to iron it, though, I sighed. Putting it on, I made a mental note that I needed to iron enough shirts for a week when we returned. I grabbed my weapon from the nightstand, and I placed it on my belt holster where it was easily accessible. Madison came out of the bathroom, ready and looking more awake. Her once wild hair was tied back at the base of her neck, reminding me to head to the mirror. My fiery red hair hung loose just past my shoulders. Madison handed me a hair tie.

"Thanks." I secured it up in a tight bun, each strand carefully tucked away. "All right, let's go." Madison smiled, grabbed the keys, and we headed out.

We arrived at the crime scene later than I would have liked. I'd let Madison drive, and she'd had no idea where she was going. Even with GPS, we got lost, twice.

"Never again, Madison!" I yelled, slamming the car door as we rushed to the crime scene. We were new to the area and had no idea what to expect. We'd received the call to head over to the Holloway building in Burke, VA for a body, but that was it.

Police cruisers and fire trucks lined the streets facing the building. The emergency workers stood around behind the police tape, their faces long and forlorn while people snapped pictures with their cell phones. I watched one woman, her face youthful and so full life, lean over the police tape. She stared at the body, studying it with such intensity that I didn't even feel compelled to stop her. It was as if she knew her. I raised my brow wondering why the cops weren't stopping her. All the officers seemed deep in conversation, more concerned with talking than the pictures of the crime scene being taken right under their noses.

"Agent Grant and Dr. Harper with the FBI." We flashed them our badges. They eyed us curiously and looked us up and down. I even think I saw one of them lick his lips.

"You've got to be kidding me," Madison mumbled under her breath. Madison and I looked at each other and rolled our eyes. This should be fun. We'd known when we'd decided to become agents, we were going to be entering into a line of work dominated by men, but since being agents and seeing it firsthand… yeah, it fucking sucked. No doubt, it would be just a taste of what would follow during our careers.

"Right this way, ladies. Watch your step," the firefighter said as held the police tape for us to duck under. His jacket hung haphazardly on his lean body, and his helmet sat crooked. His face held the wrinkles of age and the hazards of the job.

The heels of my boots clanked against the cement, but the sounds were drowned out by the guys behind us. They snickered, and I heard one of them whistle and catcall. Before I could say anything, Madison had turned around, a fire burning in her eyes.

"Listen up, jerks. I know you might not be able to think with something other than what's between your legs, but cut the shit. We can hear you. Yes, we have vaginas, but Agent

Grant and I can kick your assess any day of the week. Now, shut the hell up before I slap you all with sexual harassment lawsuits." She turned around, not waiting for a reply. She swayed her hips just a little bit more giving them something to look at as she walked away. I smiled as my steps matched hers. *That's my girl, growing a damn backbone*, I thought proudly.

The firefighter leading us stopped abruptly behind two men.

"These firecrackers are all yours, guys," he said with a snicker as he walked away. I was about to turn around and tell the firefighter to go screw himself, but then the men turned around.

I paused, taking in the men before me. My gaze zeroed in on one in particular. He was not what I expected, at all. The cop in front of me was tall, lean and muscular, and his arm muscles filled out the sleeves of his white dress shirt nicely. With the sleeves rolled up to his elbows, it displayed his olive-toned skin perfectly. My gaze landed on his unfastened tie that hung at his neck. His hips were slender, making his shoulders seem broader. *Good lord, I could fit two of myself between those shoulders*. His face was chiseled, defined and totally masculine, and his five o'clock shadow caused a delightful shiver down my spine. His dark, almost jet-black hair was longer than most cops kept it, hitting the tips of his ears.

"Detective Evan Bradley," the hot one greeted, and I cursed myself for the ridiculous shiver that again coursed down my spine. His eyes quickly focused on mine. There was a glint of something that sent another frisson down my body.

"And this is Detective Luke Adams." They shook our hands. His voice matched his physique perfectly. A Cajun drawl flowed through his lips. His lips—*good God*—his lips looked succulent.

My resting bitch face stood firm. *Don't let him know you find him attractive*, I said to myself as I tugged my shirt down, making it strain against my chest. The movement caused him to look down with a smile forming on his lips. I was so focused on him, I barely glanced at the ginormous guy who stood next to him. His partner was handsome, too. Military cut, a few shades darker, and covered in tattoos, but Detective Evan Bradley made me want to take my panties off and hand them to him. I felt like a schoolgirl with her first crush, so I shook my head to clear it. *Get a grip, Avery.*

"I'm Agent Avery Grant and this is Dr. Madison Harper. FBI." I quickly flashed my badge, and tried to avoid eye contact. Madison glanced at me, the corner of her lips twitching as she fought to suppress a smile.

"Great." Adams called over a local cop and asked him to secure the crime scene.

"Now that the pleasantries are out of the way, let me show you what we've got." Detective Bradley turned away and took a few steps toward the body. Madison nudged me, grinning. I shrugged, trying to play it off that I didn't know what the hell she was elbowing me for.

"This is Francine Dewitt. Went missing a little over a month ago," Bradley said as Adams opened the body bag. A young girl, no older than a teenager, lay inside, her body distorted, legs and arms broken and hanging limply at her side.

I didn't flinch, and Detective Bradley eyed me curiously as I put on gloves and leaned over her body, moving the brunette hair from her face.

"Interesting. Looks like she bled out somewhere else." Cuts covered her body, at least twenty I could visibly see. "These wounds are fresh, but there's no blood pooling by the sites," I commented as I removed the gloves from my hands. Madison took notes next to me, stood her ground, and looked intently at what I was showing her as she jotted down the important information.

"Observant, Agent Grant." Bradley looked at me, cocking his head slightly to the side. He studied me. Awareness sparked over my body at his ability to make me feel something intangible. I never blushed. I was never uneasy. I exuded confidence at all times. But the way Detective Bradley studied me, my control slipped. Desire pulled at my insides and want flowed through me. I'd felt passion and sexual need before, but this man…. His very presence, his words, his eyes, had me feeling that need all through my skin, down to my very bones. It was unnerving, considering we were standing above a dead body. I tried to shake the effect he was having on me, but the attraction was there, annoying little shit that it was.

"Bradley, the press is here." Adams looked at Madison. "Dr. Harper, would you mind joining me to do a press release, try to hold them off until we have more information? Figured you might have some psychological mojo you could use on them." He smiled, and it softened his appearance.

"Not at all, and please call me Madison." Madison smiled at Adams. She glanced at me and I gave her a look, begging her not to go. *Don't leave me alone with Mr. Hot Stuff,* I mouthed to her when Bradley briefly looked away. She chuckled, and Detective Bradley folded his arms as a small smile crept across his face. Madison and Detective Adams walked away to wrangle the mass of reporters setting up, ready to make up some lame story about this case.

I cleared my throat in an effort to fill the awkwardness.

"So, fill me in. I know a bit about the case but not a whole lot." I pulled out my notepad and stared at him. No matter how physically appealing Detective Bradley was, I was an agent. My job came first.

"Well, the FBI has been consulting since the victim went missing a month ago. Agent Reynolds was able to provide some background information and insight into the case. We called the FBI in officially since the victim's friend positively ID'd Jameson Cruz as her kidnapper."

I stopped taking notes and looked right at him. He pierced me with his stare, and my breath caught in my chest. His eyes were gray with a hint of silver. Gray like the moon reflecting in the sky and looming over the crime scene. His eyes were heterochromatic. One was gray, the other held a hint of blue.

I brushed back my hair, just to do something with my hands. I knew that not a single hair was out of place.

"Okay," I said, shifting my focus back to the case. "Agent Reynolds is one of the best so I trust his analysis on the case." Bradley nodded. "There hasn't been any sign of him or the cult for a few months. Why now?" I looked over the girl again. "She couldn't have died from these shallow wounds. I do see a small, deep puncture wound. They could have used that to exsanguinate her. Bleed her out."

"Yes, and then push her off the building," Detective Bradley said as he motioned to the roof. *Oh, shit.* I shifted, transferring the weight of my body between one leg and then the other nervously.

I looked up at the building. It was under construction and friggin' tall, at least eighteen-floors high. Scaffolding and construction equipment surrounded the structure, making it look abandoned and neglected. *She'd been pushed.* My heart beat faster against my chest. I looked at Bradley wondering if he could hear it. The sting of tears pressed against my eyes.

"Were there any signs of sexual assault?" I questioned.

"The ME will have to conduct a rape kit, but she was clothed when she fell, so my money's on no." A tear broke free from my eye as he spoke. I rubbed it away quickly, hoping he didn't see.

"Plus that's not really their style," Detective Bradley added. I stared at her body, thinking of a memory that seemed like it had happened yesterday.

"Momma?" I went room to room in our big house. Five bedrooms, three bathrooms, just for the three of us. Mom said it was because Daddy wanted everyone to know he was successful. That "stuff" was important to him.

"Mom?" My voice croaked as I called out for her again. Last time I couldn't find Mom, she'd ended up sick and in the hospital. Dad had said she was really sick, but that hadn't stopped him from leaving us again. He often went off to help other families. Other people. He said he was trying

to make the world a better place, but what he didn't realize was we needed him here. To make our home a better place. To make Mommy better.

After checking the last room, I grabbed my jacket and backpack and laced up my sneakers. At nine years old, I knew how to do most things for myself. I cooked. I cleaned. I even got myself up for school. I'd learned at only six years old how to use the iron, and cook with the oven. Most kids my age were more worried about what toy they could play with next, but not me. I worried if my mom would make it home from the motel.

I was self-sufficient, my dad said. "Independence and a good work ethic is what makes a good woman." I always remembered those words from my dad. It was never, "I love you." It was never words of encouragement. Just words of survival.

I headed out the door, locking it behind me, but not before checking to make sure the spare key was in my pocket. I walked a few blocks to where I knew I'd find Mom. The Cedar Motel. She'd say she was visiting friends, but I knew she went there to score drugs. I watched her once as she'd taken the needle and shot it into her arm. I'd watched her eyes roll back into her head. Her body had shuddered and quaked as the poison seeped into her.

She needed help. Something at nine years old, I couldn't give her. It didn't stop me from trying. I bathed her, made her eat when all she wanted was more drugs. I tucked her in at night and lay with her until she fell asleep while she cried. She wept for a man who cared more about his job than his family.

31

As I got closer to the motel, the familiar sound of police sirens pierced my ears. I saw the blue and red lights circling around the trees, and I squinted as my heart thumped loudly in my chest. I felt it then. Fear.

That was the first and last time I ever felt afraid. It was as if I had something lodged in my throat, bobbing and sticking each time I swallowed. I gripped the straps on my backpack as I moved closer, bracing myself.

"Kid, you can't be here." An officer looked down at me as I swerved between the onlookers. I looked at him, determination coursing through me. As he reached out for me, I ran. My little legs pushed hard against the pavement. I managed to scramble through the crowd and stood at the end of the police tape.

Her face was smashed against the pavement. Her arms were broken at odd angles, and her legs sprawled beneath her unnaturally. My mom looked how she had always told me she felt: broken, discarded. I glanced down at her hand that clung tightly to something.

"There you are! I said you can't be here!" The officer grabbed at my arm, but I managed to pull free just long enough to steal the paper from my mom's hand. The officer missed the action, grabbed my arm again, and dragged me away, putting me on the sidewalk. He left me alone with my thoughts, and I opened the piece of paper.

"I'm sorry," was all the small slip of paper said. Shoving the bloody paper in my pocket, I touched the creases and stickiness of the blood as I walked home. To my empty house. To loneliness.

"Penny for your thoughts?" Bradley's eyes fixed on me, his arms crossed at his chest. Shit, I must have looked like an idiot zoning out and looking at the large building again.

"Sorry." I cleared my throat. "Just thinking of the case," I lied, shaking my head and squaring off my shoulders. "It could be him, but we'll have to wait until the ME report comes back." I frowned. "But the MO matches to a tee from what I remember about the case because of the pentagram. Just now he's killing people."

"Yeah. That's what I was afraid of." He took out his cell and started texting wildly. He moved away from the body and I followed. I was thankful. Even though the crime scene had been secured, local police milled around. I hated being watched, even in the smallest capacity.

"Well, I better go grab Madison." I shoved the notebook in my pocket and went to walk away. Bradley stopped texting on his phone and hesitated. "Don't worry. Madison and I are good at what we do," I added, unease creeping into my mind. Maybe he thought we weren't good at what we did? Why the hell did I even care? I normally would have delivered a solid middle finger and walked away.

"I heard. You ladies were pretty badass out there with Walsh, vigilante style." He made some weird kung fu move that resulted in his leg kicking in the air and his arms flailing crazily in front of him. I smiled at the sight and let out a small laugh.

"And she smiles!" he teased, throwing his hands up in the air like he just scored a three-pointer.

"I smile all the time." I scowled at him.

His shirt had tightened and become more taut against him when he'd folded his arms across his chest, and this only further sent my body into a wild frenzy. Frustrated that he was having this effect on me, I straightened my shirt, attempting to gain some composure.

"Ms. Professional," he said as he looked me up and down. A hint of hunger lingered in his eyes as he studied me intently. He licked his lips, and I didn't move from under his stare. I looked at him, letting him know I wouldn't back down from him. My barriers, my walls, were not coming down. Plus, what was wrong with how I dressed? It was professional and didn't get me any unwanted attention.

"You know nothing about me." He seemed like a man who hid behind humor and his big gun who had the occasional on point observation. He'd been right about me being professional and it pissed me off. Because no matter how I tried to shake the way my body responded to his dazzling eyes and the way he kept touching his gun, I couldn't help but wonder how big his gun really was. *Snap out of it, Avery.* I took my hand and smoothed out my shirt again. Who did he think he was? I barely knew him, and he thought he knew me so well. Sure, he was hot. He dripped testosterone and exuded sex with every move of his mouth. And that little bump on his nose was endearing. He had probably broken his nose a few times, and I secretly wondered what had caused the breaks. But regardless of how fucking delicious he was, he didn't know me.

"I know that you're impenetrable. Like an unbreakable vault." He was right. I was impermeable. He would do well to remember that. It didn't mean I had to like that he'd guessed that about me.

"Yes, well, you're a jerk." *Wow, great comeback, Avery.* It wasn't like me to lose control and this guy, he was already under my skin. I was flustered, sweat beaded on my forehead, and I was pretty sure I needed to change my panties.

"Ouch." He grabbed at his heart. "Here." He went in his breast pocket and pulled out a card. "My information. Strictly professional of course." He winked at me and gave me a smile, his perfectly straight teeth dazzling me.

"Thanks," I mumbled, snatching the card and shoving it in my pocket.

"See ya, Grant." He waved as he called out, walking away to join his partner.

"What was that all about?" Madison asked as she sidled up next to me.

"What?" I muttered, kicking a rock with my shoe as we walked to our car.

"You think he's hot," she replied.

"He is somewhat attractive, but that's beside the point. We're working a case together." I put my hands in my pocket feeling his card between my fingertips.

"Right. You see where that got me." She flashed me her engagement ring. We both laughed.

We spent the next few hours bogged down in paperwork. No one could have prepared us for the endless forms and procedures we'd need to do once we became agents. When we finally made it home, Madison hit the bed without taking off her clothes. I wanted to do the same; instead, I ironed all my dress shirts and slacks. I hated not being prepared.

The clock read 5:45 a.m. by the time I had neatly pressed the last pair of pants. I hung them all as outfits, ready to grab and to be thrown on, or to be packed if need be. My phone buzzed, an incoming text message flashing across my screen.

Dad: Heard you have a case. Don't let me down. Everyone is watching you. What you do is a reflection on me.

My dad sure knew how to make a girl feel special. I typed out my reply, pressing way too hard on the screen of my phone.

Me: When have I ever let you down? I'd hate to have people think badly of you.

My father probably wouldn't pick up on my sarcasm; he was that dense. I turned off my phone. My dad and I barely spoke, and when we did, it was usually him telling me how I needed to make him proud, what I had to do. I didn't need that right now. Hell, I didn't need that ever. Never once had he told me he was proud of me. Never once had he hugged me and meant it for just me. There was always an ulterior motive. And yet, I worked in the field he had paved the way for me because the FBI was all I knew, and this job was all I was good at.

Smiling to myself at my silently rebellious text to my father and content with the organization of my belongings, I headed to take a quick shower.

I turned up the water to scorching hot. The heat coming from the running shower filled the small bathroom, and steam quickly covered every surface. Dampness streamed down the walls. I undressed, catching a glimpse of myself in the clouding mirror. I untied my hair and let it fall down to my shoulders. I then stared at my reflection. Freckles covered my fair skin while my unruly red hair flowed around me. Madison called me fiery. It seemed fitting. I was fire, always ablaze. I was organized, slightly neurotic in my need for order, but I was headstrong. My mother had always called me stubborn, like a fire that could never be put out. I had tried to count my freckles once when I was little. I'd gotten up to twenty-three before getting bored and going off to play cops and robbers.

I wasn't a typical little girl. I wasn't all princesses and dolls. I preferred actions figures, GI Joe. And the girl was never a damsel in distress. She kicked ass. I smiled to myself. *Just like me.* I had learned early on in life that in order to survive, I could not let my emotions show. I had to take care of myself and had to be good at everything I did. After watching my mother cave in to addiction due to unrequited love, I vowed to never love a man like my mom had loved my father. That vulnerability, that pure raw emotion was disastrous.

As I continued staring at myself, I felt at peace with my body, every part of it. I was strong. My sculptured abs were visible after years of kickboxing and MMA classes. Despite my frame being slender with few of the soft, sexy curves that Madison had, I was a hell of a fighter. My reflexes were quick and I was agile. I was always on alert and prepared for anything that crossed my path.

Once in the shower, the hot water felt good as it scorched my tired body. Almost as if it were cleansing me of the emotions that had plagued me all day. The moments of warm peace were short lived, however, as my mind wandered to Detective Bradley. Why couldn't I get this guy out of my head?

I closed my eyes and remembered the definition of his body. Goose bumps danced on my skin at just the memory of his Cajun drawl saying my name.

As the water flowed down me, it hit my center, adding to my growing wetness. I imagined Detective Bradley's hands caressing me in a similar way his deep gray eyes had earlier with lust. Heat rose within me, and I moaned when my back hit the shower wall. The contrast between the cold wall and the heat pounding my skin heightened my need. I hated when my body reacted this way. I wasn't one to feel out of control, but when consumed with desire, I no longer felt in control of my body. Sex, though, was a release. A much-needed release. It was a bit of stolen time I allowed myself to just be and to feel.

"Screw it," I said aloud as I gave in to my body's needs.

With two fingers, I gently swirled them around the outside of my thighs. The water droplets found me, further lubricating the way. I slid them in and tightened when they entered, my body almost rejecting them at first. They weren't what I really wanted, but they'd have to do, for now. I braced the side of the shower with my other hand as I stroked my clit, willing myself to climax. Releasing the side of the shower, I pulled my nipple with one hand as I slid my fingers in and out of my folds. I moaned as my body tingled and my vision began to blur. I stroked harder, faster until I was almost there. Closing my eyes, images of Detective Bradley played in my head like a dirty movie. His body on top of mine. His fingers where mine were. His full lips running down my neck.

I gritted my teeth, not wanting to lose too much control. *Easy girl.* As I pictured him again, his eyes focusing on my center, him licking his lips in anticipation, I lost all control. My body shuddered and clenched around my fingers. The release was welcomed, settling the whirlwind of emotions stirring inside of me.

With weak legs, I all but stumbled out of the shower. I toweled off and changed into my yoga pants and tank top before padding into the bedroom with my dirty clothes in my hands, the sounds of Madison's deep breathing filling the silence. I reached into my pocket, grabbing Evan's business card. *I'll need this, won't I?* I placed it on my nightstand, throwing the clothes in the hamper. Climbing into bed, the warmth of my skin was shocked by the coolness of the sheets. The gentle breeze from the open window soothed the searing heat that beat away at me. Turning over, I forced my eyes shut. I had to get this guy out of my head. He was driving me crazy, in more ways than one.

Chapter Four

EVAN

I fumbled for my keys to open my apartment door. It'd been four days since I'd been home. Mail piled at my doorstep, held together by a stretched-out rubber band. Mrs. Freidmont next door always looked out for me. She made sure no one messed with my apartment, and she always got the mail for me when I was away for a few days. I made myself a mental note to send her flowers.

When I opened the door and flicked on the light, the roaches scurried. They hovered, some of them waiting and stopping in their tracks. The ones that were smarter fled up the walls and behind the little bit of furniture that lined my crummy apartment. I grabbed the roach spray from the side table and sprayed the few that stayed behind. I shook my head. I really needed to move. It was all that I could afford, though. All my extra money went to Mia's college tuition at Santa Fe

University. She was a junior, and ever since our parents had died two years earlier in a car accident, I had looked after her.

I sifted through my mail, opening a bill from Santa Fe University: $10,500.00 due.

"Jesus." I guessed I'd be picking up some overtime. I tossed the bill on the counter and glanced at the clock: 4:00 a.m. With my stomach growling, I walked over to the fridge. Other than my bagel for breakfast, I had forgotten to eat. I hadn't had a decent meal since Airi, Adam's wife, had made Nikujaga the previous week. The meat, potato, and onion stew had been perfect with just a hint of sweetness. My stomach growled again in memory of how delicious it was. A bare fridge stared back at me. I sighed as I slammed it shut.

Slumping my shoulders in defeat, I flicked off the light to my house and locked the door behind me. Well, that was short-lived. I headed back down to my car. My baby. My blue 2014 BRZ was the only luxury I allowed myself, and that girl purred like a kitten.

I rubbed my hand down her side as I clicked the unlock button on my key fob. My fingertips tingled, sending jolts up through my body. I swear I got a hard-on just looking at her. I opened the door, gently placing myself in the driver seat. The coolness of the leather seats pressed against my back, and my groin throbbed, twitching and pressing against my suit pants. Avery slowly crept into my mind and the throbbing became more persistent. I smiled to myself, thinking of our exchange at the crime scene. She was tough and I had no doubt that she could kick my ass. Slender but fierce looking, and that hair, oh, sweet Jesus! That hair did things to me. I clenched the wheel harder. The only aspect that softened her hardened exterior were her freckles.

I grinned. There was something alluring about a woman who could hold her own. There was no weakness there. She'd handled that crime scene with such ease.

I put the key in the ignition, the soft purring of the engine rumbling under me. If I could just get Avery in this car…. I laughed. I'd have to break through that impenetrable fortress she'd built up.

I sped off, the torque sending me flying back in my seat. I turned the corner heading to grab some takeout before going back to the precinct. My home.

Chapter Five

"Good Morning!" Madison said cheerfully as she put two plates filled with food on the small table that served as our dining table.

"You're awfully cheerful this morning," I replied, taking my seat. Madison was not a morning person and I usually found myself awake first. She sat down across from me, eagerly shoveling a spoonful of eggs in her mouth. Before she could take another bite, her face dropped and she looked like she was going to be sick.

"What's wrong?" I asked as she groaned and clenched her stomach.

"I'm not sure. Woke up with a headache and I feel a little nauseous. Probably just the long day yesterday." She shrugged as she moved the food around on her plate a little bit more. Madison did look tired, but the way she looked at me let me know not to press the subject any more.

"So, what's on the agenda today?" I asked, attempting to change the topic at hand.

"Well, it's Saturday, and as long as the murders hold off, I figured we could get together with the girls tonight." I placed a grape in my mouth and juice squirted Madison in the eye.

"Ah! Man down!" Madison screamed, pretending she was falling off the chair.

"You're so dramatic," I said, rolling my eyes with a slight laugh. Madison laughed, sitting up. She placed her thumb in mouth to bite her nail.

"That's gross. Do you know how much bacteria are on your nails?" I said with disgust.

"I know. Bad habit." Madison said as she cleared the table.

I headed to our bedroom to change into my workout clothes. I needed to clear my mind. A workout was just what I needed.

"Hey, Madison!" I peeked my head from around the corner. "Want to join me at the MMA place down the street?"

"Heck no!" Madison said. "I'm still not feeling too hot."

"Fine." I finished dressing and grabbed my gym bag. "Be productive," I yelled as I opened the door to leave.

"I've got a date with the couch and some ginger ale." Madison sighed as she plopped herself on the couch. It was probably for the best I left. I didn't want to catch whatever she had.

I couldn't help but smile as I made my way to my car. I wish I could just sit down and relax like Madison. She was able to do that, disconnect from the craziness of our job and the constant need to go, which had been programmed in me since childhood. The desire and need to be connected to everything that was going on; everything but not anyone. I saw what that did to my mother and although memories of her grew fuzzier as time passed, I remembered her devotion to my father, which led to her death.

Eyes wide open at all times. No distractions. It was what I lived by.

I turned down the radio that blasted "Radioactive" by Imagine Dragons as I pulled up to Capital MMA & Elite Fitness. Like Madison, I loved music, although our tastes were different. She liked the soft stuff, the music that made you want to go down on yourself. I liked rock and heavy metal, anything that was deafening. If you really listened to some of the lyrics, the songs had meaning and depth that was masked by the loudness and directness.

I grabbed my bag and walked into the fitness center where the smell of sweat and blood immediately hit my nostrils. I breathed in deeply. It was good to be back. My body tingled, and I ached to spar in the ring. I waited at the desk for someone to help me, but after fifteen minutes of waiting, I grew impatient and headed toward the sounds of men yelling and the thump of bodies hitting the mats.

Standing in the doorway, I watched the men spar in the ring. One guy immediately caught my attention. He was shirtless, muscular and had a nice tone to his skin. I couldn't make out his face as he wore headgear, but he looked absolutely decadent as the sweat poured down his body. This guy was quick—I'd give him that—but he didn't know the art of MMA like I did. I ached even more to get into the ring and throw some weight around. There was control in fighting. The need to know your body and your opponent's body. Their moves. Their intentions. It was something I was good at. Something that made me a good agent as well.

"Hey, doll, are you looking for the women's self-defense class? It isn't until this evening." I looked over, and some young guy stood there eyeballing me. I glanced at his nametag, Todd. I smiled. He was lanky like a string bean, and the way he eyed me pissed me off.

"No, Todd. I found what I'm looking for." I motioned to the ring where two fighters were exiting.

"Oh, babe. That's a bit much for you, don't you think?" A sly smile formed on his lips. "We have plenty of lessons here for something more of your caliber." He looked me up and down as he licked his lips. I took off my jacket, neatly folding it and putting my bag and jacket on the bench behind me. Todd moved in next to me, getting a little too close. I took off my tank top, standing in front of him with just my yoga pants and gray sports bra. His eyes grew wide.

"Maybe. We'll just have to see. Care to give it a go? Or are you too scared?" I put my hands on my hips, giving him the sweetest look I could muster. He let out a boisterous laugh.

"Hey, guys!" he called out, and a few men came scurrying in from the other room. "Looks like we got ourselves a contender." They all smiled at me, lust evident in their leers.

I kept my composure, but I was dying on the inside. I clenched my fists tightly at my side.

I went under the ropes and was handed some gloves and a closed mask. "Don't want that pretty little face getting beat up, do we?" Todd said. I scowled at him as I put the headgear on.

"Hey, man. She's all yours." He patted the back of the guy I had just admired in the ring.

"Don't worry. I'll go easy on her," he said, a smile visible underneath his mask. The voice sounded familiar, but the room was still so loud and the mask muffled his voice. I shrugged as I positioned myself in the ready stance.

The man in front of me still had a bare chest, which further accentuated his toned physique. I took a better look at him now. His shorts hung low on his waist, the V shape of his groin perfectly visible. I licked my lips. This would be fun.

"All right, first to pin wins." Todd left the ring, and Mr. Hot Stuff and I squared off.

He danced around, his feet fast and nimble underneath his athletic body. I followed his lead, moving more slowly and focusing on his hands. He was trying to use his feet to distract me. *Total amateur move.*

He charged toward me, his hands up in a defensive stance. Anticipating his move, I slipped to the side and pushed his elbow out of the way. I caught his head in my armpit, and I felt him struggle underneath me. I pinched my arms tighter as they fully fastened underneath his head, cutting off his air. He squirmed, like a bug, trying to wiggle free from the grasp of a killer. I felt him slipping, and I tightened my grip, falling on my back. He was much bigger than me but getting on my back gave me the extra leverage I needed to pin him. I tightened, hard, noticing the parts of his face that I could see turning a lovely shade of blue.

My head was next to his, my mouth close to his ear. "Tap out," I whispered in his ear, my mouth brushing against it. My body tingled against his as he squirmed, trying to break free. I put my legs around his and I gripped tighter with my arms. Choking escaped from his mouth. It was arousing, having this much control over a man who outweighed me by probably 100 pounds. I tried to keep my focus on getting him to tap out, rather than the heat that continued to build up in my body.

"Goddammit, man, tap out. She's kicking your ass," one of the onlookers said. All sounds in the gym stopped, and I felt all eyes on us.

I heard the joyous sound of his fingertips against the matted floor. *Victory.*

I let him go, removing my headgear and gloves and walking over to my side of the ring. I felt loose, light and free. God, I had missed this so much.

"Hot damn. She kicked your ass, Evan," Todd said, jumping under the rope.

I whipped around and I came face-to-face with Detective Bradley. He was kneading his neck from where I'd had him in a choke hold. I froze in place, and stared at the man, who I'd had between my legs just moments prior. Granted, it wasn't the way I'd pictured him between my legs when I'd made myself come in the shower, but there was no denying he had an impact on my body.

"Agent Grant," he said with a nod, a smile forming as he nursed the wound I had left him. I shifted slightly, feeling self-conscious standing before him in just my bra and yoga pants. Not because I was uncomfortable with my body, but because his eyes roamed all down the length of me. Eagerness radiated from his eyes. I felt it, too. That hunger. It was a craving. This wasn't a need I was accustomed to. I wanted him. I wanted him, bad. Even more, since I knew I'd just had him between my legs.

"Detective Bradley," I managed to get out. Todd looked between us curiously.

"You two know each other?" he asked, grinning.

"Yes, we're consulting together on a case," Bradley said, taking off his gloves. "Seems she's full of surprises."

"You have no idea," I replied half mumbling as I stepped out of the ring. I had to distance myself from him, from the reminder of what it felt like to have his slick body against mine. I shook my head as I went over to grab my things and redress. The clearing of a throat jolted me out of my daydream.

"Nice moves," Bradley said as I put on my tank top and stepped out of the way.

"Thanks," I replied as I made my way back toward my bag. I shuffled through the bag, looking for my car keys. Where the hell did I put them? The physical closeness of Bradley and I became more apparent. His breath caressed my neck, and I barely managed to hide the shiver.

"Looking for these?" His face was dangerously close to

mine when I turned around. My keys dangled from his hand. I took a sharp breath, stood on my tiptoes, and reached out for my keys. Our fingers brushed as he released the keys into my hands and I backed away quickly.

"What are you doing tonight?" His smooth drawl coursed through me. The goose bumps on my arms stood on edge. God, what was it about a man with an accent?

"Excuse me?" I asked, distracted by his hard and possessive stare. I glanced down at his lips and my thoughts wandered to all the dirty things I could do to him. I could take his lips between my teeth, clamping down subtly, a love bite. On instinct, I bit the side of my mouth.

As if he knew what I was thinking, Bradley moved a step closer, so my chest rested against his stomach. If I moved a few inches down, I'd be face-to-face with his dick. My nipples hardened at the thought. He was gorgeous. I couldn't deny it anymore as I stood in front of him, our bodies brushing, touching, and caressing one another. I could easily stand on my tiptoes and our lips would collide, completing the pull I felt. But I had just met him, and I quickly reminded myself, just dominated him in the ring. I smiled.

"I have plans." I backed away, my nipples crying out to be close to him again.

"Let me take you out." He looked at me, the smile never once leaving his face.

"As romantic as that sounds"—I rolled my eyes—"I can't. As I said, I have plans." I gathered my bags and went to walk away. Bradley moved out of my path, surprising me, as he seemed like a man who didn't take no for an answer.

"What do you have to lose?"

I stopped in my tracks, having almost made it to the door. He was right, what did I have to lose? Other than my sanity at the thought of dating. I turned around to face him just as he put his hands in the pockets of his gym shorts that still hung incredibly low on his waist. His penis pressed against his shorts, showing just how excited he was at the possibilities. What pressed against his pants was enough to get any girl to say yes. I crossed my arms, annoyed with myself that yet again he was having an impact on me I seemed to be unable to ignore.

"I'm going to the Down Under Pub tonight with some friends around ten. Stop by if you want." I turned back around and walked away, leaving him chuckling.

"See, was that so hard?" he yelled after me. "I'll see you tonight, Avery. Leave the sparring gloves at home." I took one last glance at him as I opened the door to exit and he winked at me.

I ran out to my car, got in and turned on the AC, blaring the coolness right on my face. It felt amazing, and it slowly brought me down from the sexual tension burning inside me. Bradley was pure sex. It seeped from him even when he was being a complete ass. But he wasn't an ass. He was playful, and while I hated to admit it, I liked it. I fanned myself, adding to the coolness I needed. Maybe a good lay was what I needed to break up some of the monotony of my life. I was too regimented at times, never wavering from my routine. Yeah, I'd had guys, but never for more than one night. I wasn't loose; I didn't sleep around, but I was not the relationship-type.

There was just something about Evan, though. Something about being close to him that made my mind all fuzzy and all my inhibitions fade away. I put the car in drive and headed back to the Extended Stay. I shook my head, unsure of what I wanted. I did know that I wanted to look sexy tonight and get his attention and that required needing something other than my normal khaki pants and button-up shirts. I grabbed my cell and dialed Garcia. She'd have something for me to wear, ideally, something to drive Evan wild. It was only fair as he certainly seemed to be having that effect on me.

Chapter Six

LORELEI

"I'm just not sure if this is the life that I want. I came to you guys because I was lost and confused. My parents didn't understand what I needed." I watched Clarissa shake her leg nervously as she sat down in front of me. I had become somewhat of a legend, the ruthless one who takes no shit. It was hard to follow the teachings and take care of so many lost souls. There were so many people begging for release from a stifling life, a religion that held no purpose other than to tell them how to behave. I was swift and fierce with my judgment, but it made them stronger and helped them realize they were the facilitators of their own lives.

"Are you mad at me?" My eyes focused on the wall behind her. I didn't want to look at her as anger welled up inside of me. She was a fucking ungrateful little bitch. Jameson and I took her in, clothed her, fed her, taught her the ways of Lucifer and she repaid us, repaid *him*, by turning her back and wanting to run back to Mommy and Daddy.

I smiled. "Clarissa." I stood and walked over to her, gently placing my hands on her shoulders. "Of course I'm not mad at you." Her body relaxed at my words. A bigger smile crept across my face when she took comfort from my words. Her big brown eyes looked up at me.

"Thank God." She sighed. "The others said you and Jameson would be angry. And I'd be punished for wanting to go home, but I told them that you said I could always leave. That this wasn't a prison. And that Jameson was kind and would never hurt anyone again. He said so himself."

My grip on her shoulders got tighter. It was slow at first, a caress, turned into a grip so tight I could feel my hands turn numb. *Thank God. Thank God. Thank God.* The phrase replayed in my mind.

"Lorelei, you're hurting me," I squeezed her harder as she writhed and wiggled under my grasp. "Ouch!" Her words fueled me further. She had no right, no place to talk about God here.

"Jameson has a mission. *We* have a mission." I raised my voice. "We will sacrifice someone using all of the five elements. Then we will be free. Lucifer will fully accept us all." Trickles of blood seeped through her shirt as I rambled on. It was warm, thick, comforting to my soul as it wept for this girl who had no idea who her true god was. She needed to be taught that my husband was not weak. That he would follow through with this mission.

"Do you understand me?"

She whimpered in agreement.

"Good." I released my hold on her and walked in front

of her, kneeling down so I was at eye level.

"You'd be wise to remember that, or you"—I poked the tip of her nose—"will be his next sacrifice."

"I don't want to die," she whispered as the tears streamed down her face.

I stood up, my tall, slender body overcoming her.

"It's not dying, Clarissa. It's being set free." With that, her whimpers became sobs. Clarissa. Clarissa would be the next sacrifice. A soul needing to be set free from the shackles it had been subjected to its entire life. Once she was let go, released from a world that catered to the rich, neglected the poor, fought for all the wrong things, she could truly be at peace.

Chapter Seven

AVERY

I'd agreed to a date with Detective Evan Bradley. I gripped the steering wheel tighter as I drove home from our spar in the ring. I wasn't expecting to see him there. I couldn't say that I was disappointed either. He looked damn good with his shirt off.

My cell phone rang, distracting me from replaying the feeling of Evan between my legs. I hated that he'd convinced me to go out, but as long as I stayed in control, it'd be okay.

"Fuck." I glanced at the caller ID, my dad's name flashing over and over. The equivalent of "Hey, your dad's a dickhead" on repeat was annoying.

"Hello." I tried to sound cheery but I guess it didn't sound sincere enough.

"Always so happy to speak to your father," Dad said dryly. My dad was a lot of things, a great agent, a good shot, a phenomenal leader, but he'd definitely fallen short of being a good father.

"Well, you're always calling to lecture me on something. You'd think with me being a grown adult that would have ended but nope." I pulled into the parking lot of our home and sat in the car while it idled.

"I'm your father. It's my job to lecture. Now about this case." I heard the shuffling of papers. "Detective Evan Bradley and Luke Adams, are they any good?"

I smiled. I couldn't help it. Were they any good? I assumed he meant as agents but once again, I got distracted by a shirtless Evan.

"Hello?" The impatience in my father's voice pulled me back to reality.

"Sorry. Um. I guess. I haven't really spent much time with either of them other than last night. They seem competent. I don't foresee any issues."

"Good." I heard some murmurs on the other end of the phone. "Due to you, Madison, and Scott consulting on this case, it's getting a lot of publicity. I don't want any snags in this case. Open and close."

"Open and close," I repeated like the dutiful daughter that I was. Every time I spoke to him, I felt like a child. Like that little girl clinging to the idea of a dad who would play with her, tuck her in at night. I had no idea why I still clung to that. It never was and never would be my reality.

"Well, that's all. I'll check in." The phone went dead.

"I'm sure you will," I muttered to myself. With these higher profile cases, my dad always got involved. He didn't want any negative press. It just came with the territory though, even more so since so many followed The Beautiful

Masterpiece Killer.

I went into our apartment and found Madison lying on the couch.

"Hey! How was it?" She scooched over on the couch and made room for me. I plopped down.

"It was great. Other than the fact that Evan was my sparring partner."

Immediately, Madison laughed. It wasn't a giggle; it was a laugh that lasted minutes and had her snorting.

"Is it really that funny?" I gave her a death glare.

"Oh, man, that must have been epic. I would have given anything to see you kick his ass."

I couldn't help but smile because Madison didn't ask if I kicked his ass; she just knew.

"I pinned him. I pinned him good." Madison wiggled her eyebrows and we both laughed. "And my dad called."

Madison shuddered. "Did he say anything worth mentioning?"

"Just how we can't screw this case up. Did you know the press is on the case?"

"No!" Madison said as she made a fake shocked face. That was what I loved about her. She made me smile when I felt defeated. I tried not to let my father get to me, but he did. He always had and I couldn't help but feel like he always would.

Chapter Eight

LORELEI

"Drown her."

"What?" Jameson's eyes met mine as we loaded up Clarissa in the car.

"Water. That's the next element. Drown her," I said as I moved closer to the car.

"Lorelei...." The hesitation in Jameson's voice made me uneasy. He couldn't stop this. Not now. There could be no hesitation. No second-guessing what we were doing. We were just fueling what we had promised our god we would. Using the elements to provide him with sacrifices. That was what he wanted. That was what he deserved.

"I think we need to take a break. We can just live here in peace. Keep farming off the land." He took my hand in his. "We can have a good life. Stop the killing. Maybe have a family. And Clarissa, she's confused. You're such a good teacher. Teach her, mold her. Don't kill her."

The sentiment was cute. I'd give him that. But I didn't

want a family. I'd never desired children of my own. The vile, nasty little things sucked you dry and were ungrateful. Look at Clarissa. Seventeen years old and telling her parents that they didn't understand her. I smiled at the thought. They hadn't allowed her to have a sleepover with her boyfriend because they didn't want her to have sex. I couldn't say I blamed them. Ungrateful. Blind to what she truly had. Parents who loved her. Parents who looked out for her. Not like Jameson. Not like me. Our parents couldn't have cared less about us. Other than how we made them look. Were we obeying? If not, we were whipped with the belt, the hand, the shoe, whatever was convenient at the time. Abuse disguised as religious normality. God's calling to save the children and put them on a path of righteousness. I chuckled to myself as Jameson frowned at me.

Since Jameson and I had found Lucifer, the calling of the rightful god, we'd been able to embrace even the darkest parts of ourselves, and I had never felt freer or more able to be who I truly was.

"We need to finish this. Follow through with our plans." I took Jameson into my arms and hugged him, resting my head on his shoulders as I often did. He stiffened against my touch and didn't stroke my hair as he usually did. He was hesitating, again. I needed him. More than ever, I needed him.

"Then we can settle down. Together. Just us." I whispered the words, and his body slowly softened against me, his hands making their way to my hair. He stroked it, our breathing becoming one. I released him and rested my forehead against his chest.

Beautiful Sacrifice

"You're right, Jameson. You stay here with the others. I'll take care of her." I glanced back at the frightened girl in the backseat. Clarissa whimpered, her sobs audible through the closed doors. "I'll take her with me and talk with her. Make her see that she should stay." I took a breath. "That she should support our mission."

"That's my girl." Jameson placed a quick peck on my cheek, the hesitation completely gone. "And what if she doesn't obey?"

I knew what he wanted to hear. He wanted to know that I wouldn't sacrifice her. That I would let her go home to her family. I wouldn't. Deep down he knew that. She knew where we were; she also knew who we were. It was more than just us. It was everyone, everything we had worked so hard to achieve. She had to go. She had to be sacrificed for something bigger than this world.

"Then, of course, I'll let her go home." Jameson nodded and Clarissa stopped whimpering. It was quiet for a moment, an eerie calm temporarily coming over us.

I slid into the car and waved to him as I backed out of the driveway. I headed toward the wharf. Her pleas to let her go vibrated through the car, further fueling my desire to teach this girl about her true savior. Lucifer.

The wharf was empty under the mask of the night. All the fisherman, boaters and visitors had gone home to their fancy houses and loving families.

"Let's go." I ripped Clarissa from the backseat by her long brown hair, and she stumbled behind me.

"What are you going to do to me?" Her wide eyes

61

glistened with tears.

"I'm going to set you free." I brushed her hair out of her face as it tangled with her tears.

"God, please save me," she whispered.

Fire.

Hate.

Rage.

They all coursed through me. I was ablaze. I clawed at my arms, struggling to get the feeling out of my veins. God? Save *her*?

"You naïve, child." I bent her down in front of the water. "There is no god to save you." She glanced back at me, and another squeal escaped from her lips.

"But the devil. Well, he's here, and he's waiting for you." I took out a knife from my pants pocket. It was small but sharp enough to cut into flesh. I lifted her shirt, exposing her stomach. I pressed it against her abdomen and I watched as the red dripped down her skin. She struggled against me, threatening to mess up the thin red lines I was trying to form. I stopped as she continued to fight me. Her restraints were loose, and she stared at me, fear and confusion causing her eyes to widen. Anger built in my body, threatening to boil over.

"Give me your hand," I demanded as she stared back at me. Her shaky hand reached to me as I placed the knife inside of it. Although she was scared, I had built a trust with her that she was hesitant to break from the months of my influence and guidance. Her hesitation further ignited my strength and my own confidence.

"Carve," I demanded.

"What?" Her words came out shaky and confused.

"Carve a pentagram into your flesh." I nodded to her stomach urging her to continue.

"I can't," she sobbed.

"If you don't, I will, and I won't be kind. I'll make it hurt," I hissed, trying to instill fear into this girl.

With a shaky hand, she as I asked. I smiled in victory. She required no guidance. My training had worked. Each time the knife pierced into her flesh, her teeth clenched in pain. When she was done, the knife plummeted against the earth, and I snatched it up, placing it back into my pocket. I took her shoulders and leaned her over the water.

Clarissa struggled and kicked against me as I pressed her head closer and closer to the water. I dug my heels in, and my simple, black pumps seeped into the earth. When her face finally hit the water, the fire was gone, replaced by coolness, replaced with a soothing enveloping feeling like a blanket. I felt alive as I held down her struggling form. Her limbs flailed frantically as she reached for salvation, reached out for me, reached out to claw at the earth. Just as soon as they had started moving, those smooth, young arms stopped.

I released my hold on her, and watched her float free of me. Lifeless and light as though gravity didn't exist.

"I did it," I whispered into the air. No one was there to hear me. But I knew he was watching me. That he accepted this girl as a sacrifice. My hands shook. Not with fear, with happiness, with control. I was more connected to Lucifer than I had ever been. Hate coursed through me, fueled me, and I knew I had to continue.

Hate was all I knew. Hate was all the world knew. And only by accepting Lucifer into their lives would we be truly happy. Would the world truly be at peace.

Kneeling on the damp, fertile earth and watching the dead girl float away, I made a vow. I would complete all the sacrifices in the name of Lucifer no matter what Jameson said or wanted. I would help my husband see that this mission was important, that we must complete it to fulfill our calling, and that we were destined to be Lucifer's.

Chapter Nine

Evan

I would never live it down that Avery had kicked my ass, but I didn't care. When I'd realized it was her in the ring, I'd tried to go easy on her, but I quickly learned she was relentless. That choke hold had almost caused me to pass out. When she'd had me pinned, and I'd tried to break free, she had tightened those legs of hers around me. Instantly, my hard-on had pressed against my shorts. Her body didn't look overly muscular or strong, but she was powerful. Just remembering our limbs tangling together made me horny as hell. Who was I kidding? All those things were true, but it was her freckles that did me in. When I *really* looked at her, those freckles softened her features, and they'd captivated me from the get-go. I wanted to take off her clothes, so I could count each and every freckle on her body.

I remembered that joke about redheads and freckles: each one was a soul they had stolen. I grinned to myself as I unlocked my car door. She was obviously a complete badass and had stolen a lot of souls. The temporary loss of oxygen was worth getting her to agree to go out with me. Okay, well not specifically me, but in the general vicinity of me, with other people. I frowned. I needed to get her to agree to go out with me, alone.

It'd been at least a year since my last date. Many of the women I'd dated before couldn't hack my long hours and less than mediocre conversation. I loved to talk about my job, and it seemed murders and crime wasn't of interest to many women. So what usually happened was, I talked about the newest case I was working on, and they lost interest or heaved up their dinner, so I'd buried myself deeper in my work.

I loved only a few things in life: Mia, my car, and my job. That was it. But Avery, she knew what this job was like: the struggles, the blood and the gore we were faced with on a daily basis. And she enjoyed it, much like me. Any woman who could kick my ass and look at a dead body without flinching might just be worth adding to my list. After all, my list of loves had a little wiggle room.

On my way home to my apartment, I stopped and picked up some flowers for Mrs. Freidmont. I left them on her doorstep because if I knocked on her door, she'd be making me lunch and talking my ear off. She was a nice older woman, but lonely. But I was so exhausted and didn't think I could handle the interaction.

My dank apartment was depressing. I made a note to get something of color to add to the ambiance. Everything was beige or olive green. It looked like something out of a horror movie. The walls were covered in old wood paneling, sinking the room deeper into dreaded despair. It fit my lifestyle, so I didn't care. But the thought of bringing Avery over made me nervous and unsettled. She deserved to be in a place better than this.

I texted Mia to check on her.

Me: Hey how's it going?

Mia: Ugh! Tests suck.

Me: Haha. Study hard. I'm taking a nap. Case had me up all night.

Mia: Miss you bro. Be safe.

Me: I always am. Miss you too.

Settling myself on the couch, I fell asleep even with the sun beaming through my dingy windows. The sound of my cell phone buzzing woke me out of a sound sleep. The sun had set and dark shadows hedged in from the outside, creeping in, threatening to overtake the room.

"Bradley," I answered, sleep curling through my words.

"Hey. It's Adams. We have another body."

"Jesus. Already?" I stood and began undressing from the gym. "He sure works fast." I didn't have time for a shower, so as I continued speaking with Adams, I slid into my plain white button-up, black tie and slacks. My go-to outfit. "You're going to miss the circus." This was why I hesitated when it came to having to care about anyone but myself. Because I'd miss things, like the circus with my family.

"Yeah." He mumbled something and I heard Airi's voice. "Airi and Hana are on their way now. One second." I heard a door open and close, his car engine revving. "This one. It's just fucked-up man." He sighed. I cringed. We had to catch this guy and fast.

"Fuckin' A. Okay. I'll have to call Agent Grant and Dr. Harper." I swiped my car keys from the table and headed out the door.

"Already done."

"Thanks," I growled, anger apparent in my voice. I'd wanted to call Avery. I'd wanted to hear her voice.

"You okay, man?" Adams asked, concerned. "You sound pissed off." It wasn't like me to be easily angered or annoyed.

"Yeah, fine." I brushed off the fact that I didn't get to call her. My veins were pulsing as I walked to the car but subsided as I remembered I'd see her tonight. "Where am I going?" I turned the car on, and the engine roared to life. I didn't like bringing my car to crime scenes, but if I wanted to still go out after, she—my car—would have to come with me. *Don't worry, baby. I'll keep you safe,* I thought as I patted the console.

"Fisherman's Wharf boat ramp, on Brenton Bay."

"All right. Be there in twenty." I hung up the phone and tossed it into the passenger seat. My focus should have been on this case, on the murders that were happening in my city, but I couldn't help but think of Avery as I sped off to the newest crime scene. About how much I wanted her.

There was no use in trying to think about anything else. Because as my hard-on pressed against my suit pants, the only cure would be to have her. All of her.

Chapter Ten

Avery

I spent the rest of the day cleaning. There is only so much square footage in an Extended Stay apartment, and I bleached and scrubbed it until my hands were raw. When nervous, I cleaned, ironed, and organized. Cleaning gave me an element of control over my life. Because the reality was life often has uncontrollable aspects—like Detective Evan Bradley in all his sweaty, shirtless glory.

I was running out of things to clean when Madison came out of the bedroom telling me we had another body. Although an additional victim wasn't what anybody wanted to hear about, it gave me a purpose and something to do other than dwell on the impending night out. I went to the closet and put on one of the many outfits I had ironed the night before. I was ready in five minutes. Madison, not so much. She was lagging, and I was pretty sure I heard her throwing up in the bathroom. Twenty minutes later, we were on the way to Abell's Wharf boat ramp. This time, I drove.

We made our way into my car—my baby—a jet-black 1967 Pontiac Firebird. The vibration of the V8 engine shook me to my very core. It was like a calm stroke of the hand down the length of my body. There was a subtle rumble at first, like kisses being brushed down my face, down my neck. Then the initial rumble would stop, right in my stomach, right above my center. It was bewitching, magnetic, and drew me into a simple moment with just the turn of the key.

Madison sat in the passenger seat looking unfazed by the amazingness that was my car. As I drove away, her face turned an awful shade of green.

"Don't you dare throw up in my car." I glared at her, briefly taking my eyes off the wheel.

"Jeez. No 'How do you feel, Madison? Are you okay?'" She sighed.

"Are you okay?" Despite my concern for my car, I was more concerned about Madison. She didn't look well.

"I'm not sure what's wrong. And before you ask if I'm pregnant, I'm not. Scott and I are always careful." She rolled down the window, sticking her head out slightly. Her hair came free from its bun, and her curls began to fly free.

"Well, maybe you're pregnant." I laughed absentmindedly as the thought escaped from my mouth. "Protection is never 100 percent." I shrugged.

Her silence met my proclamation, and I glanced over at her.

"Um," was all she managed to get out as her eyes darted around the car, panic stricken.

"I was joking. Relax." I patted her leg for reassurance.

"I could be. Shit! I really could be." She started biting her nails. "I missed my period, which isn't that unusual for me because of my stress, but I don't know," she whispered faintly.

"Seriously, Madison?" My tone took on that of a mother, something I didn't even know I possessed. I slammed on my brakes, so I didn't miss the turn into the wharf. Then, I took a breath, steadying my own nerves. "I'm sorry. This is just a really big deal, a baby?" I sighed. "Did you take a test?" I looked at her from the corner of my eye, not wanting to take my eyes of the road ahead. I had no idea where we were going. It was pitch black. Her eyes welled up with tears.

"No. I didn't even think I could be pregnant, but now that you said it…." Her voice drifted off again. I took another deep breath and tried to calm my own nerves. After all, I wasn't the one who thought they were pregnant.

"Hey." I pulled onto the dirt road. Mentally cursing and hoping the rocks didn't kick up and dent my car, I pulled to the side of the road. I noticed the flashing lights of police cars up ahead, but instead of jumping out of the car, I turned off the engine and faced Madison.

"Look at me, Madison." She turned to me with tears streaming down her face. "We'll get through this crime scene then stop and grab a test before we go out tonight. I'm sure it's just a stomach bug." I grabbed her hand in mine and gave her a reassuring squeeze. She smiled as she wiped the tears from her face.

"Sounds like a good plan. What would I do without you?" she questioned as she pulled down the mirror and composed herself.

"Well, remember what you just said when I'm freaking out over something," I added with a laugh.

We got out of the car, and I caught a glimpse of Detective Bradley, who was standing in front of us, staring. Actually, drooling would be a more accurate description. I thought I was going to have to help him pick his jaw up off the ground, but then he spoke.

"Is this your car?" He placed his hand on the hood, shock evident on his face.

"It is. He's my baby. Hands off." I slapped his hand away. "You'll smudge the wax." I took the sleeve of my shirt and wiped the spot he had touched.

"You just keep surprising me." He shook his head, a sly grin forming on his face.

"I'll never understand people and their obsession with cars." Bradley and I both whipped our heads around and stared at Madison.

"Because you drive a Chevy. Crummy pieces of metal." I patted my own beautifully made, sleek, orgasm-inducing beauty. I looked at my car, the black paint shining under the reflection of the moon. The Firebird was rare, and I was used to people gawking over it but something about Bradley wanting it, touching it excited me. It was enough to chip just a piece of that wall that I had strategically built up. Cars were my weakness and maybe so was Detective Bradley.

"If you can even call a Chevy metal," Bradley added to my comment and chuckled next to me. Our eyes locked, meeting and sharing in on the joke. We stared at each other for what seemed like forever, smiling. Madison cleared her throat, and I darted my eyes away from Bradley's.

"All right, let's go take a look at this crime scene," Bradley said, leading the way as we walked toward the wharf.

The crunch of the earth beneath our feet was a welcomed distraction from Bradley as we made our way closer to the water. The wharf had barely any illumination. If it weren't for the police car lights and the moon, we would have been standing in complete darkness. Madison trudged along, her eyes seeming to constantly wander and get lost. I really hoped she wasn't pregnant. She'd been seeing Scott for a few months now. Sure, they'd known each other since childhood, and they were engaged, but a baby in the emotional mess that Liam had left would be a tough pill to swallow. She was getting better, but she still needed time to focus on herself and to strengthen her relationship with Scott.

We made it to the end of the wharf, and Adams greeted us with a warm smile and firm handshakes.

"What do we have?" I took out some gloves and handed a pair to Madison. I knew she wasn't feeling well, but I knew she would push whatever her own personal troubles were aside to get the job done. Catching the bad guys was our life and we did that at any cost. Our own feelings, our own needs came second. We both understood that. It was what made us such great partners.

"Caucasian. Female. Teenager. A pentagram was carved into her flesh before she was drowned." I looked at the body as Adams described her, and I moved her dark brown hair out of her face.

"Jesus," I murmured. "She's so young." I sighed as I

crouched down further.

"Ah, hell," Madison said, joining me to get a better look. "I agree with Adams." She took her finger and pointed to the pentagram on the girl's stomach. "Blood was still pooling to the area of the pentagram. She was still alive when it was done." She sighed. "The wound, though, I think it's self-inflicted." Adams and Bradley looked perplexed.

"See here?" Madison pointed to a part of the symbol that covered the stomach. "These are shallow which indicate hesitation." She pointed to another spot. "Now here, it looks more deliberate. More forceful. And also, straighter. These marks were done by someone with a clear idea of what they wanted." She paused, brushing her hair out of her face. I continued looking at the girl and making notes of the other gashes and injuries that covered the victim's body. Even in the darkness, blood was visible on the ground. Blow flies fluttered around the wound on her stomach, and I swatted at my face trying to keep them at bay.

"Jameson has escalated," Madison announced. "And now, he's going to need another victim for whatever ritualistic fantasy he is trying to fulfill." She stood up from the body. "Whoa," she said as she stumbled back. Adams, however, caught her arm before she fell.

"You need to sit down," I said softly.

Adams brought her over to a nearby rock, and sat her down gently. Bradley and I walked over to join them.

"So, what's the plan?" Bradley looked at Madison and me. Madison had her head between her legs and was taking deep breaths.

"Clearly we need to catch him," she managed to say between deep breaths. "I need to take a look at his records and build a profile. What happened to him in his past will have some indication of what his next steps will be." Her voice trailed off. "It was like that with Liam and Walsh."

I didn't have to see her face to know what lingered in her eyes: sadness and regret. She hadn't been able to help Liam in the way she'd wanted. In fact, he'd been the one to help her in the end, and she'd been left to put the pieces of herself back together. If anything, I knew what that felt like. Trying to build who you were as a person in the midst of a wreckage. All you could do was hope that there were enough pieces to make you whole again.

"It's okay, Madison," Adams said gruffly, surprising me with his sincerity. Many guys in our line of work would have backed away awkwardly or even used Madison's weakness as a way to prove women shouldn't be in the field. But not Adams. She glanced up at him, and her eyes glistened against the moonlight that had finally settled in.

"I'm sorry, guys. I don't know why I'm getting so emotional. This is so unprofessional." She looked over at Adams, but before he could answer, she tilted her head to the side as if realizing something.

"Why are you so understanding?" Adams looked at her and it was like it was a secret only she and Adams shared, but Bradley and I were witnesses to this moment that held so much importance.

"My wife had a difficult past. Held onto so much and it was hard for her to move on. I helped her through it." I moved closer to Madison, and I put my hand on her back. I didn't know about Adams's wife's past, but his sincerity impacted even me. I could see in his eyes he knew what Madison was going through. "Until she had our daughter, Hana, she struggled. Hana brought her back to me. It will be the same for you." His toothy smile made Madison grin.

Madison looked up at me and twirled her engagement ring on her finger. Adams was right, and his words seemed to resonate with her. She was deep in thought, and I knew their conversation was far from over.

Giving them the privacy they needed, I stepped aside to make a quick call to the office to make sure we had all of Jameson's records. I ended the call and turned to rejoin the group, but instead, I ran directly into Bradley's chest.

"*Oomph*," I grunted. His chest was hard, really hard, if I remember correctly. Which I did. Each ripped ab. Every muscle that protruded from his toned physique. I scowled. Moisture formed between my legs and I clenched them together. It didn't do anything to stop the feelings. *Mental side note: Take a cold shower.*

I backed away from him, cutting the invisible rope that seemed to connect us. He stepped closer, and our bodies were only inches away again. I held my breath. Waiting. Anticipating. He took another step closer and instinctively, I placed a hand up, and it landed naturally on his chest. He breathed in heavily, his breath catching in his throat. I felt the rise and fall beneath my hand, and I closed my eyes, listening intently to his heart as it pounded.

"Grant." I stumbled back at the sound of his voice

and opened my eyes to stare at him. His eyes held so many questions, so much *want*. What the hell was he doing to me? Just a simple touch of my hand against his chest and I turned into a mush of emotions. I squared off my shoulders and stood up straighter, removing my hand and smoothing back my hair. *Get a hold of yourself, Avery.*

He grinned, satisfaction lingering in his eyes. The guy was some evil mastermind. It was the only explanation.

"Did you need something?" I placed my hands on my hips.

"Just checking to make sure you were okay. It's dark out here."

"I can take care of myself. It's a little something called a Glock." I patted my gun.

"Something tells me you know how to use it, too," he muttered.

"I'm known to be very good with guns." I smiled as I walked away, adding just a little extra sway to my hips. "The bigger, the better," I called out as I continued to walk away.

"You're evil," he yelled after me, echoing my thoughts from earlier.

We wrapped up the crime scene around nine o'clock as dusk finally settled. Jameson had upped his game, but there wasn't much else to go on. We had no idea where he'd gone, or even where he'd been able to keep his followers all this time. I asked about Lorelei's parents' farm, but apparently that had been sold. It seemed we were at the mercy of Jameson and hoping he'd make a mistake. I hated that. He wasn't the type to be violent. Something had changed. I just wasn't sure what, and that put our case in the hands of our killer. Something none of us were comfortable with. We needed to get ahead of Jameson, and make it so he was running from us, and not the other way around.

I needed a moment to collect my thoughts. This case and the emotional turmoil of discovering the death of someone so young threatened to wear me down. I took a second to look at the water. The natural stillness of the lake brought me peace from my thoughts. There were no boats or people splashing. No sounds. No ripples. The moon glistened off the surface of that stillness, and I also noticed the perfect reflection of the stars that covered the sky. I loved the south, the vastness of the area and the nature. The south's open land, free of the typical suburban sprawl in the north, made me feel free.

Madison handled the press again. They'd finally caught wind of the heinous crimes that up until now seemed to have had no pattern to them. But looking at the violence and the pentagram that seemed to be present at every scene, it was a clear MO. They were calling Jameson the "Satanic Killer." At hearing such a name, Madison became irate with one of the reporters, going off on a tangent about psychological disorders. "He needs help, and we need to stop these crimes so no more innocent people are killed," she said. She handled herself pretty well. She was coming into her own with this job, and was good at what she did. Finally, Madison stomped back over, her eyes wide with rage.

"Those goddamn bottom-feeding reporters. Anything for a good story." She pulled out her cell phone. "Are we ready to go? It's 9:10. We can still run home and change before meeting the girls." She sighed. "We all could use the break and sense of normalcy. Whatever that is in our line of work," Madison mumbled.

"Yeah, we're good to go. Adams said the ME just took the body, and forensics is just cleaning up." I walked toward the car. "Seems they found a woman's heel print," I said, flipping through my notes.

"That's weird. Maybe Lorelei is involved more than we think," Madison commented.

"Interesting," I said, continuing to flip through the pages. "It's worth considering." I slammed the notebook shut. "Plus, there weren't any other shoe prints. Either she was really careless and Jameson hid his tracks or she did it solo."

"Could she physically hold down a body though? Isn't she smaller?" Madison questioned.

"She is. But I'm smaller and... well...."

Madison chuckled. "You kick ass."

"Damn right I do!" We both laughed.

"Soooo, I heard Bradley is joining us." Madison looked straight ahead. The corner of her lip twitched and a smile threatened to break free.

"Yes, but only because he's persistent. I had no choice!"

She rolled her eyes playfully. "Okay, Avery." She patted me on the shoulders.

Madison and I drove off, stopping by the drug store to get the pregnancy test and some anti-nausea meds for her. Regardless of what was happening, the medication would help settle her stomach.

When we pulled up to the hotel we were currently

calling home, Garcia and Marshall were sitting on the hood of their car looking ready for a night on the town. Garcia wore a black skirt, short, about four inches above her knee. A purple sequined top covered her tanned skin. Her shoes were easily five inches, and I was afraid she'd break an ankle once she started drinking.

Marshall wore skin-tight leggings, with a pale pink halter top. Her shoes weren't as tall; she was tall enough as it was. But the shoes were sparkly. So sparkly I felt the need to cover my eyes when I looked at her. These girls were crazy, but I loved them. They squealed when they saw us, and we all embraced each other in a hug. We chatted eagerly as we made the way to our room. I opened the door and watched them all pile in. My heart swelled at the sight of Madison, Marshall and Garcia together again. Although we weren't working far from each other, we were no longer at the academy, and I missed seeing them every day.

"Make yourselves at home. Madison and I will just take a minute." Both Garcia and Marshall sat down on the single sleeper couch that was in the living room, but Marshall was the first to grab the TV remote and start flipping through the channels. I headed into our room and changed quickly into the outfit Garcia brought me. It was subtle, yet sexy. I appreciated her not giving me some skirt that let my vagina blow in the breeze. I had on tight jeans and a tube top, both jet black like the color of my Firebird. Pairing the outfit with big hoop silver earrings and letting my hair down to cascade naturally around my face made me look more like a normal woman heading out for the night than an agent. I didn't bother with makeup. I just added a pink shimmer to my lips. Looking at myself in the mirror, my hair looked even wilder against the black of the outfit I was wearing.

My cell phone chirped. I glanced at the screen.

Scott: Where's Madison? I'm here in town to consult on the case. I want to surprise her.

Me: We're changing to go to the Down Under Pub. Meet us there in 30.

Scott: Roger.

This was perfect. Madison would feel better with Scott here.

"Who was that?" Madison asked, towel drying her curls from the shower.

"Just the secretary about the files. They'll be waiting for us tomorrow," I lied. *What's a little white lie among friends?*

"Did you take the test?" I put on my black two-inch high platforms. Only two inches because platforms were far easier to walk in. And I intended to have quite a few drinks this evening.

"It's on the counter. I can't look." She pulled on her lacey red underwear and matching red bra. I smiled knowing Scott would probably love taking the ensemble off.

"What are you wearing tonight?" I asked nonchalantly as I crammed my stuff into my clutch. By stuff, I meant my weapon, my lip gloss, and my wallet. It barely closed but it eventually reluctantly snapped shut.

"Probably this lace dress." She pulled it out of the closet. "It's cute but comfy. I'm feeling slightly bloated." She patted her stomach, and I glanced down, noticing a little pouch.

"Pretty," I said. "So, do you want me to go look at the test?" I went behind her and zipped up the dress before sitting back down on the bed.

"No. I need to be a big girl and suck it up." She padded to the bathroom, leaving the door open. I didn't hear anything. No gasping or screaming. *See,* I thought, *just a little stomach bug.*

She came out holding the test, a look of panic on her face. She flipped the test over and all I thought was, *Oh shit. Fuck. Dammit.*

When she said, "It says positive," I pulled her in for a hug and replied the only way I could.

"It's going to be okay."

Chapter Eleven

LORELEI

I had watched from afar as the agents riffled through the crime scene, shuffling through the leaves and dirt, looking for clues as to who committed the crime. I couldn't help the smile that curved on my lips as I looked at their disgusted faces. They disapproved. They thought I was a monster. Maybe I was, but it wasn't for the reasons they thought. It was for him. This was all for him.

We are only five days away from the full moon. So the last sacrifice had to be completed on that night. It was the only way to make Lucifer happy.

Water, air, these elements had both been satisfied by the taking of a life. Fire and earth remained and I was overcome with excitement and thoughts of who the next victims should be. The first fire was us testing our wings as we tried to bring our followers closer. The next victims had to be perfect sacrifices so beautiful and worthy that Lucifer would be our god. When this happened, no longer would people mindlessly follow the word of a god that left his people behind. A god that sat on his throne and watched from the heavens as we suffered. That wasn't a god. That was a fucking coward. I wanted to liberate people. Show them that there was someone worthy of our following.

I glanced over at my husband as he talked with one of our followers. I loved Jameson from the first time I'd seen him in church. At fourteen, my family had moved from Oregon to Virginia. My father inherited his parents' farm. Acres and acres of open land and a huge farmhouse with eight bedrooms became my father's. With not another soul for miles and miles, it was so peaceful, it was easy to settle down here, not be noticed by the FBI. His home was sold to a cute older couple, looking to settle down and retire. My parents ran once they heard about Jameson and I marrying, and the death of his parents. They were embarrassed. They didn't fucking care about what happened to me, just their precious image. Like it had always been. Go to church and be a good little girl. Play with your dolls. Get good grades. Never question anything. Well, fuck them and their lies.

Even if the FBI came snooping around, the Johnsons, who had bought the home, covered for us. They thought they could save Jameson and me, change our ways back to that of those who served the Lord. Ha! They were so blinded by their faith that they didn't see how far gone we truly were.

I knew what they were before they even opened their mouths. The Holy Bible sat on every surface of their house. They were just like our parents, followers to a religion built on lies. When they started getting too pushy, we killed them.

Buried just a few feet from my bedroom window. Buried with their bibles. I let them take their lies with them to the grave.

When I was younger, my parents always told me that any respectable family needed God. We needed a church and Pastor Cruz was there to guide us in with holy scripture. I laughed at the thought. Holy scripture. More like holy lies. If it wasn't for Jameson taking me under his wing and showing me what life truly was about, my head would be deep in a bible, talking about redemption and salvation. There was no salvation. There wasn't going to be any rapture. The only salvation we had lingered right below us and his name was Lucifer.

How could this God be worthy when he let Jameson get beaten by his father every night, sometimes to the point where he couldn't walk? It was all in the name of God, Jameson's father said. A disobedient child was evil. A wife who was disobedient was even more evil. It was lies. All of it. Jameson had the permanent scars to prove it.

We tried to find our place in his fucked-up world. And we found it in Lucifer and in Mother Nature. It fueled all things in the universe. It was no different for the underworld. Four essentials: air, water, fire, earth. We had to satisfy Lucifer by providing sacrifices in these four ways and then, then we would be *his*.

Jameson usually handled all things but lately, he had become distant, hesitant. The last victim was a challenge for him. He was struggling with his beliefs, with this path we had chosen. I couldn't let him lose sight of what really mattered.

I'd been keeping an eye on the FBI and Virginia police

over the past few days. With all the followers, it was easy to send some around to see and hear what was going on for me. They were investigating the murder of Francine Dewitt. It was clever throwing her off that building. Watching her fall still made me tingle. Air was all around her. Air had taken her life. But it was then that his eyes changed. What I saw in Jameson's eyes wasn't hope, love, or desire; it was fear. It was mistrust. It was confusion. And I knew then that he was losing his touch, his beliefs and that was why I was taking over. In any marriage when one fell, the other became stronger. I was becoming stronger each and every day.

I smiled, remembering agents Grant and Harper talking about two agent friends visiting them. It would be risky taking Grant and Harper as they were on our case, but those other two agents? It was meant to be. This path had been sent out just for me in order to fulfill my mission.

I knew they were going out drinking at a local bar. So, maybe, if they were drunk enough, I could get to them.

"I have to go run out, Jameson. I'll be back." Jameson smiled at me and kissed me on the cheek as he handed me the car keys. He was so trusting, loyal to a fault. He didn't know what I was going to do. It was a surprise to show him how dedicated I was to the cause. Our cause. I would be strong in the face of my husband's uncertainty. I would lead us to fulfill the mission. I would become one with Lucifer.

Chapter Twelve

When we pulled up to the Down Under Pub, I inwardly groaned. I suddenly didn't feel like being out tonight. Sleep tugged at me, and I just wanted to go home and curl up in my bed. I went into the bar, though, for Madison, for Garcia and Marshall. Madison desperately needed a distraction from the news that she was going to be a mother.

We took our normal table at the corner of the bar, right near the dance floor. We were all in kind of a state of shock and just simply going through the motions of a night out on the town. Garcia and Marshall were happy for Madison and her having a baby, but the unexpectedness couldn't be ignored.

"What can I get you?" The familiar blue-eye-shadowed waitress stared back at me. Her name was Doreen. She was easily in her sixties but dressed like she was in her twenties, was widowed and super sweet. But she still looked like Mimi from *The Drew Carey Show*.

"Hey, Doreen, the usual. But for Madison a ginger ale."

She eyed me curiously, but as Madison's hand instinctively found its way to her stomach, a smile formed at her lips.

"You got it, girls." She walked away, her heels slapping loudly against the wooden dance floor. Her legs were bare underneath a short, tight black skirt, and her blue varicose veins matched her eye-shadow perfectly. It didn't matter that her body showed the signs of her age. She wore her cute little outfits with a confidence many women would kill for.

"I'm so happy for you, Madison." Garcia took Madison's hand in hers.

"You're going to be a great mom," Marshall added. I looked between the girls. There was no doubt that she'd be a good mom. I agreed with that. I just saw it in her eyes; she was worried about telling Scott.

Doreen came back with our drinks quickly, and I hoped they would lighten the mood. She kept them coming, and I was feeling much lighter, much freer after about four beers.

"Guess who?" I smiled, watching Scott sneak up behind Madison and put his hands over her eyes.

"Scott!" Madison flew into his arms, and he caught her—barely—as they fell back and hit the wall. I knew Madison was really emotional after her news, but watching her with Scott, something I was used to, made my heart tug. I was always happy for them, for what they'd found. Watching her reaction, seeing the way he looked at her, for the first time, I wondered what it would be like if that were me.

"Babe?" He tilted her chin so her eyes were on his again. His eyes were filled with concern, but tenderness and love lay there as well. "What's wrong?" Madison wiped the tears from her eyes.

"Not here. Later." She hugged him again. "I missed you."

"I missed you, too." He looked back at me, caressing Madison's curls as he often did. I smiled at him, trying to settle the uneasiness in the air.

"Surprise!" I yelled out, dramatically putting my hands up in the air.

"You knew?" Madison let go of Scott and turned to me.

"Of course." She gave me a quick hug before heading back to the table. Scott and I followed, sat down and ordered another round of drinks. I needed more alcohol to ease the feelings battering me.

Scott took a sip of Madison's drink and Garcia, Marshall, and I eyeballed each other. "Ginger ale?" he asked Madison. "Want me to grab you a hard cider?" He started to stand.

"NO!" everyone at the table yelled. He jumped at the reaction, sitting back down quickly.

"Fine. Okay!" He looked between us all. "Madison, what's going on? Are you sick or something?"

She sighed. "Guys, Scott and I are going to head out. We have to talk." Madison stood, taking her purse off the back of the chair. We said our good-byes and I gave her a reassuring hug.

"He loves you. Just tell him the truth," I whispered in her ear.

Madison smiled sadly at me, the burden of the truth she carried weighing her down. It was happy news, especially for the two of them since they're so clearly in love. But Madison, her struggles, her past still loomed around her from time to time. Each day she got stronger, and I was thankful to be a part of watching her grow.

She walked away, hand in hand with Scott and I sat back down at the table, Garcia and Marshall chatting away about something. I didn't care what they were discussing. I just stared at my empty hand, wondering what it would be like to be held by someone the way Scott held Madison's.

"Here's another, sugar." Doreen plopped another beer in my hand and I smiled.

I looked at the beer and caressed the outside of the glass. "It's just you and me tonight." I chugged down the beer, slamming it on the table.

"You all right?" Garcia raised her eyebrow at me. "That's like your fifth beer."

"And I'm going to have another." I raised my hand to get Doreen's attention. "It helps me forget."

"Forget what?" Marshall asked, more concerned with her phone than with me.

"Forget that I'm alone," I mumbled.

Garcia put her hand over mine, before dragging me and Marshall out on the dance floor.

The drinks kept coming, helping me forget all the shit that made me who I was today. I danced, laughed, and I pretended. Something I had become very skilled at, even if it led to my own unhappiness.

Chapter Thirteen

EVAN

I walked further into the bar and immediately, my eyes found her. Her jeans hugged her firm ass, and her bare shoulders were covered by her cascading red hair. Sweat glistened down her body as she danced alone to the music, her body fluid and rhythmic. She was perfect.

I glided around the people, came up behind her and pressed my body against her back. She tensed at first, but as she glanced back at me, and her eyes met mine, she slowly smiled. Her eyes lit up with eagerness and desire. As she softened and her body melted against mine, Avery laid her head against my shoulder and closed her eyes.

Our bodies moved with the sultry voice of Amy Winehouse's "Will You Still Love Me Tomorrow." My entire body tingled, anticipating each sway of her hips, each moan from her mouth. My body ached for something more, though, so I let my hands roam the length of her. I started at her neck, caressing the pale smooth skin. It was slightly slick, and I had to fight the urge to lick the taunting length of her neck. As my hands drifted to her shoulders, she moaned against my ear, bringing my cock to life. It pressed against her tight jeans, directly against the crease of her ass. Her eyes opened and met mine, hunger and lust dilating her pupils.

Taking that as an invitation to continue, my hands stroked the length of her, finding their way to her side. I felt the beauty of her subtle curves. They were just enough for me to grab on to. Just enough for me to hold and toss her up against the wall. I'd have her pinned exactly where I wanted her, where I could fully look at her, touch her, become a part of her. I took her ass in my hands and she arched her back, closing her eyes. Heat radiated from her center and my already hard cock twitched. *Jesus, Avery.* This was a much different side to Avery than earlier. I wondered how much she'd had to drink. I focused on her lips as she turned herself around to face me and I pictured her screaming my name, her pink lips forming a perfect O shape as I made her come.

Her face was only inches from mine and our noses touched. We danced like this for what seemed like hours. Our hands roamed, but we never once took our eyes off one another. When the music ended, our bodies parted unwillingly, and the need to continue our dance ignited within me.

She sat down at the table her eyes still wild with lust.

"Do you want a drink?" I asked, sitting down next to her. I pushed my chair closer, placing my arm around the back of hers.

"Yes, Guinness. The biggest one they have." She took the napkin off the table and started dabbing away at the sweat.

She got to her chest and opened up the front of her top, her pale pink strapless bra showing underneath. I gritted my teeth, trying to stop myself from burying my face between those two luscious breasts.

She was clearly drunk, and I didn't want to take advantage of her, but her defenses were down, her overthinking brain less obsessive. Every time she smiled, every time she brushed up against me, our connection sparked to life. It was an attraction that burned so deep it threatened to overwhelm me. I had to bury those feelings. Not because I didn't want her, but I wouldn't take advantage of her in her drunken state. I was horny, but I had morals, after all.

I went and got the drinks, two Guinnesses. Avery was badass. No fruity drinks with frilly little umbrellas. Oh no, she was hell on wheels, a firecracker. And I wanted her, bad. It wasn't just sexually either. Yeah sure, I wanted to bury myself inside her, but I also knew I'd met my match with her. She was no nonsense and straight to the point. She didn't fall for anyone's shit. I admired that in a person, and I loved that in a woman.

When I brought the drinks back, she took long sips. She slammed the glass on the table and leaned back into the chair, her eyes drifting closed.

"Where are your friends, Avery?" I asked. She needed to go home. She was done.

"They left. I stayed." She leaned closer to me. "I knew you'd come." She smiled. She put her hand on my knee and moved it up my thigh. I wanted her to move it up just a little further and feel how much I wanted her. My eyes looked over the table filled with empty bottles.

"Okay, let me take you home." I took her clutch from the table. Damn, it was heavy. "Let's go, Avery." I put out my hand for her. She opened her eyes, and looked at me thoughtfully.

"I love the way you say my name… *Avery*." She mimicked my accent, and I busted out a laugh. "You have the best accent." She took my hand, and I pulled her close to me.

"I don't have an accent, baby. You do."

She smiled at me, and her eyes wandered over my face. "You're so handsome." She reached out to feel the stubble on my face. It was a curse really. I could shave first thing in the morning and by the afternoon, my beard was already growing back. The way Avery touched it though made me thankful I didn't shave.

"Come on, Avery. It's time to go. You've had a lot to drink."

"So what if I'm drunk? This is the only time I can just be. No worries. Nothing to organize. No one to save, and no thinking about the what ifs." She pressed her breasts against my chest and it was back. My hard-on pressed against her stomach.

"You want this too, Evan. I can feel it." She moved her hand down to my pants, grabbing my cock with it. I fought back a moan and smiled to myself realizing she called me by my first name.

"I do, Avery. You don't know how much, but not when you're drunk. I want you alert, and fully aware when I'm making love to you." Her eyes opened wide as I gently took her hand away, and held it in mine. "Come on. Let's go," I said.

I took her outside, and the clatter of her heels sounded against the pavement. When we were outside of my car, she stopped. She caressed the side of the hood, her eyes wandering over the body of the car with almost as much lust as she'd had earlier in the bar when she'd given me the once-over.

"She's beautiful." Excitement filled her eyes.

My cock hardened again as images of me fucking her over the hood of my car entered my thoughts. I could imagine her red hair covering her body and her perky ass smacking against the hood.

"Thanks," I managed to get out. I opened the car door for her and she gracefully sat down.

"I'm at the Extended Stay. The one off Main," she said as I settled in as well. She placed her head back against the seat, and I was almost jealous of my car.

"Got it."

We rode in silence, but I couldn't help but steal glances of her as she lay back with her eyes closed. In my perusal, I realized her face was heart shaped. Her hands were delicate. Her fingernails were perfectly manicured.

"My car!" she said, all of a sudden bolting up from her seat. "I can't leave him down there. Someone will definitely vandalize him." Her eyes were frantic, and I couldn't help but laugh. I placed my hand on her knee.

"Don't worry. I'll get an officer to drive it to your hotel."

"Thank you." She breathed out in relief as she fell back into the seat.

When we arrived at her place, she invited me up. I watched as she opened her clutch and pulled out her weapon before wandering off to the bedroom. *That's why it was so heavy.* I smiled to myself. Always prepared.

"Madison's staying with Scott tonight, so if you want to stay, you can." She raised her voice from the bedroom, so I could hear her. She poked her head around the corner. "I could make up the couch."

"That'd be great." I glanced at my phone, it blaring 2:00 a.m. Sending a quick text to an officer on duty I knew, I asked him to come grab Avery's car keys before bringing the car back to the hotel.

I sat on the couch and a few minutes later, she came out with sheets and a blanket in hand, and dressed for bed. She had on a long T-shirt that ended just above the knees. She wore no bra, and I could see her nipples poking through the fabric. Even dressed in a T-shirt, she drove me wild.

I jumped off the couch and helped her make it up.

"Thanks for bringing me home, Evan." She folded the blanket, leaving it on the end of the couch for me.

"Hey, anytime. Thanks for the dance." I winked at her. Smiling, she headed off to her bedroom. With a click of her door, I knew it was lights out. I ran downstairs quickly when I received the message that Officer Perry was here to take the keys. As I made my way back to her apartment, I opened the door silently. A part of me hoped she would be sitting on the newly made-up couch, naked and waiting for me to take her. But it was empty. I reprimanded myself for the thoughts. She was drunk and I could wait. I could wait until she was alert and fully capable of making the decision to let me inside her. And when that day came, it would be explosive.

After taking off my shoes, shirt and pants, I lay down on top of the sheets in my boxer briefs. Sexual need still flowed through me. Goddammit, why did I have to have morals? I rolled over as my balls screamed for release. Nothing like trying to fall asleep with thoughts of Avery Grant running through my mind. She was the star of my wet dreams and the current reason for my blue balls.

Chapter Fourteen

AVERY

"What the hell?" I yelled and pulled the blanket over my head.

"Rise and shine sleepy head." I peeked from underneath the blanket and saw Evan standing in front of me in his low-hung boxers. The perfect V of his hips caused my heart to beat faster as he stretched. If I didn't know better, I'd have thought he was putting himself on display with all of his manhood pressing against the opening of his boxers.

Last night, I'd screamed into my pillow, trying to muffle my sexual cries. I'd been *slightly* drunk, but I'd known what I wanted, and I had wanted Evan. Sexually of course. Still did. He had been such a gentleman last night and it had pissed me off. I'd wanted to get laid, to sever the sexual tension that had lingered within me since I'd laid eyes on him. I'd wanted to move on, to wrap up this case, and to be done with him. But he'd shown me he was much more than just a quick screw.

I didn't do long-term. Heck, I didn't do anything past one night. It was easier. No complications. No getting to know one another. I was organized and methodical in all that I did, and relationships were messy. I didn't like messy.

I had tossed and turned for hours, and the last time I'd caught a glimpse of the clock, it had read 5:00 a.m. It had been hard to sleep. I'd felt the tightness gather between my legs, and I'd thought about pleasuring myself, but I'd known it wouldn't be enough. And before me, there he stood, like he hadn't left me high and dry.

"Don't you know how to knock?" I flung my legs over the side of the bed irritated that I hadn't been able to work through my sexual frustration last night. Knowing he wasn't a one-night stand kind of guy, I might not ever be able to work through those feelings with him. He jumped down next to me, taking me down with him.

"Nope. I have no manners." He sprawled out, stealing my blankets in the process.

"I couldn't tell," I grumbled. I laid there for a moment. *This feels so normal,* I thought.

"Let's snuggle." Evan scooched closer to me laughing.

I snorted. "Did you just say snuggle? Seriously? Are you five?" *Snuggle?* I didn't snuggle. Snugglefuck maybe, but not just snuggling. Snugglefuck. When you pretend you are going to snuggle, but your *real* intentions are, well, fucking. I didn't like being wrapped around someone unless they were giving me some attention. Attention between my legs to be more specific. Oh, and with their tongue. I was practical that way.

"Wow, I leave for one night…." I bounced up and saw Madison and Scott standing in the doorway to the bedroom.

"Morning, Bradley." Scott nodded at him, a huge-ass smile plastered across his face. I was tempted to walk over and smack that smile right off.

"Morning." Evan smiled back, putting his hands behind his head. He was too comfortable and having way too much fun with this. I shoved him off the bed with my legs and he hit the floor with a loud thud. Madison shook her head.

"We'll be in the other room," she said as she pulled Scott behind her.

A loud laugh came from the floor. I moved over to the side of the bed ready to give Evan a piece of my mind, but before I could, he grabbed my arms, pulling me down on top of him.

"Now I have you right where I want you." Our faces were inches apart and we stared intently at each other. The moment was different than last night. The feelings clearer since my senses weren't clouded by alcohol. And those feelings not only made me sexually frustrated, but they were also tinged with panic. I was almost suffocated by the overwhelming sensation to kiss him.

"Not going to happen, stud," I said, climbing off him.

"You called me a stud." He smiled, jumping up from the floor.

I rolled my eyes.

He pressed his body against mine, his erection pressing into my back. Gently, he pushed away my hair from my face and whispered into my ear, "I think you're beautiful, Avery. I can't wait to count every single freckle on your body." His deep voice rumbled in my ears reaching all the way to my toes.

I shuddered. Damn, I wished I was on top of him again. I turned to face him, letting my guard down just for a moment. I stared at his full lips where a subtle smile had started to curve at the ends. My resolve was dissipating. The reeling of my mind subsided and my mind calmed—and then, *it* happened. His goddamn phone rang.

"Fuck," he swore under his breath. "Don't go anywhere," he growled. He left the room quickly, leaving me flustered. I took the time to gather my bearings. To focus on not doing something stupid like kissing him. I needed to get myself together. Quickly, I put on my jeans and an off-the-shoulder red sweater, trying to gain some sort of composure over myself.

I made my way out to the living room, and Madison was making breakfast while Scott sat at our small dining room table watching every move she made, his eyes filled with adoration.

"Morning, Avery," Scott said as he temporarily removed his eyes from Madison. He smiled widely. "Did you hear I'm going to be a father?" He beamed with excitement as he took a sip of his coffee.

"I did. Congratulations!" Madison glanced back at me, her face glowing. I was happy it was all working out for them. She deserved every bit of happiness that life chose to give her.

"Yeah, and you're not only going to be my maid of honor but this peanut's godmother." She placed the spatula on the counter. Her eyes welled up with tears.

"Oh, Madison!" I embraced her and then Scott. These two had become like family to me, but the thought of being a godmother made me panic. I started to sweat and my chest started to constrict. I didn't know what to do with a baby. I wasn't married. Hell, I'd never really been in a committed relationship, but Madison trusted me with her child. Her faith in me was something I couldn't understand. Since the moment I'd met her, it was like she'd chosen me to be her friend no matter how much of a bitch I was to her or how much I just told her the truth even if it hurt. I wondered why she stuck around and put up with my shit, but watching pieces of her broken life get put back together made me thankful that we had become so close. It also made me hopeful for myself.

"Are you sure that I would make a good godmother?" I glanced between Scott and Madison.

"Avery, I trust you with my life. I trust you with our child's life. I don't care that you work crazy hours or that you have to iron a shirt fifty times before you'll leave the house." She laughed softly. "You will always be one of the most loving people I have ever met." My heart tugged in my chest. Tears threatened to break free, and I quickly fought them back.

"Thanks, Madison," I said. "I'm not sure all of that is true, but I appreciate your confidence in me. And one thing is for sure, I will protect him at all costs."

"Him?" Scott asked from the chair.

"Just a feeling I have. A boy. With your eyes and Madison's hair? How cute would he be?" Scott and Madison grinned at each other. That would give them something to talk about other than me for a while. I was well versed in distracting myself and others from my emotions, and at that moment, I felt like bawling my eyes out. Madison saw things in me I couldn't see in myself. I constantly felt like I didn't know how to love. That I was damaged. But maybe I wasn't after all.

As Madison finished breakfast and chatted with Scott about whether they were having a boy or a girl, I heard Evan's voice. It was a whisper, but the frustration was hard to miss.

"Yes, Mia. Don't worry, I'll take care of it."

"Honey, when have I ever let you down?"

"Okay, I love you, too. Bye."

My heart twisted in my chest. Who the hell was Mia? He rounded the corner to the kitchen, and I hoped he would drop dead with my stare. I had no claim on him, but there was no mistaking the sexual tension between us last night and this morning. I should have known the one time I thought of doing something stupid, the guy would turn out to be a womanizer.

Scott and Madison glanced awkwardly between us, the tension filling the room. The thing with me was when I was angry, everyone knew it. And well, I was angry. I took a deep breath to try to calm myself. I wasn't one to jump to conclusions or be irrational, but there was an aching feeling in my chest. It made me uncomfortable and fuck... my rationality, it went out the window when I almost kissed Evan, a man I barely knew.

"Come to breakfast with me," Evan said. He was now dressed in last night's clothes, and his hair still looked tousled from sleeping.

"No," I said, placing my hand on my hips.

"No?" He eyed me curiously.

"Yes. That's what I said." I tried not to focus on his lips

curved into a scowl. Even looking pissed off, his lips were delicious.

Scott cleared his throat next to me and Madison slapped him on the arm.

"Um, okay then." He went to get his keys and wallet off the table and headed toward the door. I was breathing heavily, my chest heaving with each breath I took. He whipped around before he left. He held the door open, his eyes blazing.

"You know, Avery. It's just breakfast. I'm not asking for your hand in marriage." He smoothed his hair back, and with that, he left slamming the door behind him.

"What the hell, Avery?" Madison glared at me.

"Don't give me that look, Maddie. He was just talking to some woman on the phone. In my house. After I almost kissed him." I gritted my teeth. "Calling her honey!" I stomped into the living room.

"Avery—" Madison interjected.

"I don't want to hear it. This is why I don't get involved with anyone."

Madison glared at me.

"Not that I was going to get involved with him. But look… messes." I slouched down on the couch.

"Avery Elizabeth Grant. That *woman*, Mia, is his sister!" she said, laughingly.

I paused for a moment, taking a second to rearrange my thoughts, and then I groaned. Ugh. *I* had made the mess this time. I groaned again.

"How do you know?" I said.

"He mouthed it to Scott as he came out of the room."

Madison smiled as she sat down next to me. "You are soooo jealous."

"Ugh." I frowned, putting my arm across my face. I *was* jealous. Madison was right. I had been so mad when I heard him talking to Mia, I'd wanted to strangle her and castrate him for leading me on. If this was how Madison had felt falling for Scott, I didn't blame her for almost going mental. But, I reminded myself, I didn't fall for anyone. I couldn't. I wouldn't. I shouldn't.

"You have to meet him for breakfast," Madison said, standing from the couch. "Go make it right." And with that, she walked away. I knew what Madison was saying. I had to smooth it over. Not because I wanted to be with him, but because I had to work with him until this case was solved, and I'd just made an ass out of myself. He wasn't good for me. He made me feel out of control. Something I just couldn't have. My body still tingled from the almost kiss we'd shared. I bit the side of my lip as I thought of his hands all over me last night and my unsuccessful attempt to get him in my bed. He was a good guy. I knew that much about him. I had to at least apologize.

"I don't even know where he was going!" I yelled back after Madison.

"He was going to his partner, Luke Adams's house," Scott yelled from the other room.

Well, I guess that was that. I grabbed my purse and shoved the contents from last night into the bag. I'd usually spend a good fifteen minutes organizing and making sure everything had its place but I didn't have time. I ran out the door with lightning speed and got into my car before I lost my nerve.

Dammit! I slammed my hands against the steering wheel. I didn't know where Adams lived.

An incoming text message from Madison lit up across my screen.

I smiled. It was Adams's address.

Thank God for best friends.

Chapter Fifteen

EVAN

"Why does Avery have to be so incredibly difficult? Okay, so I said I liked that about her, and I do, but she's so hot and cold. I don't know what the hell she wants." I sat at the Adams's table, frustration dripping from my body.

"Evan," Airi's soft voice interrupted my tirade. "You're falling in love." She smiled at me, and then her eyes found their way to Adams. He reached out his hand and took hers in his. She was such a beautiful woman, petite, a hint of color to her skin. Her hair was always down, gently sweeping into her face and hiding the only imperfection that marred her perfect skin. A thin red line stretched from her chin to her right eye. I didn't know how it happened, and neither she nor Adams cared to share. Regardless, she was a beautiful woman, scar and all. After all, didn't we all have scars? Some of us had them hidden on the inside, and others wore them physically on their skin.

"You're delusional. It's only been two days." I sighed,

slumping back in my chair. I'd just met this woman. It couldn't be love.

"Man, love doesn't know time. You're falling hard for her. Any other woman and you would have moved on by now." He stood and put his arm around me. "Welcome to the club, brother."

"What club?" I furrowed my brow.

"The 'whipped for the rest of your life' club," Adams said with a chuckle.

"Luke!" Airi playfully screeched. I envied Airi and Adams's relationship. They seemed made for each other. I didn't know everything about their story, but I knew Airi and Luke had met when he was on a case for the CIA in Japan. I wasn't sure what had made him join the force. All I knew was their story was rough, but love had prevailed for them.

There was a large contrast between the two of them. While Adams was dark skinned, covered in tattoos with a shave close to his scalp and standing over six feet, Airi was petite. She had the biggest brown doe eyes I'd ever seen and stood at five one, and that was being generous. Her hair was a black unlike any I'd ever seen. The strands almost glistened each time she moved. She kept it long, just past her waist, and because of Luke, who made it known that he loved her hair, Airi would never cut it.

"Uncle Evan!" the little voice boomed from the hallway, and I heard the pitter-patter of her feet. She ran in and I swept her into my arms.

"Hana Banana!" I swung her around.

"I just woked up!" she said, yawning.

"I just woke up," Airi corrected, brushing Hana's hair out of her face.

"I see that." I smiled at her, placing her on the ground. She looked just like her mom, her eyes big and round. Her black hair hung loose around her chubby face, and she wore a Hello Kitty nightgown with slippers. She was so stinkin' cute it hurt.

Her eyes beamed when she saw Adams and she squealed, "Daddy!"

"Hey, munchkin. I missed you last night."

"You missed the circus." She frowned at him, and her lips folded into a cute little pout.

"I know. I'll make it up to you." He smiled.

"You better." She wagged her little finger in his face.

I sat back down, looking at Adams's beautiful family. They had accepted me as one of their own, and I was thankful. If it hadn't been for them, last Christmas I would have spent it alone in my crummy apartment, and every meal I ate would have been something fast and cheap. Looking at them, I realized that I wanted a family. I wanted a wife, kids. I didn't care whether they were boys or girls. I just wanted them to be healthy because they'd sure as hell be loved. I pictured a little girl in my mind, her hair red and wild and free, just like Avery's. She'd be stubborn just like her mother, always giving me a run for my money. I smiled. Yep, that would be the life.

"What are you smiling about, man?" Adams asked, his eyes filled with humor.

"Just thinking about having a family." I rubbed my eyes trying to free myself of the thought. I wasn't accustomed to love. I wasn't a manwhore, either, but my job kept me busy and that made love nonexistent. It wasn't for a lack of effort, but most women hated the life of a detective. Adams smiled, shaking his head.

"Yeah, you're whipped already."

"Nah, she wants nothing to do with me." I scratched at my days-old stubble. The doorbell rang, and Hana squirmed off her father, leaping to the ground.

"I get it!" she screamed, running to the door with her long hair flowing behind her.

"Hana Marie Adams, don't you open that door," Adams yelled, following closely behind her. I stood and helped Airi set the table for breakfast.

"I'm so sorry to bother you, Adams, but is Evan here?" *Avery.* The sweetness of her voice stopped my heart, even with its slight quivering. She was nervous. I barreled through the dining room and into the hallway that connected the rest of the house. Their house was a modest ranch. Three bedrooms and two bathrooms. The basement was finished, and Adams and I often spent time down there after Hana went to bed. And yes, they had a white picket fence. I stopped in the entryway. I tried to make sense out of what was happening. She was here. She'd actually come here. Adams smiled and opened the door wider, so she could see me standing there. Hana stood between him and the door and scowled as she looked between us.

"Uncle Evan, why's she here?" Hana asked, coming to stand by me. I picked her up and placed her on my hip.

"I don't know, Hana." I looked at Avery. Her eyes were filled with regret as she tugged on her sweater. "Why are you here, Avery?"

Airi shuffled in, sucking her teeth. "Children and boys, no manners. Avery, please come in." She pushed Adams out of the way and motioned for Avery to come in. "I'm Airi, Luke's wife, and this is Hana, our daughter." Airi smiled warmly at Avery, but Hana continued to scowl.

"Nice to meet you, Airi," Avery said, stepping over the threshold. She came up to me and looked at Hana, her eyes twinkling. "Hi, Hana. I love Hello Kitty," she said, motioning to her night gown. Hana's face softened, and her previous scowl turned into a big grin.

"Me too, Ms. Avery. Let me show you my room!" She tried to wiggle free, but Adams shut the door and took her from my arms.

"Not now, munchkin. Avery and Uncle Evan need to talk." Adams, Hana and Airi walked into the dining room leaving Avery and me in the hall.

I propped myself against the wall, and my eyes focused on her mouth. She was biting her lip. I was still mad that she'd dismissed me so easily earlier. But who was I kidding? I wanted her.

She stared back at me, her green eyes searching for something on my face. She was trying to read me, and I tried my best not to give away what I really wanted, which was to toss her up against the wall and show her just how mad she really hadn't made me. To show her how much I wanted her last night. My cock pressed against my jeans, and I fought back the urge to grab her hair and smash my lips against hers.

"I'm sorry," she managed to croak out, but her eyes

quickly found something else to look at. "I'm sorry I didn't come to breakfast with you but then I heard you talking to Mia—"

"Who's my sister," I interrupted. And then it clicked. She'd been jealous. I smiled at the thought. Despite the overwhelming need to be closer to her, I waited. I remembered that I had almost kissed her this morning, and that *she* had almost let me. My cock pressed even harder against my pants at the thought of her on top of me again. I tried to adjust myself discreetly but Avery glanced down and bit her bottom lip at the action. She was adorable when she was apologizing. But the way she shuffled her feet and constantly pulled on her shirt, let me know she wasn't used to apologizing.

"Yeah. Madison told me that." She frowned and joined me against the wall. We stayed that way for a few minutes— both of our backs to the wall and both of us listening to Airi hum and finish setting the table for breakfast. Hana's laughter filled the silence. My steady breathing was met with Avery's intense inhalations, the sound rocking me to my core. I couldn't take it anymore.

I slid myself in front of her, covering her with my body. My arm muscles flexed on either side of her and I let my knee fall between her legs to open her, to stretch her out. She smiled. She didn't move away, though. Just like the hell on wheels she was, she stood there, her eyes locked on mine.

"So, what you're saying is, you wanted to have breakfast with me, but you got jealous because you thought Mia was my girlfriend." My face was a mere inch from hers. She glanced down at my lips, licking hers.

"Yes," she said breathlessly.

"I haven't known you long, but I wouldn't have ever thought I'd hear you say you were jealous."

"I didn't say it. You did." She smirked.

"You're a pain in my ass," I groaned, rubbing my face.

"And always will be." She ducked under my arms. Dammit, I should have kissed her when I'd had the chance. *Again*.

"Stay for breakfast?" I asked.

"I suppose," she replied with a sly smile. I took in the beauty of the wild woman before me. She looked delicate in her sweater and jeans. The feminine nature usually hidden behind her perfectly tailored suits and practical heels was apparent. She was just Avery. Not an Agent, not the daughter of the head of the FBI. But I knew she was anything but delicate.

I devoured her with my eyes as she stood there, her green eyes sparkling at the want radiating between us. Her nipples poked through her red sweater, and I realized she wasn't wearing a bra. My breath hitched in my throat. I shook my head and put my hand on the small of her back as I led her into the dining room. The moment I touched her, heat pulsed from her and I knew she wanted me just as badly. I just had to get her to admit it. I couldn't help but think Adams was right; I'd join the "whipped for the rest of your life" club, if she'd let me. Regardless, I was fucking screwed.

Chapter Sixteen

AVERY

I sat at the breakfast table, the rumble of laughter and happiness flowing through the air. French toast and bacon filled the space, and my full stomach ached from eating too much. Airi and I had hit it off immediately. She was a strong-willed woman and took absolutely no shit from her husband. I'd liked her from the moment she'd smacked her husband upside of the head for swearing in front of Hana.

Evan kept stealing glances at me as he played with Hana. His eyes lit up every time she said his name. But each time he looked at me, his eyes widened as he took me in. I gave him a playful smile. A thrill rose within me each time he looked at me, but there was also an underlying fear and hesitation that dwelled there. I was unsure about the yearning surging through me. It was all new to me, and for the first time since I was a little girl, I was scared.

I helped Airi clear the table, chatting about their house and how homey it was. I thought in those moments about buying a house for myself, settling down and putting down roots somewhere. I was used to being tossed around after my mom died, jumping from aunt to aunt while my dad moved up the ranks of the FBI. I loved my job and would never give it up, but I desperately wanted to have a place to call home.

I loaded the dishwasher while Airi and Adams wrangled Hana into the bathtub. My mind wandered, thinking of Evan and if he wanted the same things out of life. I wondered if he wanted to settle down. He seemed married to the job like me. We were similar, driven by our careers, but a nagging feeling made me wonder if there was more to life than fighting crime. Maybe there were other things that were more important.

"Hey." A clearing of a throat jolted me back into reality. I closed the dishwasher and turned around, looking at Evan leaning in the doorway. My mouth went dry when I absorbed how good he looked. I had sexual urges often, but Evan was the only man who had ever made me consider something more.

"Can I take you out to dinner tonight?" He pushed his hands in his pockets and darted his eyes to the ground before he brought them back up and looked directly at me. A sinking sensation formed in my chest. I was falling with nothing to catch me. I closed my eyes for a second trying to rationalize my thoughts. Evan was interesting, funny, and we had a lot in common. Something with Evan seemed different and I couldn't help but think that he had some expectations that I just couldn't meet. I couldn't be that woman he wanted, the woman who cooked dinner every night and snuggled in bed. Admittedly, I was getting ahead of myself but for the first time in forever, I cared about not hurting him.

I glided across the kitchen, closing the distance between us. His eyes skimmed over me, uncertainty causing him to tense. I stood on my tiptoes, so I was mere inches from his lips and staring at the fullness of his.

"Just dinner," I whispered, my breath touching his mouth. He encircled his strong arms around my waist, pulling me in. Our lips collided and heat enveloped us. He flicked my lips open with his tongue. That sinful tongue thrust into my mouth and my own met his. I moaned against his lips, and his embrace became tighter and more possessive. My hands found their way to his chest, and I moaned louder, feeling the hardness that lay underneath his T-shirt. We broke free of the kiss, breathless.

A content smile formed at his lips. I backed away, our hands still touching. The kiss was intense. So fucking intense I felt like I was going to have a panic attack. I had to go. This was more than attraction. It was a clawing need. I had to distance myself from the surfacing desire for more.

"This isn't anything, Evan. It can't be anything more than dinner between friends, okay?" His shoulders slumped and his smile faded away. And fuck me sideways if it didn't pull at my heartstrings.

"Relax." I punched him playfully on the arm. "Pick me up at seven. Please tell Airi and Adams thank you." I reluctantly released his hand. My body craved his touch as soon as it left his embrace, but I grabbed my purse and keys and headed out the door. I could have sworn I heard him mumbling, "I'm so screwed," as I walked out the door.

He wasn't the only one dealing with those thoughts. I

just didn't know what the hell to do with them.

No sooner had I made it to my car did Adams and Evan coming running out of the house.

"There's been a fire...." Evan was out of breath.

"Get in!" I reached over and flung the passenger side door open.

"Adams. Follow us!" he yelled out the open window as I sped away.

I glanced back in my rearview mirror, watching Adams quickly kiss Airi and Hana good-bye as he rushed off to another crime scene. I wondered how he did it, kept a family and a career.

I stepped on the gas, sending Evan further into his seat.

"How does he do it?" I blurted without thinking.

"Do what?" Evan glanced at me.

"How does Adams keep a wife and kid at home with a job like this?" I shifted gears with one hand, thankful for the distraction. I wanted to reach for Evan, seek comfort in his embrace to ease my conflicting emotions.

"I don't know. I think it has to do with love." I waited for a smart comment or a laugh but neither came.

"Love," I breathed. I didn't know what love was. I knew what it was for other people. Compromise. Trust. Openness. Time. All things I didn't have. As we sped off to the crime scene, I felt further away from ever knowing anything like Adams and Airi, or Madison and Scott. This was my life. Chaos and crime. I didn't know how to do anything else.

Chapter Seventeen

LORELEI

I stood at the door and listened to the two FBI agents I had kidnapped, Garcia and Marshall. I was proud of my work. I'd lured them under the ruse of a flat tire and took them away from the crowd of people who hovered around the pub. I sedated the weak one first, Marshall. Garcia had sharp instincts, and I could tell immediately as she glanced at her surroundings when they came to help me that she was on alert. I was even more excited to have them as the last two sacrifices. They were special.

Jameson, he just didn't understand. He wanted me to put them back. Like they were an item I stole. Each day that passed he was growing distant from our cause. I couldn't let that happen. We had to finish. Together.

I listened to Garcia and Marshall talking, their backs to me and unaware of my presence.

"Marshall? Marshall?" Garcia called out to her partner. I smiled, watching it all unfold. Garcia's grief, her fear as I watched her head frantically search for her friend.

"Garcia, are you here?" Marshall whispered.

"Save your strength. Just stay still. Talk to me." Garcia affirmed she was the stronger one. She took care of Marshall. Even with her own fear and her own death imminent, she still found the strength to comfort her friend.

"I'm so sorry." Marshall sobbed. "Now look at us." I shook my head. No one would ever expect me to do this. Jameson maybe, because he'd killed his parents and started this entire thing. Not me. I'd been a silent party until recently. Standing in the background observing and taking everything in gave me insight into human nature and what made people tick. Fear and love were always the reasons.

"Hey, it's okay. It's going to be okay." Garcia managed to roll herself onto her side and scoot herself into a seated position. I moved out of the way to avoid her seeing me.

"I should have told Torres I loved him. I shouldn't have hidden our relationship. He thinks I don't love him, and now I'm going to die before I can tell him." Marshall cried harder. There it was: the love.

"Don't say that. We are going to survive, and then you can tell Torres how much you love him." Garcia's response was met with more tears.

"Did I ever tell you that I was born in El Salvador?"

"No," Marshall replied.

"I had two younger twin sisters, Lola and Tallie, who I loved so much." I couldn't see Garcia's face but I knew she was smiling; I could hear it in her voice.

"But when the civil war got really bad, Papa decided

we had to go to the United Nations and seek refuge. To come to America and have a better life."

"And you made it," Marshall said, the smile apparent in her voice.

"I made it. My parents made it. But not my sisters. They died in a fire that was started in our village the night before we were due to leave."

Marshall gasped and my heart pattered in my chest. *Fire*. The next element. This was a sign.

"And that's why I became an agent. I met a woman, Karen Andrews, who worked for the air force and was stationed at the UN when we immigrated in. She took me under her wing. She even got stationed in San Diego where my parents and I ended up living. She pushed me in school, showed me what a strong woman was, and now I'm here."

"Why did you leave then?" Marshall asked.

"I wanted more. No matter how hard I pushed myself, the accomplishments I made, the scholarship to college, it just wasn't enough. It wasn't enough to forget what happened in El Salvador. So, when I left for college, I never went back. Typical case of running away from your problems."

"Why are you telling me all of this, Garcia?" she whispered.

"Because, if I can make it, you can make it."

"You're wrong. That's exactly why you'll make it and I won't."

And Marshall was right. She wasn't going to make it. Well, neither of them were. The last sacrifice had to be strong, and Garcia, she was strong, albeit plagued by the loss of her sisters. I didn't doubt she was afraid too, but she turned that fear off to try to keep Marshall going and that was what Lucifer would want as his last sacrifice, a person who could see beyond their own pain.

Jameson came behind me and put his hand on the small of my back. He gave me a sad look and I nodded. These two were all we needed.

"Shut up with those sob stories. Nothing is going to save you." I walked over to Marshall and pulled her to her feet. Jameson gathered up Garcia and followed behind me to the car.

Jameson opened the trunk and we all stood before it. He looked at me for direction. I was in control now.

"It's time for one of you to become beautiful." Marshall let out a whimper as I held her ropes. "Yes, you. You're my next beautiful sacrifice."

"Tell Torres I love him. Tell him I'm sorry. That I was stupid to hide how I felt!" Marshall screamed to Garcia as Jameson took her from me and shoved her into the trunk. Garcia stayed quiet and let the tears roll down her face.

"You can join your friend and be there when she dies." I breathed in. "Then it's your turn."

"How? How are you going to kill us?" Garcia asked as we crammed her into the trunk with Marshall.

"Fire and earth." My lips curled into a smile as I remembered Garcia's story of her sisters. She'd watched another person she cared about perish the way. I hoped she thought that this was God's way of telling her that she should have died that night. I hoped that fear ate her alive. Because

God, he had no place here. Only Lucifer existed in this world, and he was coming to take her home.

"We need to do this," I said to Jameson as we sat in the car outside of the church.

"This is getting crazy, Lorelei. We should just pack up our stuff and go." He sighed as his eyes took in our surroundings. Cars were all around us, the service having just started moments ago. "The FBI is involved and you just had me help you drag out two FBI agents and shove them in our trunk. It's just a matter of time before they find us," he said, his voice barely a whisper.

"I know, Jameson. But this is our calling. Our one mission in life is to worship a god worthy of our intentions. What better way to honor him than to burn the church that started this all?" My eyes ached with need as I glanced at my husband. He looked so innocent in this moment, so frightened. In the past few days, he had changed. He'd become less invested in the need to kill, in the need to fulfill our task. He shook his head vehemently at my words.

"I'm done." Jameson leaned in closer to me, taking my hands in his. "We could be so much more than people invested in hate. Invested in death."

"Says the guy who killed his parents." I sat back in the seat of the car.

"I killed my parents so I could be free. I'm free now. *We're* free now." He kissed my hands. "Just come away with me. We can start a family. Live out our lives in peace."

"What about worshipping Lucifer? We can't just desert him. He wouldn't be happy." It was my turn to try to talk some sense into him. This had been our mission since day one. Worshipping Lucifer. Giving our all to someone worthy of our following. Not God. God who allowed Jameson to be beaten by his father in the name of love. God who subjected him to things no child should have been in order to save Jameson from his sins.

That was why we needed to do this. Jameson's father ran the church. Devoted his time to a god who was a coward, just as much as Jameson's father was a coward. He was a man who hadn't loved his only child. So many people were lost and looking for guidance, and we had developed quite a following. They kept coming. Many had been lost in a religion that oppressed them just like ours had. But with Lucifer, our followers could be free. They could feel what they wanted. Dark thoughts could be welcomed. That darkness was human nature. And we needed to embrace our human nature.

My eyes met Jameson's, and I knew he was close to defeat, to giving in to my words. Because he knew, deep down, I was right. We had to finish this.

"Fine," Jameson said as he opened the car door. "But after we complete this, I'm done."

I nodded. I watched him from the rearview mirror as he grabbed the gasoline from the backseat and the fast beating of my heart sounded in my ears. The blood flowing in my body tingled in anticipation at the thought of burning the church to the ground.

I heard singing coming from the church. "This is the

day" vibrated out of the doors that seemed so daunting. I remembered being a young girl, stepping in front of this church for the first time and wondering whether these doors were meant to keep people out, or to keep people in. My dad had rushed me in, because heaven forbid we were late for church. I held my head down low like I often did, being the dutiful child that I was. Then his eyes met mine. The boy who knew and experienced so much in his twelve years on this earth. What I found in Jameson, what he taught me, was that those doors, they were meant to keep people in. Once you were inside of the realm of this church, you could never break free.

As the memory threatened my resolve, I gathered the chains from the back of the car and headed to the front of the church. The doors felt heavy in my hands and my stomach turned sour. The creaking of the door made my unease deepen but as the heads turned and looked at Jameson and me, that sour feeling turned into rage. Jameson looked at me and shook his head, willing me with that simple movement not to go any further, but I had no intention of backing down now. I was no longer that eleven-year-old girl cowering behind her father. I was in charge. I held the reins.

"Everyone sit the fuck down and listen." Jameson scurried in front of me, pushing the preacher down on his chair. Gasps and cries ricocheted off the walls as I ran to the few exits, barricading them all.

I moved to the pulpit, all eyes on me, even Jameson's, as I looked out on a parish that followed a man who I knew did not live a godly life. He had cheated on his wife, multiple times, drank to excess, and lied. He was a fraud, a liar.

"You all…" I gritted my teeth, my voice cracking with each syllable. "…you all worship a false god. Show up every Sunday, say a few I'm sorries and think your sins will be absolved." I laughed. "You couldn't be more wrong. Lucifer is the only way to be free." I walked off the pulpit, Jameson trailing behind me, yelling some sort of directions at the people. An elderly woman fainted, and sobs pierced my ears, fueling me even further.

A younger woman ran in front of me, cutting me off. She pulled on the doors that I'd tied closed with chains, sobs racking her body.

"What are you doing?" I asked. "Are you trying to escape?" I turned her around to face me.

She whimpered, closing her eyes. Everyone was quiet, all eyes on me.

"Open your eyes." She shook her head. I knew people feared me; it was something I was proud of. People did what I said because they were scared of what I would do if they didn't. I wanted to know why she was running, what made the fear so significant that she was willing to put her life on the line. Was it survival? I wanted to survive. I longed to live a worthy life not filled with the lies I'd become accustomed to during my youth.

I brushed her long chestnut hair out of her face. "Open. Please. I won't hurt you." I meant it. I wasn't going to hurt her. Her false beliefs, following the wrong god, that was hurting her. It was what would get her killed.

Slowly, her eyes opened.

"There is no escape. You *are* going to die today." She whimpered. "It isn't because of me. It's because of you. Your choices. The god you decided to follow. It's all wrong! It's all a lie!" I had backed away from the girl, sobs coming from the entire congregation. The girl ran back to her seat, clutching her body, holding herself close.

"Stay here. Don't anyone try to leave," I demanded as I exited the church, the doors slamming behind Jameson and me. There was nowhere for them to go. Nowhere for them to hide. They were at our mercy.

"I'll set the fire. You draw the pentagram," Jameson said as he bypassed me.

It was time.

It was time for one of them to die.

I watched Jameson as he grabbed the gasoline from the car. He was so powerful. His muscles straining against his shirt as he covered the gasoline over the earth and church. I wanted him to embrace his power completely, not cower from it and be ashamed of what we needed to do.

I drew the pentagram on a piece of wood I found and placed it far enough away from the church where they could still find it. Drawing it was easy. I could do it fast and with detail, but it wasn't enough anymore. After I had felt that girl's life leave her body, simply standing, watching, talking, wasn't enough for me.

I had to do more.

I found a large branch and shoved it in through the handle of the doorway to the church. When the church burned, they would all burn with it. I smiled as I walked back to the car and opened the trunk. I knew which of the two women I would choose. The weak one. The one who cried the most. Their eyes met mine, and I had no remorse for what I was about to do. It needed to be done. Garcia fought against her restraints, trying to prevent me from taking Marshall. She was strong, making the car move with each shake of her body. Fire burned in her eyes already. But there was something else lingering in them that almost looked like acceptance. It was strangely calming, watching her seemingly embrace her death. But that all changed when I reached for her friend, the one who whimpered and cried for her life. It was sadness I had never seen before. I had seen sadness, despair. This was more. It was regret, a pain so deep that it intrigued me. She would be the last sacrifice. So beautiful and damaged.

I dragged the weak, sniffling woman from the trunk and toward the church, using the extra rope I took from the car and tying her to the tree that stood close. I grabbed some extra gasoline from the vehicle and doused her and the tree in the liquid. Walking back to the car and buckling myself in, I waited for Jameson, contentment surging through me.

"You ready?" he asked as he slid into the driver seat.

"Oh, yes. I'm ready."

"Are you okay?" he asked as his eyes searched my face. I knew I looked crazy. I could feel it. Everything tingled. My entire body felt like it was buzzing and floating on a high that didn't exist except for the fact that I had built the moment up in my mind. Each surge of energy, each ping of excitement let me know that burning her alive would be epic.

"I just wondered if I could do it…. If I could be the one

to set the fire?" I was tingling still, the sensation threatening to overwhelm me. I wanted this. I wanted to be the one to take the lives of these church-going people. People who were clouded by their need for a god who didn't care about them despite the "love" that was preached about.

"Are you sure?" He shifted in his seat. My jaw ticked for a moment liking that he thought I was weak, but I knew he loved me. That he cared for me.

In my excitement, I couldn't speak, and I just nodded as I took the lighter from Jameson's hand and stepped away from the car. Placing the lighter to the ground, I ignited it. It caught quickly and I stood and watched as the church became enveloped in flames. Leaves, trees, people, all of it burned. Transfixed, I was unable to be torn away from the flickering flames.

I heard Jameson calling my name, but I couldn't move. I didn't want to move. Then I heard it: the screams and the pounding of fists on the walls of the church. I closed my eyes in bliss before glancing back at the tree. Horror wrapped around the face of the green-eyed woman who was tied there.

Jameson's face dripped with horror as he dragged me away, his eyes transfixed on the woman burning alive, as if he were just realizing what I'd done. He opened the car door and threw me in, but all I could do was smile at him.

He knew.

He knew what I'd done to that girl. How I'd drowned her.

He knew I'd tied that other woman, the FBI agent, to the tree, leaving her there to burn alive.

And he knew I wouldn't stop there. I couldn't stop there.

I had to fulfil our mission.

I looked at the church again wanting to see it crumble to the ground. But all I saw was the face of Lucifer smiling at me and I knew that I was close to fulfilling my mission. To being one with the only god who had always been there for me.

Chapter Eighteen

AVERY

Adams followed behind us, his car's siren blaring and masking the sounds of my loudly beating heart. My throat felt coarse and dry, and the sweat on my hands made the steering wheel slippery. I struggled to keep a grip on it. *Keep it together, Avery.*

Evan held on to the seat, his grip causing the whites of his knuckles to show. We hadn't talked since we first left the house but his hazel eyes swept over me, a mixture of both excitement and fear radiating from him. I winked at him as I shifted the gears of my car. I was driving fast, the engine of the Firebird roaring with each press of the gas.

My heart stopped beating when we pulled up to the church. It was Sunday morning, and cars lined the full parking lot.

"Service had started," I croaked as Evan and I exited the car.

"I know," he said. We both took in the scene as we

rushed forward to see where we were needed.

The muffled sobs and screaming were overridden by the sounds of rushing water coming from the fire hoses. Firefighters and paramedics ran around the scene, and people ran from the building, falling to the ground like flies.

"Avery!" Madison ran to me, her hand covering her mouth and nose to block out the smoke. Scott jogged behind her, concern apparent on his face.

The fire blazed high. With each drop of water that tried to erase the horrific scene in front of me, the building let out a threatening creak that suggested it was about to cave in. I looked around at the people. The scene was a chaotic mess that seemed to stretch on for miles. The minister crouched in front of his church, his shoulders rising and falling as he forced his tears and his anger deeper inside. I recognized the action. I had to do the same often in my life. Several firefighters were needed to drag the suffering leader away from his dying flock and away from the heat of the blaze, but within minutes, the older man sat dejected in a nearby ambulance.

The disaster in front of us had been caused by pure hate. There was no other way to describe it.

"This is so sad. I just can't—" Madison said. "Apparently the door was barricaded with a log. If the firefighters hadn't gotten here as soon as they did…." Her voice trailed off at the thought.

"We should help," I replied. I wanted to go to the survivors. Some were being treated in ambulances. Others sat, covered in soot and ash, by picnic tables on the far side of the parking lot. But all, all were huddled together, praying to their god.

God. I wasn't sure I believed in him. Was God even a *him*? I didn't know if I'd even really thought too hard about it. Especially because I didn't know if I wanted to believe in an all-powerful being who could and would protect us, keep us from suffering, and help ensure we found happiness. With my history, could anyone blame me? At nine-years-old, I'd buried my mother before having my father shuffle me around from home to home. My best friend and partner had been kidnapped, beaten, and barely survived her father's psychotic behaviors for a second time in her life. And not that long ago, I'd been there when a good agent had succumbed to his mental illness and taken his own life.

No. No, I wasn't sure *at all* if there was a God. How could there be when that being just let this shit happen as he or she sat on his or her ass and watched people struggle?

"I can't go," Madison said, leaning away from Scott and giving his arm a gentle squeeze. "The smoke wouldn't be good for the baby. I'm supposed to be on modified desk duty." Scott nodded. "I'm going to stay back and help the paramedics." I heard Scott breathe a sigh of relief. He bent over and kissed her on the forehead. A simple motion of gratitude for keeping their unborn child safe.

"Good idea," I said as Evan, Adams, Scott, and I rushed over and helped get people to safety or to medical personnel who could help with their injuries.

The flames slowly subsided, their once red and orange hues dimming into a muted grayish white cloud of smoke and ash. Everyone was sent to the hospital and just a few cruisers remained. Crime scene investigators snapped their cameras wildly. The arson squad was leaning against their truck, and I heard them talking about how gasoline was used as an accelerant. It was intentional. There was no doubt in anyone's mind.

"Look." Madison brushed away some debris from the ground and exposed a large wood piece. I glanced up at the church. The building was still standing, hanging on by a thread, "a thread of faith and hope," many of the parishioners had said. We all gathered around to look at the satanic symbol that had been carved into the wood that was left on the ground. This was different than the pentagram we saw on the drowned woman. The five-pointed star was joined by an image of a goat. Horns adorned the head of the goat, and two bodies hung from either horn. The dead eyes of the hanging victims seemed to stare right into each of us.

"Man," Adams blew out a breath. "Jameson is escalating. This isn't like the others. Even from before," Adams remarked as we all stared in silence at the artwork in front of us.

"Isn't that supposed to be a male goat?" Bradley asked.

"You're right. I wonder why it's a female. That has to be symbolic," Madison added. "I can't shake the feeling that Lorelei might be involved way more than we anticipated."

I was beginning to think she was right. The heel print, the goat on the pentagram, it was all pointing in her direction.

This case was different than a lot of the cases we'd heard about at the academy. It wasn't a simple find and apprehend. We needed to get into Jameson's head. We needed to figure out his background and why he was so troubled. Adams took out his phone and started taking pictures from various angles.

We walked around the side of the church only to find a singed tree.

"I guess this is where they found the body on the tree. Burned beyond recognition." Madison went to touch the burned tree, but Scott took her hand in his.

"I can't help but feel like he's trying to tell us something." Madison let go of Scott's hand and touched the tree with hers. "It's still warm," she whispered. "I need to look at his files, like now. There's *something* we're missing."

"That's a good idea," Scott said, moving closer to her.

"Hey, I think it's time we give Garcia a call and she if she can consult. She studied something like this in college. Religion and criminal justice, I think?" I questioned.

"You're right," Madison said absentmindedly, seemingly lost in thought. "Give her a call for me, please? We could use all the help we can get."

"Sounds good." Adams sighed as he joined us again. "Bradley, want to head to the station? The files were sent over this morning. We can all tag team them and get a profile going," Adams said.

"I'll text Torres," Scott said, taking out his phone. "He's supposed to have this week off, but I'm sure he wouldn't mind helping." Scott sent a quick text.

We all walked in silence back to our cars. I handed Evan my keys, and his eyes lit up like a kid on Christmas.

"I need to make a call. You dent my car, I cut your balls off," I said before blowing him a kiss. He chuckled as he opened my door.

I called Garcia as he put the car in drive. Her voicemail picked up on the first ring, and I left a message asking her to call me as soon as possible. I tried Marshall, and again had to leave a message.

"Huh. That's weird." I shrugged as I ended the call.

"What?" Evan glanced over at me, taking his eyes off the road for a minute.

"Garcia and Marshall's phones went straight to voicemail. This job...." I sighed, resting my head against the back of the seat. This case had me on edge. Okay, I had to be honest with myself. It wasn't just the case. It was me. *I* was on edge. I looked over at Evan. I never let anyone drive my car, not even Madison, but there was just something about him that made me want to take down all of the walls I'd built around myself. We were dealing with satanic cults, sure, but the thought of what Evan was doing to me. Well, that scared me shitless.

Chapter Nineteen

EVAN

I couldn't help but steal glances of Avery as we drove to the precinct. Her brows furrowed, and I knew she was deep in thought. I was sure she was overanalyzing everything: the crime scene, Garcia and Marshall not picking up their phones, and whatever was going on in her head where we were concerned.

We were far from anything; she made that clear by saying we were strictly going to dinner as just friends, but after she'd shown up at Adams's door, I'd been hopeful that maybe she wasn't too hidden behind those walls. From the glimpses of desire I'd seen in those pretty little green eyes of hers, I knew there was a part of her that wanted me just like I wanted her.

When we finally made it to the precinct, dusk had settled in. The cool September breeze blowing in through the windows of the car had replaced the hot, humid afternoon sun. Virginia wasn't as humid as Louisiana, though. Louisiana had that sticky air that clung to someone like wet clothes, air that was enough to take a person's breath away each time they stepped outside.

I missed Louisiana, especially since my parents were gone. All I wanted to do was move back into my childhood home and put down some roots of my own. A month earlier, I'd been offered a position at the Shreveport Police Department as lead detective, but I still hadn't replied. I'd been in constant contact with the department. They had given me another week to decide before moving on to someone else. The position would mean a little more money, which would be nice, but something had kept me here. I glanced over at Avery again. Maybe that something was her.

"What are you thinking about?" Avery's voice interrupted my thoughts.

The car idled in my designated parking spot right in front of the precinct. Okay, it wasn't mine per se, but everybody knew that if they parked there, I would have words with them. I took the keys out of the ignition and handed them to her. I allowed my fingers to brush against hers and linger much longer than they were supposed to. My entire body responded each time we touched. My hands grew sweaty and my heart skipped a beat. My groin twitched and I tried to focus on something else other than how badly I wanted her. It was like everything I needed was wrapped up in Avery. I know she felt it too. The way her eyes darted to our fingers as they touched. I wasn't dreaming; Avery and I were meant for each other.

"Just thinking about the heat. My parents. Mia." I looked right at her. "You."

She laughed. "That's a whole lot to be thinking about at one time." She sighed. "What were your parents like?" she asked, ignoring the fact that I had said I was thinking about her.

I shifted in my seat. I hadn't talk about them in forever. It was just too raw. The loss became too real when I started to put into words how they'd meant the world to me and then been taken. But something inside of me wanted to share with Avery everything about my past. To lay my heart out on the line and just hope what I said wasn't too much for her.

"They were the best." I smiled. "The most devoted parents. My mom was a school teacher and my dad a cop. He was so proud of me when I joined the force." I clenched the steering wheel beneath my hands, pieces of my heart tugging at the thought of them. God, I'd loved them so much. "Their love for each other was just as strong as the day they met. So strong, in fact, that the night they were killed in that car crash, they died holding hands." Avery let out a small gasp. "I always wanted a love like theirs." I paused for a moment, trying to sift through the emotions. I did want a love like theirs. That forever kind of love. The kind of love that didn't care whether you had morning breath or that the size of your waistband had gone up over the years. The kind of love that pushed through all boundaries. Their love had been more than just a marriage. Marriage was a piece of paper. Their love had been fate. "Mia and I were lucky to have them. Now, all we have is each other."

"You seem to really care about your sister," she commented as she glanced out the window, smoothing out her hair.

"She's my life now. I take care of her the best I can. I tried to keep the house in Louisiana, but with my parents' debts, me living here, her college tuition and trying to live on a cop's salary…." My voice wandered off. Avery surprised me by taking my hand in hers.

"Hey, you do your best. You've stood by your sister when many men would have just walked away and worried about themselves." She gave my hand a quick squeeze before pulling away. No matter how many times I spoke about my parents, it was like it just happened. I smiled at her to show her how much the comment had meant, and she blushed a little at the attention. *Damn, but she was beautiful.*

"Enough about me. What about you?" I sat up in the seat.

"What's to tell? I work for the FBI. My mom died when I was nine. My dad's the deputy director of the FBI, so I was passed around from aunt to aunt a lot growing up. Not so much love and devotion. Just obligation." She shrugged as she listed off her past like it was her grocery list. I realized it was going to take a lot more than being a shining knight to win her over. Her lack of attention and love from her father growing up made her literally shrug in the face of love. Winning Avery Grant over was going to be a lot harder than I thought.

"Your mom died when you were nine? Wow, that had to be hard." I looked into her eyes, and I caught a flicker of sadness, which was quickly replaced with a hardened stare that could have only been developed with years of practice. Years of practicing how to not feel anything.

"It was. But I managed."

The silence hung in the air. There was so much that wasn't said. So many unanswered questions. But the way Avery kept adjusting herself and staring nervously out the window, I knew not to ask anything else. Her mother was clearly a tough subject. I didn't want to push her away by being too eager.

"She killed herself." Her words pierced through the silence. I looked at her trying to offer comfort, so she could continue on with her story. "She became addicted to drugs shortly after I turned two. My dad was always gone. Too consumed with climbing up the ladder of the FBI to care about his family. So my mom and I were left behind a lot. She dealt with it for a while, but it became too much. Drugs became her outlet to forget." She took a breath.

"Avery, you don't have to tell me this." I took her hand in mine and gently caressed it with my thumb.

"I know, but for some reason I want to share this with you." A small smile spread across her face.

"She started leaving me home alone when I was five. I didn't mind. I learned how to take care of myself early on. I knew something was wrong with her. I told my dad and whoever would listen, but everyone kept saying I was just a kid and had an overactive imagination." She let out a soft laugh. "Well, on October fifth, the year I turned nine, she jumped off the roof of the motel where she'd go to score drugs. Never once did she think about me or what I would do without her. She just jumped." A single tear escaped her eye as she clenched her fists at her sides. I wiped the tear away and took her face in my hands.

"Avery, she was struggling. It had nothing to do with you."

"I know that, Evan. It's just that night has shaped me into this hardened, unemotional being. I don't want to feel anything. Ever. Because the pain I went through in losing her was just too much for me to bear."

Understanding of why the thought of us was so hard for her registered. She'd never let anyone in. "And that's why the thought of us being anything but friends scares you." It all made sense. It wasn't that she didn't want to be with me. She was afraid to feel anything for anyone, for fear that she would lose them.

She nodded.

All I wanted was Avery to agree to be with me. Her walls were secured tight but the fact that she'd opened up to me, ever so slightly, gave me hope that maybe with time she would see that being with someone didn't make her weak. I didn't know what else to say. I wanted to tell her that I would be there for her, but I knew that I was coming on too strong, too fast, so I let my physical impulses take control. Taking her face in my hands again, my lips found hers. Passion and need swirled through our interlaced tongues. Everything Avery was afraid of feeling, I felt with our kiss.

A knock at the window made Avery moan against my mouth. I looked up, and Madison's bright eyes and full-faced smile greeted me.

"Time to get to work, you two."

Avery's forehead rested against mine, her breathing uneven and staggered. She reluctantly pulled away from me.

"Come on, Evan. Let's go do what we do best. This emotional shit is for the birds." And with those words, the moment I'd had with Avery was gone.

Chapter Twenty

The smell of sweat and coffee hit my nostrils as we entered the precinct, and the ringing of telephones and the shuffling of paperwork filled the running commentary in my head. I shared something I had buried deep with Evan. The fear of becoming what my mother became. I cringed, thinking how spot on he was about me when we first met. That I was hidden behind my professional demeanor. I felt Evan's hand brush against the small of my back. My mind was replaying everything that just transpired between us in the car, over and over again causing me to stiffen at the feeling. My eyes shot to Evan's and he smiled at me, that crooked smile that showcased how kissable his lips were. I remembered then, my mind temporarily releasing my fear and anxiety. I remembered the kiss, the parting of my lips with his tongue, the gentle nibble on my lip with his teeth. My body slowly softened against his touch as he rubbed my back with his hand.

Adams opened the door to the musky conference room.

Filing boxes lined the walls and a beat-down conference table filled the middle of the room.

"Here we go, guys. It's not much, but it'll get the job done," Adams said as Evan and Scott dragged in a few chairs from the other room and we all quickly took our seats.

I glanced around at the photos that hung on the walls. The pictures of dead bodies on display for all of us to see. The burned church, the pictures of Lorelei and Jameson. This was the life I chose. A life of death and struggle. A life of heartache. Madison grabbed the files from the center of the table, her eyes stopping at me. She wiggled her eyebrows playfully between Evan and me, and Scott laughed as he sat down next to her.

"All right." Madison opened the file and tried to shift my focus. "Does someone want to write on the board while I talk?"

"I'll do it." Adams stood up and barreled over to the whiteboard that had been shoved behind some boxes. With ease, he lifted it, and carried it to the front of the room, making it visible to everyone.

"Here goes nothing," Madison mumbled to herself.

Madison read Jameson and Lorelei's files aloud as Adams frantically wrote the information on the board. A lot of the things we already knew: his overbearing minister father, who shoved religion down this throat and beat him and his mother up constantly. And Lorelei, the girl who had flown into this life at the most opportune time. He'd been falling apart, and she'd helped put him back together. They'd fallen in love, and Jameson was able to convince her of the hate and wrongness of the church. The lies and deceit that often plagued many religious beliefs and caused them to crumble were the motivating factors for both Jameson and Lorelei. They obviously didn't despise all religions as they'd both found whatever it was that they needed in Satanism. It was darker though, allowing their true colors to show through. Their desire to kill.

Lorelei had moved around a lot until her father, who had moved for work every few years, settled the family in Burke, Virginia. The town became her home. Jameson became her home.

It seemed like the typical childhood rebellion to everyone else, but I knew better. It was deeper than that.

Jameson killed his father and mother at the tender age of twenty-one, his obsession with all things devilish started. He started his cult. For Jameson at least, the cult wasn't a rebellious phase. He was truly psychotic and slowly losing sight of reality. I knew what Madison was going to say, that he hid behind the cult because of killing his parents. He felt guilt, something he didn't know how to process. But by taking Lorelei under his wing, falling in love with the quiet, shy, rule-breaking woman, it seemed to have helped.

"Lorelei was such a good kid," Scott commented as he read more of her file. "Straight As, always obeying her parents, but then she met Jameson and she changed. Her grades slipped and she was constantly missing school. She rebelled. She became the rebellious one."

Madison took out a picture of Jameson and Lorelei holding hands and smiling at each other and placed it on the board.

"They look so in love," I blurted out. Evan glanced at me and winked. I shifted focus back to the picture in front of me. *Love.* That was what seemingly made Lorelei follow Jameson. He let her live, no boundaries. Again, it seemed the cycle I had seen repeated often. Someone loved another person so much, it made them do unspeakable things. Just like my mother, who I was fearful of becoming all because of how I felt about Evan.

"He has a personality disorder," Madison confidently stated. Scott and Evan eyed her curiously, while Adams nodded in agreement.

"Hear me out. I know it's easier to just say he's crazy, and leave it at that, but his view of things changed more significantly once he met Lorelei. His drastic change of commitment to the church, and his obsession with Lorelei and making her believe that the god they had known was wrong and the devil right." Madison took a breath. "Once he killed his parents, his delusions and beliefs took on a deeper meaning. He believes he has to do these things, commit these sacrifices in order to satisfy his new god. It doesn't matter if it doesn't conform to societal beliefs. It is right to him. He made this all up in his head to prevent his guilt of killing his parents from eating away at him." I couldn't help but inwardly grin. I knew that was what she was going to say.

"And his new god is?" Evan asked.

"The devil," I said as I stood from my chair. Silence hung in the room as I walked over to Adams and took the marker from his hand.

"Look, what we have so far are sacrifices. They aren't

just mindless killings. They are serving a purpose." I wrote down all of the killings so far and drew the connection to religion. The names of those who lost their lives tugged at my heart, but especially the Jane Doe—the woman who had been burned beyond recognition. Her name stood alone, unknown.

"Man, that's just crazy," Evan mumbled. "And how the fuck does Lorelei just blindly follow him around like a lost puppy dog? Maybe she's the one behind it all."

Scott snorted. "I doubt that. She seems so fragile, like she is following him. Maybe she's helping him now. Their relationship is so strong that she's willing to do anything for him?" Scott said. "I mean, I'd do anything for Madison." Scott looked at her lovingly.

"Plus those female shoe prints at the second crime scene." Adams added.

"I agree that he's a killer, but he doesn't see it that way. He sees his crimes as a necessity. A means to satisfy his connection with the devil. Now, the way in which the sacrifices are happening are significant. I just can't put my finger on it." Madison took the marker from me and I sat back down as she wrote down each victim's name and how they'd died. Madison squinted her eyes as if that might help put what was staring right at her into perspective. "And Lorelei... I agree that there is something about her. Something specifically that must make her stay. Love sometimes is all it takes." A loud clearing of a throat shifted my focus to the gentleman who had just entered the room. Agent Torres stood in the doorway and I couldn't help but smile. He had become like a brother to me in the short time that I had known him.

"It's the four elements of life. Think about it—air, water, fire, earth. They are what makes the world exist. Without these, we are nothing." He moved to the chair and sat down. "It makes sense. He is trying to sacrifice these women through all four of these essentials. This would then make the devil happy, and he would be blessed by him, if you will."

"Who's this guy? Is he your prodigy, Madison?" Evan snickered and Adams chuckled next to me.

"I'm Emmanuel Torres, Reynolds's partner." He leaned forward and shook Evan's hand.

"Glad to have you, man," Evan said with a nod.

"You're right. It makes perfect sense," I added. "But that means there's only one left before he has completed what he needs." I brushed back my hair in frustration.

"When will it happen? Who will his next victim be?" Madison thought aloud. "And what is Lorelei's role in all of this?"

Scott came up to Madison and embraced her in a hug. "Those, my dear, are the million-dollar questions."

Chapter Twenty-One

AVERY

I tried to engage as much as I could in the conversation about Jameson, but my mind kept drifting between the case and the remembered feeling of Evan's lips against mine. He made me want things I'd never known I wanted. A home. A relationship. All those images had crashed into my mind when his lips had met mine. I had been scared at first, but I was surrounded by happiness, and I didn't care anymore. I felt each barrier, each wall I had strategically placed around myself start to crumble and fuck me, it was terrifying. I scrambled to place my walls back up, but each time he looked at me, each time he gazed in my direction, said anything to me, I felt like I was losing myself. Falling, falling, falling....

With his body so close to mine, I could still feel the heat radiating from him, a sign that his passion for me was burning even when it should be contained. My own body was on overdrive, like it was a runaway freaking train. I couldn't control the impulse to take him, fuck him so hard that he couldn't remember any other woman besides me. Our bodies spoke to each other even when we sat in silence, even when we talked about the deaths of innocent people.

"All right, guys. There isn't much else we can do tonight. We should wrap it up and get some rest." Madison yawned as she placed the marker on the whiteboard.

Murmurs of agreement filled the room. Everyone's eyes held the tiredness and burden of the day as the clock blared 12:30 a.m. The hustle of the precinct was now a low rumble as tired officers dragged themselves home to their families.

"I'll be right back. I have to go grab something," Evan said as his fingers touched my back. Just that simple touch sent my body whirling with thoughts of him between my legs, of me between his. I watched as he walked away, the tight pants hugging his ass just right. I couldn't help but think how I'd love to take a bite out of that. I shook my head, trying to clear it from the sexual desires that refused to leave. I brought my hand to my cheek and felt the heat, the need as it coursed through my veins.

"Where are Garcia and Marshall? Thought they'd be here to help." Torres asked me.

I heard what he said but my brain was still focused on Evan's ass.

"Hum?" I asked as I glanced up at Torres. We started walking out of the conference room as he repeated his question.

"I tried to call them, but no answer. Guess they must be busy on a case they are working on," I replied.

"Huh, I tried to call Marshall, and she didn't answer either. It isn't like her."

I gave Torres a wide smile. "So, you and Marshall…."

I nudged him with my elbow as we exited the building. The muggy air hit us, making it hard to breath. What I wouldn't do for a breeze.

"I don't know what you're talking about," Torres said as he shifted uncomfortably from leg to leg. Torres was a private guy. No one really knew much about him, not even Scott, but the way his mouth had twitched when I'd asked about him and Marshall let me know my hunch had been correct.

I looked at him with understanding. I was trying so hard to fight my pull toward Evan. For the first time in forever, I understood what it was like to feel something for someone deeper than a casual screw.

"Don't worry. They're just busy." He nodded, still trying to not give any of his secrets away. The look in his eyes told me everything he didn't want me to know. He loved her.

"Hey." Madison and Scott came up next to us and joined the conversation. "We're going to head back to the hotel. You good by yourself tonight?" She eyed me curiously. I knew she was wondering if Evan and I would be staying together, but I didn't know where we stood. After the exchange in the car, I felt closer to him than ever, but I was new to all of this mess.

"I'm fine, thanks. See you tomorrow morning?"

"Not until around twelve. We have the baby's first doctor's appointment tomorrow." She and Scott beamed.

"What? Congrats, man!" Torres grabbed Madison and Scott into a quick hug.

"Yeah, sorry, things got kind of crazy. I meant to tell you," Scott said sympathetically.

"No worries. I'm happy for you two." He placed his

hand on Scott's shoulder, quickly squeezing.

"You staying at the Marriott?" Madison asked.

Torres nodded in agreement.

"Follow Scott and me. We're staying there, too." Contentment and happiness radiated from her.

"See you later, Avery," Madison gave me a quick squeeze. "Just let it happen, okay?" she whispered into my ear.

I said my good-byes to Scott and Torres, and I watched as they all walked away.

Madison's hand was intertwined with the man she loved the night before their first baby appointment. Torres held his cell phone in a tight grip, and I knew he was waiting and hoping for Marshall to call or text him.

And there I stood.

I didn't know which way was up or down. My mind was struggling to comprehend the emotions that battered at me. My body didn't give a damn though and wanted Evan, and it wanted him bad.

I walked toward Evan as he spoke to Adams. And what I saw transpire between them overpowered me with such a strong sense of love, of partnership. Evan's hand rested on Adams's shoulder. It was such a simple gesture but all that it meant, all that it carried, radiated from them both as I headed toward them.

"Hey, man. It's okay. We have plenty of help. Especially now that Torres is here. Go. Be with your family." Evan patted Adams on the shoulder. Adam's face was long and forlorn as his hand barely made it into a wave as he sprinted away.

"Is everything okay?" I asked, watching Adams run to his car after grabbing his things and throwing me a quick smile.

"No. No. He's good. It's just Hana's sick." He sighed, looking back at where Adams had just been. "Poor kid."

"Oh, that's too bad. We should send them something," I started to say and then gulped. I'd said *we*. Like *we* as in a couple *we*.

Evan pulled me into his arms. My head rested on his chest as he smoothed back my hair. I listened to the pitter-patter of his heartbeat. The sound was quick and it pounded against the wall of his chest. I gently placed my hand above his heart. He glanced down at me, and a full smile settled across his face like it had been there all along. Just for me.

"You're so thoughtful. *We* should send them something."

I grinned into his shirt.

"I like the way you said we." He pulled away and looked down at me.

Emotion flashed in his eyes as he looked at me. He pursed his lips, readying himself to say something, but that something never came. I hesitated, wanting to ask what he was going to say but it seemed as if he were struggling, pushing back his thoughts. Just when I couldn't take it anymore, waiting for him to speak, he kissed my forehead. I'd seen Scott do this to Madison a lot, and it had confused me. It just seemed so silly. A kiss on the forehead? But oh hell, the moment he kissed my forehead, my panties filled with moisture, and my head reeled with thoughts of Evan and me tangled between my sheets.

"Let's go back to my place," I said confidently. Madison was gone for the night with Scott and there was nothing holding me back anymore. My eyes held the same desires his did. This was it. There was no turning back.

"I won't argue with that," Evan said as he took my hand. I stiffened at first, but Evan gave it a quick squeeze as if he knew my struggle. I was ready to sleep with him. My body had responded to him since I met him days ago, but my thoughts seemed to be propelling me for something more. Something more I wasn't sure I knew that I could even do. But as I looked down at my hand intertwined with his, rightness settled in my chest. They fit perfectly and I couldn't help but think that I sure could get used to this.

Chapter Twenty-Two

Evan

Avery was by far the strongest woman I had ever come across, and that was saying a lot. In the law enforcement field, women had to be extra tough and go above and beyond to prove themselves. The few women in the field I had tried to get to know were softer. The others were the women who were in it for the glory, the title, not the love of the job. Avery wasn't like either of those categories. She was tough, and she loved her job. Avery and I had that in common. The love for what we did.

Avery had the hardness, even the callous nature that was nearing unapproachable, but she wanted love. She wanted to be loved so badly, it hurt me to watch as she struggled with her emotions. Listening to the story about her parents, it was no wonder she distanced herself from all things emotional. It was just easier, and I knew exactly what that was like. Drowning myself in my job was simpler than facing what had happened to my parents. Coping had become a distant thought, and I'd learned to just bury my emotions. But Avery made me want to bare my heart and soul to her. To tell her all my deepest, darkest secrets.

She let me drive her car again, and as we drove to her place, I knew this was it for me. *She* was it. There would never be anyone else who could compare to Avery. All my girlfriends in the past, if you could even call them that, seemed like minor steps on my way to her. I wanted to tell Avery I loved her. Right now. Right there. And I didn't care how absurd that sounded. Sure, we'd just met a few days ago, but I felt it deep in my core. Every time I looked at her, I could see our future, fighting crime side by side and making love every night like our lives depended on it. Every time she said my name, I wanted to hold her. So yeah, this was it for me. It was the type of love that went down in the history books. The type of love that would last a lifetime, through all obstacles, through all hardships. I knew, though, that just getting her to say there was a *we*, was quite a feat. So, for the time being, my love would be something I would keep to myself. I just didn't know how long I could. But the last thing I wanted to do was scare her away when I had just found her.

"We could always just go to your place?" Avery asked as she smiled seductively. "I want to see where Evan Bradley lives," she teased. Her demeanor had changed. Before, I had known she wanted me, but since then she was completely relaxed, her body leaning into me as I drove. She reached out and put her hand over the hand I was using to shift the gears of her car. Her lean fingers slipped in between mine and glided in and out. Who knew that something so simple could be so incredibly erotic? I wanted to stay in that moment forever, but the thought of her in my apartment made me sick to my stomach. She knew about my past and my financial responsibilities because I'd told her in the car earlier, but I just didn't know how much of that I wanted her to see.

"My apartment isn't really Avery worthy." I cleared my throat as I spoke. I half hoped she wouldn't hear.

"What's that supposed to mean?" She tensed against me, and her hand jerked away from mine. I briefly took my eyes off the road and glanced at her. Her eyebrows were furrowed and her lips pressed so tightly together they'd almost disappeared. *Ah, shit.*

"I'm far from high maintenance, *Evan*," she mocked. "You think I care that you don't have money? That you have to work overtime just to make ends meet? Is that what you think of me? Some shallow woman?" She moved closer to me as I stopped at the red light, shifting the gears. I knew her eyes bore into me, and I wasn't even looking at her. Hell, I was too scared to look at her. I thought her stare alone could probably kick my ass.

"Well?" she asked, urging me to reply. I glanced at her from the corner of my eye. Her arms were draped across her chest, lifting her breasts. I gulped. God, how could a woman be so scary and hot at the same time?

"It isn't that. I just…." I gripped the steering wheel. "You just deserve better than what I have to offer. My apartment is a pit. I don't want you to see that. To have to experience that." I sighed. "You just deserve better." I gently pressed on the gas pedal as the light turned green and tried to refocus on the road.

I felt her soften a little, the tension in the air slowly breaking.

"Evan, I don't care if you live in a cardboard box. If this, whatever this is, has a chance of working, you have to let me be a part of your life. All of it. The good and the bad."

I pulled into the parking lot of a Walgreens. I couldn't focus on driving with this conversation. I cut the engine and turned to face her. Avery appreciated no nonsense and was always straight to the point. That's what I was going to give her. My honesty, my frustration.

"Really, Avery? Whatever this is? And I have to let you in? Coming from the woman who wouldn't even give me the time of day? That's rather hypocritical." Love? Yes, this was absolutely love. She was single-handedly infuriating me and turning me on at the same time. I took my hand off the wheel and adjusted my hardened cock. As she looked down at my length pressed against my pants, her green eyes sparkled, and she bit down on her bottom lip.

"I suppose I deserved that." She let out a small laugh. "Listen, we both have to learn to open up, let people in. I know *I* do, and I'm not asking for your whole life story. I'm just asking to go to your apartment."

I groaned. She was right. I couldn't keep her from my apartment forever.

"Fine," I grumbled as I turned the car back on. "We'll go to my place."

"Thanks." She smiled and sat back in her seat.

"But you owe me. Big time." I smiled. I couldn't

believe I was opening up this part of my life to a woman I barely knew. I'd never wanted so much for a woman to like me or want me. As I glanced at her, I couldn't help but push those hesitant thoughts aside as I considered a few ways she could repay me. Mostly involving her lips on mine, her hips grinding underneath me. Ah yes, if that was how she repaid me, payment wouldn't be so bad.

Avery's eyes burned with need as she licked her lips.

"Oh, I will absolutely repay you." I found myself shifting gears and increasing my speed. Now, all I could think about was getting her in my bed.

Chapter Twenty-Three

AVERY

The carefree flirting back and forth between Evan and me continued the entire ride. I didn't know his apartment would be such a sore spot for him, but I knew this was a huge step for him to take me there. Honestly, I didn't care what his place looked like or if he had no money to his name. I had enough to last me a lifetime, and it didn't matter. I still chose to live at the Extended Stay. My mom had had a hefty inheritance. Half a million sat in a bank account with my name on it. That was the only thing she'd left me. Well, besides the potent wounds of losing a mother at nine-years-old.

Even though I had the money, I hadn't touched it. Twelve years ago, when I'd been eighteen, it had been released to me. I'd already been in college, for which I'd received a full scholarship, and I was doing just fine on my own. I figured the money was supposed to make the feelings of my mother's loss go away, but it didn't. Every month when I got that statement in the mail, it was just another stab in the heart. Just another reminder that I was motherless.

We pulled onto Lafayette Street, I did a quick check to make sure my door was locked. Lafayette was one of the worst streets in Burke, Virginia. Sneakers hung from every telephone pole, and the rows of tightly packed houses and apartment buildings looked barely put together. Street lights flickered on and off, masking whatever was hiding in the shadows. Tons of shootings, drug busts, and prostitution stings had been uncovered on Lafayette. I looked over at Evan, but his eyes remained on the road. As for our flirtatious banter, yeah, that was long gone. Silent tension filled my car.

He came to a stop at an apartment building. Out of all the complexes on the street, his was probably the best. It was an all-brick building standing tall at about six stories. Clothes hung on the balconies, and many of the windows had bars covering them. Were those bars to keep people in or out? I wondered to myself.

Two young teenage boys stood outside of the double door entryway. Smoke billowed from their mouths as their gold chains hung low on their necks and flickered with the street lights. Their pants were so low I could see their boxers, and the way they stared at my car made my hand reflexively go to my side to touch my gun. Just to make sure.

"Let's go," Evan said, cutting through the silence like a dull knife. I opened my door, and my boots crunched against the pavement. I glanced down and a used condom and a broken beer bottle were lying next to my shoe. Evan stood in front of me, his hand stretched out for me to take. I took his hand and looked him in the eyes. I tried my best to show him that this was all okay. That I wasn't judging him. I wasn't judging him. Instead, I thought how he deserved so much more than the cards life had dealt him. *Didn't we all though?* I thought as we made it to the door where the two young boys stood.

"Avery, meet Jamal and Andre," Evan said as he took the two cigarettes from the boys' hands. "What did I tell you about these things? They'll kill you."

"Nah, Mr. Evan. Can't kill me anymore than those assholes out here. Always trying to a pick a fight."

Evan stomped on the cigarettes and let go of my hand.

"Nice to meet you, gentlemen," I said with a smile. These kids obviously looked up to Evan. Maybe his being in this area would do some good. So often, these young adults got roped into a life of crime just to survive. They too deserved so much more than what they had been born into.

"Hey, so that's Ms. Avery's car. Keep an eye on it?" Evan said. "I'll be free in a few days, and I'll take you guys to the market. Will you be okay for food until then?"

"Yeah," Jamal and Andre said in unison.

"All right, don't let me catch you guys smoking again." He looked back at them as he put his key into the door and opened it, guiding me inside.

"Yes, sir," Jamal said with a nod. I smiled as the doors slammed shut behind us. Evan pulled on them to make sure they were locked.

"You ready to climb five flights of stairs?"

I nodded and glanced around at the surroundings as we climbed. I tried to breathe through my mouth because it smelled like urine and weed. Paint peeled from the walls, and just like the street lights outside, the hanging overhead lights flickered off and on. Screaming voices vibrated through the walls as we ascended the stairs. Each creak of the stairs and screaming voice I heard made me want to tell Evan to pack his stuff and come home with me. We could work out the rest later. I wanted him to have the life he deserved. The comforts of home and not worrying about money, about work, or about supporting his sister. I wanted to be the person to give him those things. I stopped walking suddenly as that realization hit me like a hurricane. I wanted to take care of him. To be his partner in life. I repeated the thought several times in my head as I stood stock still at the top of the stairs.

"This is me." Evan's voice rumbled through me, jarring me from my thoughts. He'd stopped in front of a cracked, faded brown door and grabbed the mail sitting on the ugly gray carpet. He slid his key in reluctantly and then pushed the door open with his hip after jiggling the door knob.

As he opened the door, he flicked on the lights. I took in the apartment. The barren walls and the stains covering the carpet were the first to grab my attention. The apartment looked unlived in. There were no touches of home, no pictures adorning the walls. It was just a place. Void of anything but a worn-out couch, which looked old enough to have been my grandmother's, two end tables and a coffee table which together made up the living room. Plain beige curtains hung at the windows.

"Make yourself at home." He sighed as he threw his keys on the broken countertop island that was in his adjoining kitchen. "I'm going to change." I watched as he walked away, and my heart began beating loudly in my chest.

I traced the countertop with my fingertips as I walked on top of the squishy carpet leading to the faded tile floors of the kitchen. Everything was clean despite the tattered state of the place. I sauntered into the kitchen and opened the fridge. It was bare except for a few beers lining the white shelves. I grabbed two and popped them open on the counter.

On top of the countertop was tons of opened mail. A letter sat partially opened on the top of the stack. I didn't want to snoop, but it was addressed to Detective Evan Bradley. It had already been opened, so technically, it wasn't snooping, right? I quickly scanned the letter. I felt my mouth go dry and my heart leap in excitement for Evan. He had been offered a full-time detective position in Shreveport, Louisiana—his hometown. The letter was dated over a month ago. Why hadn't he taken it? I heard his bedroom door open, and I swiftly moved to the living room, plopping myself down on the couch. The faded furniture dipped and moaned under my weight.

Evan came over and grabbed the beer from my hand.

"See you found my stash." His lips curled into a small smile. He was tense, his shoulders rounded and his face held a permanent scowl. Why had I made him bring me here?

"I can sniff out beer a mile away," I said as I pulled my feet underneath me on the couch.

Evan sat next to me, and the couch protested with a loud popping sound.

"This damn thing." He punched the cushion with his fist.

"Hey." I took his fist in my hand. "It's okay. This is where you live. I'm totally okay with it."

"I don't care if you're okay with it, Avery. I'm barely okay with it, and I'm also barely ever here. I'm at the station mostly or Adams's house. I just…." He sighed, slouching back into the couch.

"You just what?" I leaned in to get closer to him.

"I just wanted to make a good impression. I really like you." He sat up and moved closer to me, so our faces were only inches apart.

I breathed in deeply. He was worried I wouldn't want to date him after this? I smiled. Oh Evan, I was in too deep to let some apartment scare me away. He smiled at me.

"Why are you smiling? You're freaking me out." He laughed.

"Like I said earlier, I don't care if you live in a cardboard box. Girlfriends are supposed to support their boyfriends no matter what." Oh God. I could interview serial killers and shoot a gun with perfect precision, but uttering the word girlfriend made me want to vomit.

"What?" I asked, patting down my hair. Did I look funny? I was new in the relationship department. Maybe I shouldn't have said what I did. Fuck!

He tilted his head to the side as he studied me.

"Am I your boyfriend?" There was no distance between us now. Our lips were practically touching.

"I don't know. Are you?" Why did I have to be sassy? I wanted to fucking scream, *Hell, yes!* but I had to make him work for it. Just a little bit. I was still scared I'd royally fuck this up, but seeing Evan for who he really was made some of those worries disappear.

He growled as he leaned next to me on the couch, his lips crashing down on mine. I arched my hips as I pressed my body further into his. *Oh, God.* Yes, he was my boyfriend. He was whatever the hell he wanted to be. But at that moment, I wanted him to make love to me. I moaned as he released his lips from mine.

"Yes," I said breathlessly.

"What was that?" he asked with a cocky-ass smile. He slipped his fingers into the back of my pants, grabbing my ass with his bare hand. He moved his hand further down my cheek, lifting me slightly off the couch. His fingers teased the outside of my ass and clit, the moisture touching the tips of his fingers. I said a silent thanks to myself for wearing loose pants today. Easy access and all.

"What would a good boyfriend do, Avery?" His voice was low and deep, his accent causing little goose bumps to form all over my overheated body. He released his hand from my pants. I grew wetter as his voice vibrated to my very core. Not once did he take his eyes off mine. They were hooded and I leaned in close again, so our lips were brushing against each other. But I didn't kiss him. I lingered there, letting my tongue trace the outline of his lips.

"He would take his hands and roam over every inch of my body. *Slowly.*" He groaned as my tongue lashed out and licked his lips one more time.

I moved to his ear and I continued to whisper, "Then, once he got to know every curve, every freckle that covered my body, he would lick me, lap me up like I was the sweetest thing he'd ever tasted." I nibbled on his ear.

"And then," I said, drawing out the tension, "he would make such sweet love to me, I wouldn't even remember my own name."

My eyes found Evan's, and a devilish smile greeted me. His body tensed and his hard thickness pressed against my stomach. There was nothing I wanted more than to get us both to the point of climax. I wrapped my legs around him, his muscles flexing as his hardness pressed against my core. All I wanted was to give us what we both needed. I could already visualize the moment when our climax would crash over us in a cataclysmic moment of pure ecstasy.

I played at the hem of his shirt before pulling it over his head. His muscles were taut as I licked my way down his body, gliding slowly over each part of him. Every inch of my body touched every inch of his as we came together. When I got to his dick, I gripped the outside of his pants with a pressure that had him grinding his teeth. He was ready for me. I put my hand underneath the fabric of his pants and rubbed my thumb along the top of his shaft gathering the precum on my finger. I removed my hand from his shorts and slowly brought it to my mouth, tasting his warm saltiness between my lips.

"Mmm. Even better than I expected." His body relaxed and his eyes turned more carnal, filled with such intensity I thought I would come from his gaze alone.

I loved sex. I loved the feeling of having a man buried deep inside of me, but this, these feelings that had taken me over, were unlike anything I had ever experienced. I wanted to make Evan happy. I wanted him to feel each stroke of my hand against his cock, each thrust of my hips against his. I wanted him to feel my need for him as my nails raked into his back and marked him as mine.

Before I could do anything else, Evan was on top of me, his muscular body pressed against mine. My nipples instantly hardened, and they ached to be touched by him. He quickly grabbed my pants and dragged them down my legs. Before I could react, I heard the tearing of my panties as he ripped them with one hand and threw them across the room. They landed on the stained carpet, and I couldn't have cared less as I clenched my thighs together in anticipation.

I looked down just as Evan's face found its place between my legs. Kisses were brushed against my thighs and I arched my back, seeking contact from his lips on my lower body. My nails dug into his back as he licked between my wet folds. We were as close as two people could be but I couldn't get enough. Every nerve in my body felt exposed as the neurons fired and tingled and screamed in ecstatic pleasure with each brush of his lips. I wiggled underneath him. I wanted more. Much, much more.

"Stay still, baby." He pressed my stomach down and held my hips with one hand, which only added to the tension and the liquid warmth pooling through my lower body. My eyes rolled into the back of my head the moment his thumb found my clit, and his tongue licked the length of me. I let my mind roam free, and I enjoyed the moment when my release came. *No, not enjoyed.* That was too tame a word. I bled for that moment. I let go. I escaped to a place where only Evan and I existed. And that episode in the shower just a few days earlier? That was nothing to the cataclysmic event I had just experienced.

Chapter Twenty-Four

Evan

Watching Avery's body quake as she came was the most exquisite thing I had ever seen. Her hair had come free from her bun and fell wildly around her blushing face. Her moans had been soft at first, but with each lap of my tongue, she had grown louder and louder. Her fists had ripped at my hair as her body shuddered and pulsed, and she'd come in my mouth. Her eyes were glazed over, barely focused on my face as I casually sprinkled small kisses up her toned thighs and flat stomach. I was hard and ready for her, and I knew she was wet for me. It took me a moment to roll on the condom, and when I moved on top of her again, I didn't waste another second. I positioned myself at her opening as I looked into her lust-filled gaze. This first time, I wouldn't be gentle, and she was wet enough that I wouldn't need to be. I thrust to the hilt, and the action caused her to jolt and scream. But not in pain, no. She cried out in pleasure. I moaned as my mouth ravished hers. Instinctively, her hips met mine as I pushed myself further inside of her.

Everything was in unison. We were in complete rhythm, warmth and pure heat overcoming me.

"Baby, I'm right there. Come with me." I took my fingers and teased her clit. She stopped moving to hold on to the moment. Her eyes hooded and filled with desperate need.

"Evan," she said, panting and stilled. "We've got to switch…. I need—"

I knew what she needed. I struggled to get off her, the need for release pounding at me. I sat on the couch as she eyed me seductively, removing her shirt. Her firm tits were showcased for me, and as if my cock wasn't hard enough, it seemed to expand at the reveal. Her nipples were perky, pink and hard, like little candies, and I wanted nothing more than to suck on them, to taste their sweetness. She moved closer to me, her body fluid and sensual like when we'd danced together. When she straddled me, I gripped her legs tightly, my fingers digging into her flesh. She gently placed my cock in her wet pussy, and her moan joined in with the slick sound of our bodies meeting.

"God, you're so big," she cried as she stretched to take me all in. She rode me, her chest brushing against my mouth. I took her nipple in my mouth, gently nibbling as her hips continued to gyrate, pump, and take my cock deeper and deeper into her.

"I'm coming, Evan." She picked up momentum as our slick bodies glided together. I tried to keep myself under control, but as I watched Avery's body take over her normally regimented mind, I was at the brim, ready to explode if she moaned one more time.

"Oh God," she cried out, her body convulsing on top of me. My own release wasn't far behind and I shuddered, feeling the condom fill with my cum.

Avery slowly slid off me, and I could see she had done it reluctantly. Our bodies ached to be close to each other again. I craved her touch, the feeling of her skin against mine. The moment might have ended, but I had high hopes for many more such moments. I looked down at where Avery still lay on the couch. Her lips were turned into a satisfied smile, and beads of sweat glistened down her face. She was stunning. The most beautiful woman I had ever seen.

"What are you thinking?" I asked as I rolled off the condom. I tied it, placed it on the arm of the couch, and pulled up my pants. Avery gathered her pants and shirt and put them on, her smile getting wider.

"I have no underwear." She let out a small laugh. "You owe me a pair."

I pulled her down into my lap and kissed her quickly on the lips.

"Yes, ma'am," I said.

"I'm starving," she said as she moved from my lap and her stomach grumbled. "Let's go get something to eat and head to my place." She finished picking her pants off the floor and redressing.

"Sounds good." I turned off the lights to my apartment, opened the door, and ushered Avery out. I didn't want it to be over. The time I had just spent with Avery was single-handedly one of the best nights of my life. As I watched her step outside of my apartment, I grabbed her arm and tugged her against me.

She smiled as her chest met mine. The rise and fall of her breasts touching me made my dick hard. I wanted nothing more than to be inside of her again, to feel her orgasm release around me. I crashed my lips on hers and she moaned, her tongue flicking in and out. We were masked by the dimly lit hallway, but the bright light from Mrs. Freidmont's apartment danced across the carpet as I heard her door open.

I reluctantly released Avery as she breathlessly smiled at me. I took her hand in mine and guided her over to the partially open door. "Hello Mrs. Freidmont," I said as I stood in the hallway.

"Oh, Evan, is that you?" She sounded surprised to hear me, but I knew she'd been listening and waiting for me the entire time.

"It is." I nodded with a smile. "Mrs. Freidmont, this is my girlfriend, Avery. Avery, this is Mrs. Freidmont, my neighbor."

"Pleasure to meet you, Mrs. Freidmont." Avery released my hand and extended hers for a handshake.

"We're practically family!" Mrs. Freidmont screeched. "We don't shake hands. Give me some sugar!" Her door flew open further and Avery was pressed into her embrace. Avery seemed so tiny compared to Mrs. Freidmont, who was a big woman in every sense of the word. Being a southerner like me, she loved everything fried and had the high cholesterol and diabetes to prove it. She was also dark as night with beautiful black skin and she had a soul as light as the sun. She was kind and strong, and she went to church every Sunday. She also looked out for me. I think I reminded her of who her son could have been when instead, he was serving time for armed robbery.

I laughed as I watched Avery try to shimmy out of her big arms. I had been caught too many times in the same situation, and it was hilarious to watch someone else wiggle underneath her.

"Why, Evan, I never thought I would see the day someone would make an honest man of you. And she's pretty to boot. I can't wait until there are little Evans running around. Oh, with her pretty fair skin and those adorable dimples." She pointed to Avery's face. "Evan, did you see her dimples?" Mrs. Freidmont had her hands on her hips as she looked Avery over, and Avery didn't seem to be willing to move. She just smiled wide, a slight blush to her fair dimpled cheeks.

"That, I did," I said, grinning at Mrs. Freidmont. "They're adorable. Just like her." I led Avery away from Mrs. Freidmont and placed a kiss on her forehead.

"Ain't that just the sweetest thing." She sighed. "You all need to move out of here. She's too pretty to be hanging around the likes of these places." She pointed between us, a scowl forming on her face. "Don't worry about me, Evan. I'll be fine. But you, you just move on out of here."

"She's an FBI agent," I said nonchalantly.

"Well, my word! She can kick your ass, can't she?"

Avery laughed next to me. "I sure can. You should have seen it the other day…."

"All right, now. Enough razzing me. We need to go get something to eat. Good night, Mrs. Freidmont. Keep an eye on my mail for me, will you?" I gave her a side hug and kiss on the cheek.

"I sure will." She beamed at Avery, her face threatening to crack with happiness.

As we descended the stairs, I heard the closing of her apartment door and her muttering, "I thought I'd never see the day that boy would settle down." I couldn't believe it either. I never thought there'd be anyone who would complete me so perfectly. I watched as Avery ran down the stairs in front of me, her fiery red hair loose from the normally tight bun she kept it in. She looked back at me, a smile lighting her face.

"What?" she asked with way too much attitude.

"You're perfect. That's all." I opened the door to the outside.

"Well, aren't you just the charmer this evening. You already got in my pants, Evan." She was such a tease.

"Damn. Mr. Evan, you got lucky?" Jamal still stood in the same spot.

"Jamal," I growled at him. "Behave yourself."

"I'll be back this week. Take care of yourself, and get to school on time. I'll call your principal and ask." I stopped and opened my wallet and handed him a twenty-dollar bill. I really couldn't spare it, but I knew he'd been lying about food earlier. His and Andre's moms were crack addicts and were barely able to keep a roof over their heads, let alone purchase food. I did my best when I could, and I'd made sure they never starved, even if that meant I went without.

"Thanks, Mr. Evan!" he called out to me as I ran to meet Avery at her car.

"You're such a good man, you know that, Evan?"

Avery's eyes locked on mine, and I swear I saw tears pressing against her beautiful green eyes.

"I try," I said with a smirk as I slid into the passenger seat. Avery started the car and buckled her seat belt.

"No, you are." Her tone had turned serious and I struggled to find words to touch upon what she was thinking. I didn't want to focus too much on feelings, on what I thought we could have. That talk had to be on her terms, when she was ready, but before I could form anything into a coherent thought, she spoke again.

"Buckle your seat belt, stud. Let's go get some food." Tonight seemed to be the night for stolen moments, small snippets of time that were too perfect to last. I saw it in her eyes and the way they sparkled. I saw it in her lips as they tried to curve into a small smile. I knew she had similar thoughts to mine. What she didn't know was that I could wait for the moment when she would finally embrace her feelings. But as long as I saw hope in her eyes, I would wait for her to understand that maybe taking a chance with me wouldn't be that bad. As I sat back and watched this complex dichotomy of a woman, I hoped there would be no more stolen moments, just pieces of time that forever fused themselves together.

Chapter Twenty-Five

"Madison, we're over here!" I yelled across the parking lot as she and Scott got out of the car. Evan and I leaned up against his car, which had been picked up by one of the officers from Adams's house. We'd spent the night at my place, ate Chinese take-out, and made love three more times before we were satisfied enough to sleep. It was different with Evan. He took care of me. It wasn't just about him busting his load. Instead, he cared about what I wanted, about what I enjoyed. I'd never come so hard, or as many times as when I was with him. Our bodies were in sync like they had been made for each other. When we were rolling around in the sheets, my mind wasn't focused on anything other than what was going on in front of me and what was being done to me. It all seemed so right. As Madison and Scott joined us against the car, their bright faces made me even happier and a sense of comfort washed over me. *Jesus, what the hell was happening to me?*

"How'd the appointment go?" I asked as Evan put his

arm around me. I glanced up at him and he looked at me, willing me to say something to protest his physical sign of affection. I didn't stiffen at his touch and oddly I didn't say anything. I didn't want to. My mind was quiet for once. Scott smiled widely and Madison twirled her hair as she often did when she was nervous. "It was good. I have to wait to see the doctor, so that might be a few more weeks, but everything else seemed to be going well." She sighed. "I'll have to take it easy though. Definitely no more church fires for me."

"Desk duty." Scott coughed, teasing Madison. "We want to visit my mother and tell her. Since Madison should definitely be on desk duty anyway—"

"Go tonight," I interrupted. "There are a ton of us on this case and it would give Evan and I some time to see what we have for leads." Evan squeezed me tighter and I began to feel suffocated by him near me. It wasn't that I didn't want to be close to him, to have him hold me; it was just different from last night, when our bodies did the talking and we were alone. I wiggled free, pretending to adjust my shoe. *Much better.* Madison snapped her fingers as if remembering something as she released her hold on her curl.

"Oh! I almost forgot! Get this. The nurse mentioned the full moon." Evan and I stared at her blankly. She took a deep breath as she realized she would have to explain. "So, the full moon happens every twenty-eight days, right?"

"Right," Evan and I said in unison.

"So, it clicked when she started talking about the full moon. I think Jameson and Lorelei have been using the four natural elements to kill their victims. Just like Torres said. Air, water, fire...." She listed them off by counting on her fingers. "The only one left is earth. I think that they are waiting until the full moon to sacrifice their last victim." She took in a big breath.

"That makes sense. It would mean more if they timed it according to the moon phases. I heard you were brilliant, but it seems they didn't do you justice," Evan said to Madison as she smiled.

"So where does that leave us?" I asked.

"We need to figure out where they might be and who their next victim could be. We need to stop this before it happens." Scott said.

"Easier said than done," I mumbled. "I do agree though. I tried Garcia and Marshall again this morning, and it still went straight to voicemail. We could really use their help on this case." I sighed. It wasn't like them to not keep their phones on or charged. Something just wasn't right.

"That's weird. Maybe try their office? It's been a few days." Madison found her stray piece of hair once again and twirled it between her fingers.

"I'll call," Evan said. "I know their boss. I worked with him on a case a while back. Why don't you and Madison try to reach out to the ME and get some more information on the bodies? She has the body that was attached to the tree as well and is working on getting a positive ID. I have a hunch that was the intended victim. There also might be some information that hasn't been included in the report on the woman who was found on Gateway Plaza. Maybe that can lead us to where the victims were kept." He paused and smirked. "Careful, though,

I heard the ME's a real hardass." He laughed.

"What morgue? Who's the ME?" Scott questioned as he flipped through the screen on his phone.

"Her name's Dr. Wilson."

"Oh, Shit," Scott mumbled. Madison punched him playfully on the arm.

"Take it you know her?" Evan smiled.

"Yeah, you can say that." Madison laughed lightly. "I hoped it'd be her morgue. I'd love to see her." Dr. Wilson had been the one who'd stormed through and given Scott and Liam a hard time when Madison had been drugged during the investigation of her father. The doctor was little, but damn was she fierce.

"Madison and I will handle Dr. Wilson," I said, shaking with laughter over Scott's fear of such a small woman. "Scott, you stay with Evan and start looking at potential places where Jameson and his gang of misfits might be hanging out."

"You don't have to tell me twice," Scott said. "Torres should be on his way as well." He kissed Madison and then quickly left.

Evan pulled me into him, and I tensed.

"Don't pull this shit with me now, Avery. You're my girlfriend, and I can hug you and kiss you whenever I please."

"Oh, is that so?" I teased, relaxing as I whispered in his ear. I liked him a lot. But PDA, it was new for me. I hadn't even had a chance to talk to Madison about what had happened, and well, I guessed it was safe to say the cat was out of the bag.

I kissed him quickly on the lips and grabbed Madison's

hand as we walked toward her car. I was so flustered that I was about to let Madison drive.

When we got into the car, my breathing was staggered and uneven. I wasn't tired. I was in such great shape, I could run a mile in six minutes flat, but Evan, he did things to me with his sexy little accent. On its own it made me feel like I couldn't breathe.

"Okay, spill," Madison said as she started the car. Her eyes were full of wonder, and I knew I couldn't get out of giving an explanation.

"We're going steady. He gave me his letterman jacket." I rolled my eyes.

"Smart-ass," she said with an equally exaggerated roll of her eyes. Then she beamed at me. "I knew it though. You guys carried that tension around, and that cloud threatened to strangle everyone."

"What? I didn't say we had sex!"

"You didn't have to. The way he just held you... girl, he is *so* familiar with your body." She wiggled her eyebrows. I rested my head against the back of the seat as she drove. God, was I that transparent? I had fallen, and not only had I fallen, but I'd fallen really fast. Even when I'd tried to keep my distance from him, I couldn't, and only days later, I had a boyfriend?

"Oh, you've got it bad." Madison smiled, but she kept her eyes on the road.

"Got it bad?" I questioned.

"You actually like him." Her tone had shifted from playful to serious, and my heart thumped in my chest. I did like him. That was my current issue. I never liked any man for any length of time. I didn't need to care about anyone else other than myself. Everything I knew about relationships had been picked up from the dysfunctional one that my mom and dad had. I saw some through Madison and Scott's relationship, but it wasn't exactly conventional either. But their affection, their devotion even through hundreds of miles of distance was something that even made me want to swoon. They'd had a whirlwind romance, but they also had a past together. That was what made them stronger. *Something I don't have with Evan.*

"Avery, it's okay. I know it's scary. Trust me." Madison took one hand off the wheel and grabbed my hand in hers. "Love doesn't know when it's convenient. It just sort of walks right into our lives. But when love does walk into our lives, we can't turn our backs on it." She gave my hand a quick squeeze before she let go. She was right. God, why did she have to be right?

At her words, my heart pounded so loud I thought Madison must have been able to hear it. I turned on the radio hoping to drown out the emotions that were overwhelming me. "At Last" by Etta James filled the car, and Madison laughed. I laid my head back against the seat again and closed my eyes. Even the universe was trying to convince me. The question was whether I was going to listen.

Chapter Twenty-Six

Evan

"Good afternoon, sir. This is Detective Evan Bradley with the Burke, Virginia PD."

"Hey, son. How's it going? Long time no talk!" I heard the assistant director's chair creak.

"All is well. Thanks." I hadn't wanted to call him, but Avery was worried about Marshall and Garcia, and I knew he would be able to get ahold of them.

I hadn't spoken to him since that last case, one that knocked us all on our asses. A drug ring had been active right here in good ol' Burke. It had been a hell of a case, and it had left two of our officers and an FBI agent wounded in the line of duty, but we'd managed to shut them down before it got any worse. I glanced at Scott who motioned to his watch to hurry the phone call up. We'd made our way back into the dingy conference room and started mapping out the possible places Jameson and Lorelei could be. We'd also been waiting for Torres to show, and since we had some new information about the timing of the murders, we wanted to act.

"That's good. Sounds like you're in a rush. What can I do for you?" he asked.

"I was just wondering if you could help me get ahold of Agents Marshall and Garcia. We are in need of their assistance for a case."

"Haven't heard from them. They were off duty this weekend and aren't due to come in until this evening." He paused. "Now that I think about it, I tried to call Garcia last night and it went straight to voicemail. Marshall too. Is everything okay?" Assistant Director Collins asked. I didn't know what to say to him. I didn't want to lie but I wasn't 100 percent sure what the hell was going on either. My eyes darted to Scott.

"Thanks. I'm not sure what's going on yet."

"I'll try them again and put some feelers out to some other agents. If nothing pans out, I'm having their phones tracked. I'll be in touch," he said as he I hit End on his phone.

"Fuck." I started to pace. My mind was reeling with the information that I just received. This was not going to be good. I opened my mouth to speak.

"Hang on, man." Scott came up behind me and placed his hand on my shoulder. "Settle down. Torres is here and should be a part of this conversation."

The door squeaked open and Torres entered the room. His suit was wrinkled and his five-o'clock shadow looked like a permanent fixture on his face. He seemed like the type of man who was always put together, and I had to wonder what was bothering him.

"What's wrong?" Scott asked as they sat at the worn conference table.

"I haven't heard from Marshall in days." Torres's eyes darted between Scott and me.

"I know." Sadness filled my voice.

Scott and Torres's eyes snapped to me, but I continued pacing. "Assistant Director Collins just told me he hasn't heard from them since Saturday, when they left to come here." I stopped in front of the conference table, leaning my body down against it.

"What the hell? It's Monday morning." Torres slammed his fists on the table. "Didn't he think it would make sense to reach out to find out where they might be?"

"Apparently they didn't have to report in until this evening. But he hasn't been able to reach them either," I commented.

Torres swore under his breath.

"Am I missing something here?" Scott questioned. "Are you and Marshall a thing?"

"No." He looked down at his hands, and a pregnant pause filled the room. I pulled at my shirt collar, the weight of his answer suffocating me with its tension.

"Well, yes. She wasn't ready to tell anyone. But we've spent all that time together, with you and Madison, and we just clicked. It just happened. Now, something's happened to her and I've been fucking too far up my own ass to realize it."

"What do you mean?" Scott stood.

"I just have this feeling." He stopped talking. Scott and I stared at him, and we waited for him to finish his thought.

But he just looked at us. His shoulders slumped, and defeat was written on his face.

"They came here to meet Madison and Avery. Marshall was mad I couldn't get away from my obligations to come down with you for the week we had off, so she ignored me all Saturday morning, but then, that evening she was talking." He paused. "We were having an argument on the phone and she had to quickly get off. Something about someone having a flat tire and Garcia was going to help them." He ruffed the bit of beard that was starting to form on his face.

Scott sat up straighter in his chair.

"Torres, why the hell didn't you tell us this yesterday?" he asked angrily, flinging his arms up into the air.

"I didn't put it together until this morning. I thought she was super pissed at me and ignoring me." He slammed his fists on the table. Torres stood up and paced.

"Jesus, I'm an idiot."

"Calm down, man," I said to Torres.

"Okay, we'll figure this out, Torres. What else did Collins say?" Scott asked me as he crossed his arms over his chest.

"He said that they are setting up the IT guys to track their phones. Hopefully the feature is still enabled, and we can find out where they are located, but you know how it works. If the phone isn't on, we can't track it. That's what we're working with right now."

"Jesus." Scott ran his fingers through his hair. "Madison and Avery are going to flip."

This guy looked like he belonged on the cover of *GQ*

with his sandy blond hair touching right at the tips of his ears and his bright blue eyes, but he chose the life of fighting crime. I knew I wasn't bad on the eyes, but I was a man's man. I had darker features and a hardness about me. I liked to fight and get in the mess, and Scott always seemed to be deep in thought, analyzing everything. He and Madison were perfect for each other. They'd protect each other at all costs.

"We're not going to tell them," I said as I straightened myself up.

"What?" Scott gripped the sides of the chair as Torres shook his head next to him.

"Bad idea, man," Torres mumbled. "Madison and Avery will kick your ass when they find out."

"I know, but listen. I'm not saying we won't tell them. I'm just saying hold off until we have more information." I sat down across from them, leaning forward. "Madison has already been through so much. Avery is just, well, Avery." Scott and Torres's lips both hinted at a smile with that comment. Avery was a firecracker, and with this news, she would storm the whole goddamn city until Marshall and Garcia were found, and we still didn't know if they were in danger or what the fuck was going on. All I knew was that it was strange that they hadn't checked in.

I knew this wasn't a good idea myself, but I figured waiting until we had more information would be the best. In the short time I've known Avery, I knew what her reaction would be. She would want someone's head on a stick.

"I don't like hiding stuff from Madison, or Avery for that matter. They deserve the truth," Scott said as he eyed

Torres and he nodded in agreement.

"They are stronger than you think, Bradley," Torres replied.

"Hold up." I stood up. "I'm not saying they aren't strong. I'm just saying we need more information before we drop a bombshell like this on them." Scott still shook his head while Torres stared at me.

"Torres." His eyes refocused on mine. "Wouldn't you want to gather more intel before telling Marshall something like this?" Scott grunted and Torres sighed.

"We can't keep it from them for long though. A day tops," Scott said.

"That's all we need in order to do a little investigating. They will have their hands full today with Dr. Wilson and we can go to the Down Under Pub and check surveillance."

Torres and Scott nodded in agreement.

"Thanks for trusting me."

Scott and Torres mumbled their acceptance.

I couldn't risk that Avery would fly off the handle and jeopardize this case. I had to have all the facts lined up before I let her know what was going on. Maybe then we had a better chance of finding Marshall and Garcia. Now, if I could keep her at bay for just one more day.

My phone vibrated in my pocket with an incoming text message.

Avery: Hey, stud.

I grinned as I went to type out a reply. It vibrated again in my hand.

Avery: Any word on Marshall and Garcia?

I clutched the phone tighter in my hands. This was going to be harder than I thought.

Chapter Twenty-Seven

By the time we pulled up to the ME's office, Evan still hadn't texted me back. *It's fine,* I kept telling myself, but my anxiety for Marshall and Garcia grew. I had tried to call them again and still received no answer. Madison had tried to talk it out with me logically, but in reality, she was more concerned than I was. I could tell by the way she gnawed on her fingernails. That particular habit was so disgusting, but as I'd watched, I'd almost wished I had some bad habit like nail biting or hair twirling so I could calm my fried nerves.

When we entered the waiting room, I immediately regretted not bringing my jacket from my car. I had my long-sleeved button-up shirt on, but the ME's office was kept cold. *For the bodies,* I reminded myself. I shuddered at the thought. I was used to seeing dead bodies, blood, you name it, but my mind was reeling with different thoughts than usual. Emotions tugged at my depths, and I didn't know whether to cry or laugh. I was used to being in control of everything, and the past few days had taken me out of my normal, comfortable routine.

I glanced around the room as the lights flickered and a buzzing sound filled the air. Madison moaned next to me and shook her head, obviously lost in thought about what went on here. I approached the empty desk and gently tapped on the bell when the buzzing sound temporarily ended.

"Be right there!" The cheerful voice vibrated through the halls. It was like an echo bouncing off the pale, empty walls.

A petite woman with fashionably gray hair and sparkly red glasses came through the swinging doors that connected the waiting room to the rest of the office. She wore a white lab coat covered in splotches of blood. Her black spiky heels gave away more of her personality, and I knew she was tough shit. She was an ME after all, on her feet all day long and I knew for a fact heels like those were not comfortable. She walked with such confidence and determination that it was clear they didn't bother her. She was a force to be reckoned with.

I glanced at the name embroidered into her lab coat. *Dr. Wilson.* So, this was the infamous Dr. Wilson. From what I'd heard, she had nearly kicked Scott's and Liam's asses that night she'd found them fist fighting like a bunch of teenage boys after Madison had been drugged by her father. Scott had said that Dr. Wilson hadn't laid a hand on them, or even raised her voice, but she'd been "scary," and looking at her now, I knew exactly what he meant.

"Madison, my dear. You look wonderful," Dr. Wilson said. She shuffled over to Madison and placed two kisses on her cheeks, careful not to touch her with her coat. Madison and Dr. Wilson had kept in touch since, and the way Madison spoke about her, it was obvious she saw the doctor as a mother figure. They'd chatted and had lunch together as often as their hectic schedules would allow.

"This must be Avery." She walked over to me and gave me a kiss on the cheek. Physical attention of any kind always made me uneasy, so I tried my best to stay still. I knew I felt like a statue. Every muscle in my body tensed under her touch.

Dr. Wilson gave me a knowing nod. *God, how could she do that?* She looked at me only briefly, but it seemed she saw all the way down into my soul. I shifted my weight. She smiled and went back over to Madison.

"So, how are things? How's your uncle?" I thought I caught a glimpse of a blush forming when she mentioned Assistant Director Harper, Madison's uncle. He had been the one to send Dr. Wilson over to check on Madison when she'd been drugged by Walsh.

"He's okay. I haven't seen him since my graduation. It's hard finding time with our crazy schedules and him mainly being in New York." Madison frowned.

"Yes, I know how that is," she said with a sigh. I nudged Madison with my elbow and wiggled my eyebrows. I couldn't help but think there was a thing going on between Dr. Wilson and Madison's uncle. She held back a smile and nudged me back to shut me up.

"Actually, I have some news, and I'm glad I get to share it with you in person," Madison said. "I'm pregnant!" Dr. Wilson gasped and took Madison into the biggest bear hug.

Love and happiness flowed from Dr. Wilson, and suddenly, my own feelings hit me like waves in a storm as they crashed against me. I thought about my mother. About how I was so alone. *If I ever have children, who would I go to? Who would be happy for me?* I felt selfish for even thinking these thoughts because Madison had lost her mother too, but standing, looking at her and Dr. Wilson, I wanted my mother. I wanted the woman she had been before she'd become addicted to drugs and ruined her life because my father couldn't see beyond his obsession with his work. But I would never have that. I would never have a mother or a father who devoted their time and their life to their child. I had myself, and I had my job.

My job. I have my job. I recited this phrase over and over in my head. *How can I have been so fucking blind?* I shook my head as I realized I had become the one person I had always resented: my father.

"Avery!" Madison's loud voice pierced through my thoughts.

"Yes. Sorry, I was thinking," I said as I looked up from where I stood. Dr. Wilson and Madison held the double doors open waiting for me to join them. Had I been that distracted that I hadn't heard Madison calling my name?

"I noticed," Madison said sympathetically. With her eyes, she asked me if I was okay, and I gave a curt nod. "Come on. It's time to see the bodies."

I dragged my feet behind me and reluctantly followed. The waves still flowed and pulsed through me as I walked deeper into the building. I tried to push them back, but they still lingered, and I knew that they weren't done with me yet.

Madison and Dr. Wilson chatted in front of me as Dr. Wilson's spiky black heels clicked against the concrete floor. We entered through another set of swinging doors and were greeted by two rows of bodies that lay on the metal surgical tables. Most of them were covered by a white sheet, but three of them were exposed. Dr. Wilson stopped in front of the first.

"God, that's so awful." Madison shook her head and looked away briefly. Dr. Wilson eyed me curiously as I continued to stare at the badly charred body without a hint of emotion. I pulled back the sheet to get a better look at the remains. There wasn't much of her left. She was unrecognizable, but there was no mistaking the fact that she had once been beautiful. Her essence seemed pure, full of life, and the shape of her cheekbones and the structure of her face seemed familiar.

"Any ID on this victim, yet?" I asked as I placed the sheet back over her body. Madison's phone rang again. "I'll be right back. Doctor's office." She scurried out the double doors.

"None yet. She came in last night and I just pulled the blood work. It takes about forty-eight hours for an ID, so I should have it back tomorrow."

"Forty-eight hours? This is an active case. Surely, it can be expedited," I said matter-of-factly.

"Usually yes, but with all the recent deaths, and this being a smaller town…." She rolled her eyes. "Well, we always get the shit end of things."

"Wow." I shook my head in disgust. We had a serial

killer who needed to be apprehended and politics were getting in the way. I had a feeling if this case were in Boston or New York, resources would be at our fingertips.

"I know. Trust me, I've tried to put through expedited requests, but nothing yet. I've only received the normal bullheaded response."

"Anything else?" I moved over to the next body. I knew we'd get nowhere having a pissing match with upper management. My father being one of them. I glanced at the woman on the table and recognized her as Francine Dewitt, the first victim.

"Nothing yet. She will be harder to find any evidence on due to being burned, but this victim here, I noticed a few things." I took out the small notebook I always carried around in my back pocket. I removed the pen from the lining and shifted my mind to focus on the body in front of me.

Dr. Wilson took a breath.

"Under her fingernails, I found residue." She pushed up her glasses with her finger and put on gloves to hold up the victim's hand. "It had traces of soil on it, so I sent it out for sampling." I jotted down the information, but turned to glance at Madison when I heard the double doors swing open. She came back in without saying a word about her doctor's call and stood right beside me.

"Let me guess. Forty-eight hours?" I said snidely.

"What's going to take forty-eight hours?" Madison asked.

"The results for the blood tests to ID the burn victim and the drowning victim, and the soil samples."

"Unbelievable," Madison mumbled as she shuffled to the next victim. She put gloves on and took the hand of the drowning victim in hers. "Looks like there is residue under her nails as well." Dr. Wilson looked from over her glasses and smiled.

"Seems there is, Dr. Harper," she said proudly as she worked to gather the evidence. "I will send those off today as well. Thursday, we should get all the information back."

"That's just one day before the full moon," I reminded Madison.

"At least we know the timeline and aren't just sitting twiddling our thumbs. We can still try to piece information together and work the profile." Madison removed her gloves and was texting on her phone. Although she was talking about the case, her face stretched in a full smile. We weren't going to get any more information off the bodies today. It looked like we would be playing the waiting game.

"What did the doctor say?" I asked.

"That everything looks good and she wanted to schedule a follow-up appointment." She beamed. "We'll get to hear the heartbeat and see the baby." Instinctively her hand went to her stomach.

"Oh, that's so great!" Dr. Wilson said as she put the cap on the vial that held the newly found evidence.

"Yeah, I was just texting Scott to tell him. He's been so worried about everything. Me, the baby, my job." Madison folded her arms over her chest to comfort herself.

"It is all a big change," I said as I checked my phone for any messages. There weren't any, which pissed me off.

Scott, Evan, and Torres were together, and I knew Scott was texting Madison. Why wasn't Evan texting me back? Okay, I sounded like a jealous, needy girlfriend, and I hated myself for even thinking that way. I shook my head to whisk the thoughts away.

"Are you going to move to be closer to him?" Dr. Wilson's question made Madison's eyes get big and wide.

"I-I-I'm… n-n-not sure," she stuttered. Madison hadn't stuttered out of nervousness in a while.

"You should move," I said, surprising even myself with those words. Madison looked at me and tilted her head to the side.

"I should move?" Madison asked, her face a mask of confusion. She played with the stray curl that always seemed to find its way out of her ponytail.

"Yes, you should. You guys should move. His mom lives out in Connecticut." I nodded my head in confidence. "You're lucky to have a family who loves you, Madison, and wants to be with you. Don't let that go." Heat rose in my body. What the hell was coming over me? Usually, I'd be telling Madison not to restructure her life for any man, but there I was telling her to up and move.

"What about you?" Madison asked. Dr. Wilson pretended to be focused on something with her microscope. The way her eyebrows scrunched and danced around her face gave away the fact that she was too busy listening to our conversation to be really concentrating on what was in front of her.

"Me? I'll be just fine. I'm married to the job,

remember?" I shrugged as I glanced at my phone, which had started to vibrate in my hand. I saw Evan's name pop up on the screen. *Finally.* Madison kept talking while I clicked on the message. I heard nothing she said. I was too focused on the words and reading them.

Evan: I can't stop thinking about you. Your face, your freckles. The way you can kick my ass with just your words. You're everything I ever wanted Avery.

Evan: 75 BTW.

I texted back a reply.

Me: 75. What does that mean?

What did he mean by seventy-five? My phone buzzed in my hand almost instantly.

Evan: The amount of freckles you have. I counted last night and I kissed every last one of them.

My heart stopped in my chest. He'd counted my freckles?

"Are you even listening to me?" Madison glared.

"Uh." I tried to think of something to say, but it was useless. I hadn't been listening, and she knew it.

"You know what, Avery?" Madison said as she put her hands on her hips. "Maybe you should take your own advice for once. Just tell Evan you like him." She sighed. "You aren't alone. Even if I move to Connecticut, you are still my best friend. My soul sister. My partner in crime. And Evan, well, he's your soul mate. Your other half. Just like you said to me. Don't let that go because you're married to the job."

I let her words sink in. As usual, when it came to love, she was right. I didn't know what to do. What to say. I couldn't talk to him without being a complete bitch in order to hide behind my emotions. I was good at building more walls around myself. But I couldn't help being a bitch or building those walls because in a very short time, I had come to enjoy being with Evan Bradley, and that terrified me. It was a need. And when you needed something, and that something got taken away, you'd be left broken, afraid, confused... rejected. It was a feeling I had known my whole life. Only a few people had broken through like Madison who'd come into my life. Her friendship had shown me that I was worth more than being married to the job. Worth more than being a good agent and catching criminals. She had shown me, and was telling me again, that I really was worthy of Evan's affection.

"You're right." I was stubborn. Madison knew it. I knew it. I was sure Evan was catching on.

"I do like him. I'm just scared." I squared off my shoulders and owned up to my emotions. I, Avery Grant, was scared. Not scared of being shot, dying, any of those normal things. I was scared of my feelings.

And with that, Dr. Wilson dropped her act of paying attention to some scientific breakthrough on her microscope and turned to face me with a great big smile. Madison's eyes brightened and she skipped over to me and gave me a quick hug.

"It's okay to be scared. That's what makes life so exciting and worth living," Madison said with her almighty wisdom.

I smiled but that fear buried itself deep. I didn't even know *where* to begin. I knew I had to start somewhere. At least own up to my feelings. Not just for him but for myself as well. To prove to myself that I was more than an agent. That I was a woman worthy of love.

Chapter Twenty-Eight

EVAN

The rest of the day went by uneventfully as Scott, Torres, and I chased dead ends. Adams took a sick day, poor Hana had to stay at the hospital for a heavy dose of antibiotics to kill her pneumonia. People kept calling in to the precinct claiming they'd seen Jameson or Lorelei. It was one of the things I hated about the job; the mass panic that happened when murders and crime escalated. People started seeing things that weren't there, which resulted in the phone ringing off the hook at the precinct. That was exactly what had happened.

We spent most of the day talking to people about what they'd seen. That always ended the same. Simple cases of misidentification. The last woman who'd called in had told us Jameson was holding her hostage. The task force was sent out, but when we'd arrived on the scene, it had been an absolute shit show. The woman's boyfriend had been there smacking her around, and her kids had been screaming and crying. It had been a fucking mess. Now, I had a stack of paperwork a mile high due to a domestic violence dispute that hadn't brought us one step closer to catching Jameson.

Not to mention, we had gotten nowhere on figuring out what had happened to Garcia and Marshall. They should have checked in. Oh, and the cell phone trace? Yeah, that had been a huge no go.

At least Madison and Avery had had some luck, but of course, the small-ass town made it near impossible to get evidence any quicker than forty-eight hours. It was going to take that long to get all the residue samples and identifications of the victims we were waiting on, and that put us all in the position of sitting on our asses waiting for the full moon. That more than anything made me think about moving back to Louisiana. I still had the job offer to work for Shreveport's police department sitting on my counter. They wanted me to run things, and even though it was a small town, being in charge would mean I'd have access to changing things and ensuring the process was a smooth one.

My thoughts of home cut off abruptly by the ringtone on my phone.

"Bradley," I answered. It was William, the owner of the Down Under Pub.

"Tapes are ready. Come on down," William said.

"Excellent. Thank you. We'll head over there right now." I hung up the phone and continued driving.

"It was William from the pub. He wanted to let us know we can get the surveillance tapes tonight," I said as I made a U-turn to head toward the Down Under Pub.

"Great," Scott said from the passenger seat, but he was

texting on his phone, and he seemed a little distracted. "Hey, do you think you guys could hold things together for the night and tomorrow?" Scott asked as he put his phone back in his pocket.

"Definitely, man. Doesn't seem like we have anything to do but look at the tapes and just sit around and wait," Torres said from the backseat.

"Yeah, no problem," I said. "You two going to go see your mom?" I asked. "Connecticut right? I heard it's nice out there."

Scott smiled at my comment regarding his childhood home. "I think so. Maddie got a call from the doctor's office saying she's healthy and already made the next appointment. I can't wait to see the baby, hear its heartbeat." Scott smiled again as he took off his glasses and placed them in his breast pocket.

"She and Avery will meet us over at the bar. They're wrapping up some paperwork."

I stifled a groan. I had paperwork too. I glanced at the clock on the dashboard. It was only 4:00 p.m. After we finished up at the bar, I could head back to the precinct and tackle it, but all I wanted to do was to take Avery back to her place and make love to her again. Last night had been amazing. While she'd slept, I'd counted every single freckle on her body and kissed every last one of them. That was the only time that sassy ass mouth of hers wasn't running and the only time she wasn't trying to overanalyze things. Everything had been so rushed our first time, I'd barely had a chance to see her fully, to really look at her.

I wanted to undress her. Sure, I had gotten to do that last night but I wanted to do it slowly, take my time with each piece of clothing, peel it from her body with ease and precision. She deserved the attention as I fucked her with my eyes. But it was more than that. So much more. I didn't want a simple screw. I wanted to hold her, cherish her, lap up every ounce of whatever she was willing to give and bottle it up and carry it with me. Always.

On second thought, maybe that paperwork could wait until the next morning.

When we finally made it to the pub, William told us to order some dinner and drinks while he finished gathering the tapes, on the house of course. We eagerly sat down at what Scott had called their "usual table" in the corner and ordered burgers and sodas. What I really wanted was an ice cold beer. I wasn't used to having other guys at my back other than Adams. It was nice to have them with me, chatting and shooting the shit, waiting for the food to come.

For a Monday evening, the place was packed. Bodies flirted on the dance floor, taking up every inch of space. They masked the view, so it was nearly impossible to see the bar. People waited impatiently for their drinks, and a few murmurs of impatience ricocheted off the walls.

"It must be college night," Torres said between swigs of his drink. I glanced at the bar again and noticed the shirts and sweaters all riddled with the words *University of Virginia*. The giggling girls and the smell of heat and sweat added to the ambiance. I agreed with Torres. It was definitely college night.

"Let's just eat and get out of here," Scott suggested as he motioned for Doreen to come over.

"Hey, sexy. Where's your girl? Decided to go for a real woman?" Doreen purred as she sidled up next to Scott. Tonight, she had on a hot pink halter-top dress with lipstick to match. Scott shook his head and laughed.

"She's on her way, Doreen. Any way we can get this food in a hurry?" Scott asked.

"Anything for you." She winked and walked away. Doreen was something else. She was crude, but she was fun and harmless.

Less than fifteen minutes later, Doreen came back with our food, and we devoured it, barely saying a word to each other. I glanced at my phone and checked a quick text message from Avery.

Avery: Stuck in traffic. Be there in 15. :*

She used a kissing face emoticon? I was afraid my face was going to crack with the big-ass smile that stretched from ear to ear, and I ran my fingers over the keys of my phone to type out a reply. Maybe make a comment about how I couldn't wait to spend the night with her again, but before I could, I heard movement near our table.

"Are you guys cops?" I looked up from my phone to see three college girls standing next to our table. Scott shifted uncomfortably in his chair, and Torres looked unamused. The girls were hot. Not just your average hot, but supermodel, Gisele Bundchen hot. The way Scott kept clearing his throat and running his hands through his hair, I knew he thought they were hot, too. As the tension rose in the room, I had a

GEN RYAN

strange feeling this wasn't going to end well. My mind shifted
to Madison and Avery. They would be here any minute. I had
to get these girls to leave.

"Yep," I replied, trying to give them the hint we weren't
interested with my one-word answer. It didn't matter to me
that they were tall, thin, and fantastically gorgeous. I had a
fantastically gorgeous woman, and none of these girls would
ever compare to Avery.

"That's awesome," the middle one said. I didn't know
what her name was, and I didn't care.

"I'm Felicia by the way." I inwardly groaned. Now she
had a name. She and her friends pulled up chairs, and her blue
eyes sparkled as she sat down next to me. Her green-eyed
friend, who looked like some Indian princess with her long,
dark braided hair and ebony skin cozied up to Torres and the
other one, well, she'd found her place next to Scott. Her boobs
were enormous and clearly fake. Just like the bubblegum
pink lipstick that was all over her plastic lips. The girl's body
probably cost more than I was worth.

Scott shot me a look that was everything I was feeling.
Trapped and totally screwed.

"This is Yvette." She pointed to the girl next to Torres.
"And that's Cassie."

"Nice to meet you, ladies, but we are rather busy," Scott
said as he took another swig of his drink.

"Doesn't look like it. You guys look lonely," Cassie
said as she crossed her long legs, hiking up her already too
short miniskirt.

"And single," Yvette purred as she pointed to her ring

finger. Scott coughed, choking on his soda.

"We aren't single," Torres said matter-of-factly as he sat back into the chair. He folded his arms across his chest. I grabbed my soda and sipped it slowly, trying to give myself something to do. *Why couldn't this be something stronger?*

"If you aren't married, you're single," Felicia said, a coy smile forming on her full red lips. She took my beer out of my hand and downed the rest. I nearly lost my shit. I was just about to say something when I glanced over at Scott. He had put his glasses on as he read a message on his phone. His hair fell into his eyes, and Cassie went to sweep the strand of hair away.

"Don't touch me," Scott said from clenched teeth. Torres sat up in his chair as a wide smile spread across his face. The girls sucked their teeth, shocked that someone would tell their friend to keep her hands off them. It was apparent these girls weren't used to getting shot down.

"Excuse me?" Cassie said, her mouth wide open in shock.

"I think you heard the man." We all whipped our heads around, and there were Madison and Avery. Avery's arms were crossed over her chest, and her face was beet red. Madison clenched her fists at her sides as she looked between Scott and Cassie.

"Who the hell are you?" Cassie asked as she stood up from the chair.

"I'm that man's fiancée." Madison pointed to Scott. "So, if you don't move your ass away from him and take your little friends with you, there is going to be a problem." Cassie laughed.

"You're his fiancée?" She looked Madison up and down. "You're fat." *Oh fuck.* Cassie scrunched her nose. Scott shot up from his chair and grabbed Madison just as she went to lunge at Cassie. Shit was about to get real.

I was half paying attention to Felicia as I listened to Madison growl like a damn lion. Scott whispered something in Madison's ear that seemed to calm her down. Felicia rubbed my arm, and then it happened and well, it seemed to happen in slow motion. Avery grabbed Felicia by her arm and pulled her out of the chair. Felicia looked up at her confused as Avery motioned for her to step outside. The people on the dance floor separated and watched as Avery and Felicia hurried across the floor to the side door that led to the alleyway.

We all rushed after them, barreling through the crowds of people who were gawking at the scene unfolding in front of them. The cool breeze blasted our faces as we exited out into the alleyway. The buzzing of cars whipped through the air. As the door slammed behind us, Cassie jumped and Madison tried to lunge at her again.

I watched as Avery and Felicia spoke. I don't know what Avery was saying but Felicia was white as a ghost.

"Man, you'd better stop her," Torres said as he stood back and watched. "Before she does something stupid." We all just kind of stood there, watching Avery scare the life out of a woman who was much larger than she was. I think we all had the same thought. We were too fucking scared to stop her.

"I'm sorry. I didn't know," Felicia sobbed as Avery turned her head to me, smiled and rolled her eyes.

"It's all right. Just have enough respect for yourself to stop hitting on a man when he says he's not interested," Avery added.

Color returned to Felicia's face and her eyes widened. "I don't need relationship advice from you." She looked at Avery up and down. I watched as Avery went rigid.

"Avery, it's okay." I went up behind her and wrapped my arms around her shoulders. She softened and slowly diverted her eyes from Felicia. Avery took a deep breath and closed her eyes, gaining her composure.

"You fucking bitch." Felicia spat the words in Avery's face, her fire returning. Avery tensed, her hands forming fists at her sides. Strands of Avery's red hair broke free from the neat bun.

Taking a deep breath, Avery let out a sigh. "She's not worth it," Avery whispered as she unclenched her fists and walked away from Felicia.

Torres shepherded Cassie, Yvette, and Felicia, escorting them to their car; mostly for their own safety rather than gentleman's courtesy. Madison and Avery still looked like they were out for blood as they huddled together, their faces contorted into a scowl. As the girls got further away, Scott and I both released Madison and Avery.

"I can't believe you guys let those little girls sit with you," Avery commented, trying to regain her composure. She let her hair down all the way, and she smoothed out her shirt. Her hair was so beautiful and full when it was down. I wished she'd wear it down more often. It made her seem softer and kinder. Traits I knew she tried to bury, but that were so much a part of her.

"Can't blame them, Avery, for trying. These are some good-looking men," Madison said as she hugged Scott. He smiled as he played with her hair. He tiled her chin and kissed her gently on the lips. She blushed and snuggled in deeper to him.

I chuckled.

"You're crazy, you know that?" I said as I grabbed Avery into a hug. She tensed briefly, but softened as I moved her hair out of her face.

"I wanted to ruin her pretty little face." Avery shrugged. "But composure, decorum, FBI rules, yadda, yadda, yadda." She snickered.

"Why?" I tilted her chin up so she could look at me. "Did it matter to you?" I wanted her to say it. To say that over the past few days I had grown on her. That maybe she cared more than she let on. Sure, those girls had been hot, but they weren't Avery. No one would ever come close to her.

Something that looked like confusion or hesitation flickered in her eyes. I softly placed my lips against hers and kissed her slowly, trying my damnedest to stifle any hesitation that was lingering. I didn't know what I was expecting but it wasn't this. There weren't tongues darting out. We weren't grasping at each other's bodies. The kiss was different. It held so much. It held the words she couldn't say: she cared.

As I released her lips, her eyes opened and the flicker of confusion and hesitation were gone. I saw, for the first time since I'd met Avery, something that looked an awful lot like happiness.

"Yes, it matters to me," Avery said as she walked away. I trailed behind her, the most contented fucking smile plastered on my face and I didn't give a damn who saw it.

"Hey, we're going to head to my mom's now. Get the eight-hour drive over with. We should be back in a day or so. Keep us updated on the case, okay?" Scott said as Madison and Avery moved to the side to chat.

"Sounds good, man. Drive safe." Scott patted my shoulder.

"By the way, Torres just texted me. He took a cab back to the hotel."

"Got it," I acknowledged.

"Are you ready to go?" Avery asked, releasing Madison from a hug.

"Yep, are you done trying to fight people?" I teased.

"Never," Avery said as she kissed me on the cheek.

With Madison and Scott off on their journey to Connecticut, I ran back inside to grab the tapes from William. He was slightly pissed off that there had been yet another fight because of Madison and Avery at his bar. Another fight? I'd have to ask Avery about that one.

As I walked to my car, I glanced up and saw Avery sitting across the hood of the Subaru. Her hair still hung loose and past her shoulders and the moon reflected off the redness of her hair. I remembered the first night I'd met her and how I'd daydreamed about making love to her on the hood of my car. I smiled.

"What are you smiling about, stud?" Avery asked as I approached her.

Against my better judgment, I threw the tapes in the car. I should have headed right to the station to watch them, but my mind focused on the hot redhead sprawled out on the hood of my car. There were no leads on the case. Sure, Torres had a hunch, but I didn't work on hunches. I needed facts. Scott and Madison were taking a day off. What would happen if I took a night off, too?

I walked back to Avery, and I pushed my body between her legs and ravished her mouth. My tongue darted in and out, and I gently tugged on her lower lip with my teeth. Avery fell back against the hood of the car, and I was on top of her. I couldn't stop. I didn't want to stop, and the soft mewing noises coming from her mouth let me know that she didn't want me to stop, either. I had nothing to say to her. Not now. Everything I had to tell her had to be done with my body. Avery opened her eyes and the lust there let me know I was doing a hell of a job showing her. My mouth found hers again, and I knew by the way my cock pressed against my pants that I had to get her home, and fast before we were arrested for indecent exposure. *Yep, I'd be taking the night off.*

Chapter Twenty-Nine

GARCIA

I kept my eyes closed, listening to the sound of my own heart beating. I was alive. I was thankful for that, but Marshall. Oh, God, what happened to Marshall? I hoped that maybe she survived, that I'd get out of this and see her smiling face again, listen to her arguing with Torres and try my best to give her relationship advice. I'd give anything for that.

The door opened and I kept my eyes shut, praying that whoever it was would leave me alone.

"I know you're awake." I opened my eyes and stared at Jameson. He looked like I felt: beaten, scared, broken.

"Are you thirsty?" I nodded as he brought a bottle of water to my lips. He was different than I imagined he'd be. He seemed kinder, more understanding than Lorelei.

"Why are you giving her water?" Lorelei barged through the door and slapped the water out of Jameson's hands. He sighed.

"She hasn't had water in days. She'll dehydrate,"

Jameson argued.

"So? She isn't our guest. She is here to fulfill our mission, not to test our hospitality skills." Lorelei moved toward me and I pulled myself up on the beam I was tied to.

"Oh, you think you're so tough?" Lorelei laughed. "I bet you thought your friend was tough. What was her name...?" She cocked her head to the side. "Ah, Marshall."

"Don't." I shook my head. "Don't bring her into this."

"She was brought into this when I burned her alive."

I couldn't keep the tears at bay anymore. I let them fall silently.

"Don't cry, sweetie." She grabbed Jameson's hand. "It was for Lucifer. It's all for Lucifer."

Her delusions were far worse than I could have imagined. She'd turned to Lucifer, the devil. Lorelei rubbed her face, pulling her hair and pacing the floor. She was coming undone, trying to stay focused on her task.

"This will be your last night alive because tomorrow, you will be sacrificed." Lorelei walked away, slamming the barn door behind her.

"You don't have to be afraid, Garcia. It's going to be okay." Jameson smiled at me.

"Desiree," I croaked.

"What?"

"My name is Desiree," I said.

"Okay." Jameson walked toward the door and paused. "Desiree. That means desire."

"It does."

"I beseech you therefore, brethren, by the mercies

of God, that ye present your bodies a living sacrifice, holy, acceptable unto God, which is your reasonable service."

"Romans 12:1?" I asked. For a man who had given up on God and turned to Lucifer, he remembered scripture and recited from the heart. It was in his eyes, his hesitation. He was struggling with disowning a god he once knew so intimately. "You don't want to do this anymore, do you?" I asked, hoping to engage him in conversation.

He glanced back at me, sadness slumping his shoulders.

"Jameson honey. Let's go." I heard Lorelei's voice again.

"Get some sleep, Desiree. Tomorrow's your big day." His voice was filled with sadness as it broke with his words.

The door closed behind him and once more, I was alone with my thoughts and demons. I pushed them back though, as much as I could. I hoped that I'd get another moment with Jameson before I became the final sacrifice. I understood his struggles, his conflict with the church and God. I'd lived it when my sisters were taken from my family. When we were subjected to violence, rape, famine, all because of where we lived. I also knew that the hate you felt toward a god that you thought was supposed to protect you was dangerous and could lead you down the wrong path, just as it did Jameson and Lorelei. But if I could reach him, I knew I could bring him back.

Chapter Thirty

EVAN

"How's Hana?" I smiled at Avery's question. She had only met Hana once but she seemed taken with her. Hana was like that though; she just wrapped everyone around her little finger.

"She's better," I said, turning down the music. "They're staying at the hospital so she can get the IV antibiotics. It's quicker and more effective."

Avery nodded. "Have Airi and Adams been there since yesterday?"

"Yeah. They don't have any family here so it's just them. And neither want to leave her."

"Let's go there. Give them a bit of a break. They can at least run home and take showers or something."

"Seriously?" I came to a stop at the red light.

"Yeah." She nodded with a small laugh.

"I just figured you'd want to finish up the case and all that stuff."

Avery eyed me curiously. "There isn't much we can

do right now. We've combed through everything and are just sitting ducks. Waiting."

"Yeah," I said, anxious for the light to turn green. "I know you want to wrap this up." I paused. "Damn. I do too"

"Evan."

I quickly looked at Avery. The sternness in which she said my name gave me alarm.

"What I really want to do is fuck you right in this car." My dick twitched. Did Avery really just say that? "But we can't always get what we want, can we?" She had the most devilish smile on her face.

"I think we can get what we want. It's only fair. I mean, you can't say that to a man and then not follow through." I shifted and started driving again.

She laughed. "I'm going to follow through. I will have my way with you later. But…" She hesitated and I dreaded what was going to come next. "…Adams and Airi need to know they have people who care about them. Family is important." The way she solemnly said those last words tugged at my heart. Well hell, when she says it like that, it made me feel bad for thinking otherwise.

"I agree. Let's go for a visit." Avery smiled and turned up the music. She hummed along to the song, seemingly carefree for the first time since I met her.

When we arrived at the hospital, Adams and Airi were surprised to see us.

"Man." Adams slapped me on the back as he pulled me into a quick hug. "You didn't have to come. I know this case is keeping everyone busy."

"That's what friends do," Avery said. "Plus we're waiting on results."

Adams nodded. "Damn forty-eight hours," he mumbled.

"Language!" Airi scolded.

"So we came here so you two can take a break. Go get dinner or something," Avery suggested, sitting next to Hana on the bed.

"Ms. Avery, do you want to color with me?" Hana looked even smaller in the big hospital bed, her voice crackly and sleepy.

"I'd love to color with you." Avery swung her feet on the bed, snuggling closer to Hana. She handed Avery some crayons and the two started coloring.

Airi put her small arms around my waist. "She's perfect, Evan".

I knew Avery couldn't hear Airi but she chose that moment to look up at us and she smiled, her green eyes sparkling. She was perfect, every damn thing about her. As I watched her with Hana, I saw flashes of what our life could be like. It'd be a while until we got there but I was a patient man.

I sat and watched Avery and Hana color and watch TV. I knew she worried about being a godmother to Madison and Scott's baby but watching her with Hana, she was going to be amazing.

Avery and Hana colored and played dolls for a bit before Hana finally fell asleep. Avery stayed in the bed the entire time, enjoying the bit of normalcy.

"Hey." Adams stuck his head in, Hana snoring peacefully on Avery's lap.

"Hey." Avery smiled and stroked Hana's hair. "Guess she was tired."

"Guess so." Airi held up Hana's head as Avery shimmied out from the bed.

"You ready to go?" I stretched out my body from the past hour of sitting in the stiff hospital chair.

She moved closer to me and whispered, "Yes, I have a promise to follow through with." A sly smile formed on her lips.

"Call if you need anything guys." I grabbed Avery's hand practically dragging her to my car. I did my duty as a friend and now intended to satisfy Avery in every way imaginable.

When we entered her house, it was silent. Not the uncomfortable silence, just the all-knowing kind. The kind that held the promise of something great. For the first time it seemed Avery was content.

"Follow me, stud."

I trailed behind her as we went into her bedroom. She pushed me gently down on the bed and stood in front of me.

"Sit," she demanded.

I couldn't take my eyes off her. Her hands moved to the hem of her shirt, gently circling the rim before making its way over her head. I reached out for her and she swatted my hands away.

"Patience." She didn't smile or take her eyes off mine. She reached for the button of her pants, unclasping them and shimming her way out. Though not before turning around and giving me a magnificent view of her round, perfect ass.

Avery turned around and stood before me in a red thong and matching bra. I wanted to touch her. To see if she felt as hot as she looked because hot damn, she was on fire.

My aching dick was painful and I was afraid I'd come just from looking at her.

"I'm dying here, Avery. Please," I begged and she grinned at me. That cock-tease grinned at me. It wasn't one of my finer moments, but seeing her slowly undressing, I couldn't keep my shit together.

"I'm going to make you come, Evan. You can't touch me. That's the rule." I gulped because I knew she'd do it. I knew she'd hold me true to the promise of not touching her. I just wondered if I could handle it.

She slid her panties down her toned legs and moved to release her bra. Her newly released firm breasts stood at attention, taunting me. Slowly, she removed my pants and my dick sprang out.

As if knowing what I needed, she glided over to me, wrapping her legs around my waist. She straddled me, my dick pressing against her opening. I went to grab her hips and pull her down but before I could, she ripped open a condom and slowly rolled it on my throbbing cock. I groaned at the sensation, just the quick touch of her hands on my shaft making me want to moan with pleasure.

"Easy, stud. I've got this". She gently slid herself down my shaft, the most delightful moan escaping her lips. The sound of her slick center filling the silence.

"Can I kiss you?" I couldn't believe I was asking permission but she seemed to need to be in control, and fuck me, I'd do anything to not have this end.

"No." She groaned out more, her hips moving quicker and faster.

"Fuck, Avery, you feel so good."

She yelled my name and I took a deep breath trying to keep myself from releasing. I didn't want this to end. Ever.

"God, Evan, you're so deep." She moved herself up and down, back and forth, her slick wet folds seeming made for my dick. It was the best sex I'd ever had and I wasn't even touching her. I just watched her, felt her, and experienced each part of her body taking what was hers.

"I'm falling for you, Evan." I couldn't even respond; I came so hard so fast I was pretty sure I wouldn't see straight for the next hour. Avery didn't move from my lap. She just sat there, breathing heavily as I took in her words.

She was falling for me.

I smiled. If she only knew how much those words meant to me.

"Baby, I've already fallen," I whispered into her hair.

She faced me, relief apparent on her face as she smiled at me. This was it. This was all that I needed to be happy. I knew now why I didn't take that job in Shreveport. Being with Avery was my new home. My new forever.

Chapter Thirty-One

EVAN

The sun danced off Avery's freckled body. I lay in bed and looked at her as she rested on her stomach, her back completely bare and exposed. The sun accentuated every part of her. She appeared so vulnerable, completely unaware that I looked at her so intently. Her guard was down, and I brushed her red hair out of her face to focus on her freckles. Her face held a small smile, and she looked peaceful, calm and happy.

The clock flashed noon, and I silently eased out of bed. I checked my phone and flipped through some messages from Torres. He was at the station working on some leads. I didn't want to wake Avery, so I headed out to the living room and put in the tape from the Down Under Pub, silently thanking the Extended Stay for the outdated VCR and DVD combo. I made myself some coffee, sat down on the couch and watched as drunk people staggered across the screen. It was the same thing for what seemed like forever, but I glanced down at my phone and saw only twenty minutes had passed. Sighing, I stood from the couch and headed to the bathroom.

"You've got to be kidding me!" I jumped, practically zipping my manhood in my pants at the sound of Avery's voice.

"Motherfucker." Avery's voice grew louder and there was no longer just a hint of the frustration I'd caught before. It was full-blown anger. I ran out of the bathroom and saw Avery standing in front of the TV with the screen paused.

"What's wrong?" I asked as I slipped my arms around Avery's waist. She spun around, her eyes blazing and anger burning me to my very core.

"You knew." She punched me square in the face and I fell onto the couch.

"Knew about what?" I held my face in my hands, adjusting my jaw as I stood. Fuck me, Avery could punch. I watched her quickly shake out her hand as she paced.

"About Marshall and Garcia being taken." Avery clenched her fists at her sides, and I closed my eyes quickly, bracing myself for another punch. When it didn't come, I opened my eyes and pushed myself back into the couch a little more. I felt around on the couch for my phone. Where the hell was it? I'd left it right there. And then, it all clicked.

"You have my phone," I stated.

"Yes, I do." She held it out to me, and I grabbed it. "Torres texted while you were in the bathroom, and I checked it. I thought it was something important about the case. He was wondering if you found the proof that Marshall and Garcia were taken." Avery pressed play on the remote control.

"What do you see, Evan?" Her voice was calm and

even. She didn't raise it and that was scarier than if she'd screamed bloody murder. Actually, I would have preferred that. I had seen some shit in my day, been in some precarious situations, but I had met my match.

I tried to calm my frazzled nerves as I tore my eyes away from the woman who, just a half hour ago, had been sleeping peacefully next to me. I stared at the TV screen and what I saw, made my heart rate quicken. I began to sweat and I knew that I had blown it.

"I thought it would be better to wait to tell you when I knew for a fact." I took a breath as I watched the scene unfold in front of me.

Lorelei was sneaking behind Marshall and Garcia. Everything seemed fine, but then, like a whirlwind, Garcia fell to the ground and Marshall joined her not too soon after. I looked at Avery's face, her eyes glistening with tears watching her friends fall to the ground. I fucked up. I fucked up badly. I should have listened to Scott and Torres when they said this was a bad idea. But I had only wanted to protect her, to shield her from the worry until I was certain.

"Avery." I went to stand and head toward her, pushing aside the tug of doubt that I shouldn't even try. I had to do something. I had to *say* something. She shoved me again, her red hair flowing like fire around her reddened face.

"No, Evan. You can't kiss your way out of this one." She cursed under her breath and yanked her cell phone from the table. Every movement she made was fueled with hate, but when she looked at me, her eyes were hooded and filled with something beyond hate. Something much more meaningful and gut-wrenching: disappointment. "If I hadn't been so wrapped up with you and your fucking gorgeous body and fantastic accent, my friends might still be alive." I cringed at the words. "I should have known it would end like this. It would end before it even started. Just when I convinced myself that maybe I should give my feelings some consideration, you go and prove me right. That relationships are just messes." She took a deep breath. "So fuck this shit and fuck you for thinking you know what would be best for me."

"I'm sorry. I just…." I had my tail between my legs, scrambling to fix the mess I had created.

"I don't want to hear your apologies." She held up her hand to halt me from continuing. "I'm getting dressed and heading to the precinct. I suggest you do the same if you care anything about my friends and seeing they make it home safely." Avery slammed her bedroom door, the vibration shaking the generic stock pictures that hung on the wall.

"I'm an idiot," I admitted. "A goddamn idiot." I gathered my things and headed to the bathroom. I shifted my mind to focusing on the case, bringing Marshall and Garcia home safely. Because that was my only hope for forgiveness.

Chapter Thirty-two

AVERY

"Fucking son a bitch! I can't believe I let some hot body distract me from my job, Madison!" I cursed into the phone as I quickly dressed. "Garcia and Marshall are out there, and we had no clue! No clue! I was grinding against him, practically throwing myself on his dick!"

"I just can't even process this right now." Madison paused on the other end of the phone. "Marshall and Garcia, taken." I could feel her emotions through the phone. I heard her sniffle, and Scott's gruff voice offering soothing words.

"What are we going to do, Avery?" Madison asked. "I can't lose anyone. Especially not so close to…."

"God, Madison. Don't you think I know that? Don't you think that I can't lose anyone else either?" My voice was loud, much louder than I intended.

"Avery, that's not fair. Don't take this out on me. I'm hurting just like you." Her words meant something, sure. I knew I shouldn't take it out on her, but everything she said made me hurt worse.

"We are going to catch Lorelei and Jameson and bring Marshall and Garcia home." I paused. "I have to bring them home." My voiced shook with emotion that was foreign to me. Fear? Sadness? I didn't know these feelings. I'd pushed them aside whenever they'd surfaced but I couldn't, not with this. No matter how hard I tried to fight back the tears, they flowed silently but freely. Madison whimpered and the guilt threatened to suffocate me. All the doubts I had about Evan, about relationships in general, all made sense. It was all true. I didn't belong in a relationship. I was an agent through and through and that was all I'd ever be.

"Avery?" Madison hesitated. "Are you okay?"

"No, I'm not okay. Fuck!" I slammed my fist on the steering wheel as I continued to drive to the precinct. "I just can't think straight. I'm crying. Fucking crying, Madison. I haven't cried since my mother died." I paused. "Yet my heart aches. It aches for Marshall and Garcia. It aches for my mother, who fucking took her own life and gave in to drugs. For my father who only wants a trophy daughter." I took a breath. "It aches for love that I know I won't ever have. Damn, it even aches for you, Madison."

"For me? I'm here, Avery. I'll always be here for you." Madison's voice filled with compassion and concern. I tried not to focus on that. I didn't deserve her compassion. Not after I'd let two of our friends get captured because my head was too far up some guy's ass.

"But you won't always be here. You're moving."

"Why didn't you tell me you didn't want me to move?"

she asked quietly.

"So what? So you could stay with me and we could be old maids together and adopt cats?" We laughed. "No, Madison. You deserve happiness."

"You do, too," Madison said softly. "We're good agents, Avery. We'll bring them home." There was resolve in Madison's voice, a determination that replaced the sadness. I wanted to believe her, but something held me back from putting faith in her words.

"I want to believe you, Madison. I do." I shook my head. "Listen, I just pulled up to the precinct. I'll see you when you get here."

"Okay. About eight hours to go." I hung up the phone without any gesture of good faith. Without any words of hope, or goodwill. I felt mentally beaten. I had been in fights, scraped by to prove myself. But my usually strong mind struggled.

I stayed in the car for a moment, closing my eyes and trying to steady my breaths. It was difficult. My chest ached, my hands shook, and I felt out of control. It was no use. The only cure for my emotions was to find Garcia and Marshall and bring them home. I opened my eyes, my hands still shaking and my heart thumping loudly in my chest.

"Fuck it," I said aloud. I was going to go in there and solve the case.

And I'll kill anyone who gets in my way.

Chapter Thirty-Three

GARCIA

I tried to keep my head upright but I was so tired. My head lobbed to the side every few minutes, cracking and straining with each movement. I wasn't afraid of Lorelei. I was prepared to die. To see my sisters again because only in death could we be together once more. But I wanted to die with my eyes open, looking into the face of the woman who decided that God was a lie. I knew he'd be waiting for me. Regardless of the fact that I'd turned my back on the church, I believed, with every ounce of who I was, I believed I would be safe, pain free, and loved when I left this earth.

I wasn't left alone with Jameson again, though. Lorelei saw to that. She had someone drag me out to the field after a night of restless sleep, and I'd been sitting under the sun, waiting for my death ever since.

Strong and forceful footsteps against the ground neared. I was ready. I straightened myself up, the bark of the tree rubbing against my already raw and broken skin. But the face I saw wasn't Lorelei's. It was Jameson's. I gulped loudly, the fear that I had pushed aside surfacing ever so slightly. I understood Jameson but I wasn't Madison. I had very little training in psychology. I did know he was second-guessing everything he had built, his followers, his worshipping Lucifer.

"Desiree." Jameson knelt down in front of me so he was eye level. I looked at him, the years of torment permeated on his youthful face. "I don't want to kill you, but I have to." He sighed and sat down next to me.

"You don't have to do anything, Jameson. Lorelei is confused. She thinks that Lucifer is god and that by sacrificing all these people, that what? She'll be happy?"

"No!" He raised his voice. "That she'll be free. That all this shit that religion tells us is true, that all the lies we were forced to believe, it would all go away. That we would have the truth."

"Jameson, what truth?" He looked over at me, his eyes red-rimmed and puffy.

"The truth is that there is a god. You know that. I know that. Lucifer, he's in your mind. Someone you made up to make the horrible stuff you've thought and done seem not so horrible. Sure, religion can be fake, superficial, and money-driven, but it can also be so fucking beautiful and so real that it gives life purpose."

Tears streamed down Jameson's face and I wanted to smile. I thought maybe I had gotten through to him. That my words resonated with him and made him realize the error of his ways.

"You're right." My heart beat faster. I did it. I talked

him off the ledge. "I was a confused boy. My father beat me. My mother let him. I blamed God for letting it happen. "

"I'm sorry that happened to you."

Jameson laughed. "Yeah. Sorry. That's what everyone said to me. But there wasn't anything they could do because it was discipline. It was okay. It was good for me. He was a minister. He knew what was right for me." He clenched his fists at his sides. "He didn't know shit. He knew control, order. He didn't know God. He was the one who knew Lucifer. The devil was in my house more than the Lord. I can see that now. Clear as day."

I smiled. He was going to be okay. Jameson could see the truth and I was going to survive. Relief washed over me and I closed my eyes, relishing in the moment.

"But it doesn't matter." My eyes darted open and my chest sank.

"What do you mean it doesn't matter?" I asked in a panic.

"You still have to die." He stood from the spot next to me and looked down at me. Sadness was in his eyes and I knew he meant what he said.

"For Lorelei. She doesn't understand things like we do, Desiree. At least not yet. I have to follow through with this. I love her. She was there through my darkest times. She believed in me. She helped me. Now, I have to help her."

He walked away, leaving me tied to the tree awaiting my death. The sun grew brighter, a ray of sunshine hitting my face. I rested my head back, letting the sun warm me for what I was sure would be the last time.

Chapter Thirty-Four

AVERY

I swung open the doors of the precinct and all eyes came to me. The sounds of telephones and chatter still filled the air, but the moment I walked in, the atmosphere shifted. I knew it was because I wasn't as composed as I usually was. My shirt wasn't pressed. My hair wasn't tied back. I looked batshit crazy. I felt it too. I felt everything coursing through my body. My blood was boiling. I swear it was. I was hot to the touch, and my hair flew all around my porcelain, freckled face.

Torres poked his head around the corner from the conference room we usually used. His eyes widened when he looked at me, and I shook my head, indicating for him not to open his damn mouth.

"Torres," I screamed. "Get me all the case files on Lorelei. We need to be focusing on her now."

He stumbled back slightly. It was like he knew he should move, but he didn't. He just stood there like a deer in the headlights.

"Did I stutter? Get me the goddamn files. Marshall and Garcia are out there! We have to find them." The precinct went quiet. Some cop in the corner chuckled and mumbled, "Cuckoo," as he shuffled through his papers. I couldn't help myself. I really couldn't. He'd given me all I'd needed to kick his ass.

I stormed over to his desk and flung his papers off with one swift motion of my hands. He stood up and I looked up at the man, who was easily over six feet tall.

"What the hell you... you crazy bitch!" he yelled. People crowded around, and I glanced back and saw Torres trying to get through the crowd.

"Avery, don't do it," Torres yelled from behind me.

"Do what?" I smiled shyly, and I peered at the man's name tag. Officer Stetson.

"Don't hurt him. It's not worth it." I glanced at Torres. He was right. I took a deep breath and brushed back my hair. It didn't matter much, but as I breathed in through my nose and practiced some of the relaxation methods Madison had taught me, I felt better. I smiled at Officer Stetson as I turned away from him.

Officer Stetson snickered. "Like she could even hurt me," he mumbled as I took a few steps. It was loud enough, though, for me to hear it, and a loud gasp came from beside me. I guessed my reputation had preceded me. All the calmness, all the relaxation techniques I had just worked through and applied.... *Yeah, screw it.*

All I heard was Torres's voice behind me as I kneed Officer Asshole in his balls. He stumbled back and fell to the floor with a loud thud. I marched closer to him, the sounds of yelling voices all around me. It didn't matter, though. I heard nothing but my desire to kick his ass running through my head.

"Avery." My arm tugged from behind me as I wound up my fist to pummel into Officer Stetson's pretty little face. That'd teach him to call a woman a bitch again.

A more aggressive tug this time just pissed me off even further. So I did what any normal woman who had just been called a female dog would do. I turned around and braced myself to punch him. What I didn't expect was *him*. My Kryptonite.

"Evan." His name came out breathy and lingered ever so slightly at the tip of my tongue. I released the ball of tension that was in my fist and took a deep breath. I glanced back as moans hit my ears. Torres and some other officers were helping Officer Stetson off the floor.

"Come on, Avery. Let's go to the conference room. We have a case to solve." Evan held his hand out to me. I glanced at it, and his gray eyes bore into me. I could only glance, though. I didn't look at him. I couldn't. I knew my resolve would dissipate. I couldn't help but remember his hands all over me and his hands not all over me. Me in control, taking what I needed. A small smile crept across my face, but it was quickly replaced with thoughts of sorrow and doubt. The emotions were my only companions.

The simple gesture of his hand was a peace offering. If I took that hand, it would be a symbol, an indication—no matter how slight—that I didn't hate him. That there was hope. My heart was saying to screw all fucking logic and take that hand. To not overthink every little damn thing. But after what I'd discovered, what he'd hidden from me, I didn't know anything beyond the need to get my friends home. So I did what my father had done my entire life. I walked away, leaving the gray-eyed man, who had, whether I'd admit it or not, stolen my heart, all alone.

Something about me walking away from him this time seemed so final. I'd made my choice. Tears welled in my eyes. I'd borne witness to my mother's love for my father. I'd seen it eat away at her, little by little, until she'd turned to drugs, to something that would make her feel again.

I couldn't let that happen to me.

I *wouldn't* let that happen to me.

I wasn't Madison. I couldn't see beyond my own pain. I'd caught glimpses of what her life would be down the road. She would be happy because she had come to terms with her past. She had been given a chance to move on. I hadn't been. I'd been given a mother who had killed herself—not a mother who'd sacrificed herself. What had I been left with? A father who cared more about fighting crime than his only child.

I made my way to the conference room, Evan and Torres trailing behind me. My phone rang, drawing my mind away from the pity party that had formed in my head. The distraction was welcomed because being in my own head wasn't a pleasant place to be.

Especially now.

"Grant," I answered without looking at the caller ID.

"Avery, it's Dr. Wilson. Is Madison with you?" Dr.

Wilson's voice was distant, and I caught a hint of what I thought was a whimper almost.

"No, she's on her way back from Connecticut." She sighed into the phone and I could have sworn I heard her crying. "What's wrong?"

I motioned for the guys to hurry up into the conference room, and they took their seats by the table eyeing me with every ounce of anticipation I felt. My heart rate quickened and my composure, which was already shot, completely went to hell. I paced, waiting for a response. It seemed like an eternity.

An endless moment in time.

"It's the blood work. It came back." My heart stopped and I held my breath. I stopped pacing, and I knew then that one of my very best friends was no longer with us.

"It's Marshall. That charred body… it was Marshall's." Dr. Wilson tried to remain professional, but the staggering and soul-felt nature of her words rocked me to my core.

"No," I said simply, as if those words would make Marshall's death disappear. I couldn't feel my legs. Numbness enveloped my entire body. I was frozen in place. I stumbled, and my back hit the wall behind me.

"I'm sorry, Avery," Dr. Wilson said.

"And Garcia?" I replied, stealing a glance at Torres. His eyes widened and he sat up to the edge of his chair. Evan hung his head, diverting his eyes from me.

"None of the blood work matched hers."

"Thank you, Dr. Wilson." I went to hang up the phone, but she called my name.

"Avery, wait. There is one more thing. Those soil

samples came back with a match to a rare type of seed that is only found in certain areas of Western Virginia."

"What areas?" I asked, trying to shift my focus back to the case.

"Burke and Craigsville." The feeling slowly came back into my legs. It was the break we'd needed. Burke was where Lorelei's family farm was.

"Thank you. We'll be in touch." I glanced at the two agents in front of me. Both looking lost and scared as their eyes searched mine for an explanation. I knew Torres was worried about Marshall, but Evan... he was worried about me. *About us.* About what this meant. I shook my head, a small smile creeping on my face. Not for humor, but for the fact that the gods, or whoever was upstairs, royally hated me. This just solidified my very lonely future even further. I hadn't been able to keep my mother safe. And I couldn't keep my friends safe.

I bypassed Evan in the chair and went right to Torres as I placed a hand on his shoulder.

"Marshall is dead," I whispered to him. I wanted to hug Torres, pull him in and cry for my friend who had died a horrific death. Instead, Torres—a man I had grown to know, trust, and respect—crumbled, his tears flowing freely.

In that moment, I'd wanted to console him, but truly, I envied him. Envied the fact that he was so in tune with his emotions that he could freely show them. I glanced at Evan right as he looked away from me. Evan didn't bother offering me any words of condolences or tales of happy endings. Evan moved closer to Torres and whispered something in his ear.

He patted him on the back and Torres lifted his head and wiped away the tears that had fallen for the woman he had loved. Whether it was in secret or not, the tears he had shed were real.

Whatever Evan said to Torres consoled him. He offered him words of comfort that I couldn't give. Evan was almost a total stranger to Torres yet brought him comfort when I couldn't. I stared at the two men who had shared a moment so close and intimate that I envied them. I wanted to be them. I wanted to be a part of that shared moment. But just like always, I didn't want to feel. I didn't want to let anyone in.

"What about Garcia?" Torres asked, his voice quiet, hesitant.

"There is no sign of Garcia, so we can assume for now she is alive."

"Fucking pieces of shit!" Torres said as he stood and punched the wall where I had almost let myself crumble and fall. I clenched my fists at my sides, the heat rising in my body and I knew my cheeks were red. I just wanted the raw emotion like Torres. I fought it all back. Now wasn't the time. Yet, when was it ever a good time for me to *feel*?

"What else did the doctor say?" Evan looked in my direction as he asked this question. His eyes refused to hold mine.

"The soil samples were for a rare seed. For a tree that only grows in certain areas of Virginia. Burke was a match."

I texted Madison and I let her know about the development with the soil samples. Marshall's death was not something I could text her. I just had to find the courage to let my best friend know that she had lost someone else. No. That *we* had lost someone else.

Adams finally showed back up and was put in charge of organizing a task force to head out to Lorelei's parents' farm. Torres helped because we needed manpower due to the acres of land that needed to be explored. I wanted to give him time to grieve, but time was of the essence, and that was what we did in this job. We pushed aside what we needed to get the job done. I was left alone in the room with Evan who hadn't even looked at me since he'd last spoken.

I shuffled through paperwork and checked my phone mindlessly. I caught Torres crying silently, grieving by himself instead of finding comfort in me, his friend. I was grateful for that though. I didn't have to try to know how to deal with feelings. Instead, I could continue to try to take my mind off Garcia and Marshall. No matter what I did, it was my fault. Deep guilt crept into my bones.

I had let this happen.

I heard Evan's chair squeak, temporarily ending the silence that had enveloped the room. Then I felt it. The pull of him against my back. The attraction and nearness of him causing the nerves in my body to stand on end. His breath brushed against the back of my neck, and he leaned forward to get closer to me. His lips grazed against my ear.

"Avery." His voice was a low whisper with a hint of sadness. I didn't turn around. I didn't acknowledge his presence. My body wanted to move toward him. It fought with my mind, wanting to run to him and seek comfort in his arms. I waited for him to say something, but it never came.

The closeness slowly drifted away and I felt more alone than I ever had. I was left with the scent of him, one I had become intimately familiar with over the past few days.

Where he would normally have reached out for me, he didn't. He walked away, and I knew he wasn't going to come back.

Chapter Thirty-Five

EVAN

"Adams, did you call it in?" I asked as Torres and Adams sat at my small desk, which was overflowing with the paperwork I had neglected over the past few days. His ear was pressed to his phone, and he placed his hand over the end of the receiver to reply.

"Yeah, they'll be ready in twenty so we can head out now. Torres is just filling Scott in." Adams released his hand from the receiver.

"All right, Scott. See you in a bit." Torres ended the call and stood abruptly from the chair. His body looked worn-out, and his suit was wrinkled. Adams stood as well, looking for whatever was to come.

"Ready?" He looked over my shoulder. "Where's Grant?"

"Conference room," I said quickly as I maneuvered around Torres and grabbed my keys off the desk.

"At least she's still alive." Torres stared at the ground,

his eyes filling with emotion. I knew he'd loved Marshall, but she was gone. The loss of her was taking its toll.

"Wish I could offer you some words of encouragement, but after what just happened, well…." Torres glanced at the floor again as he stumbled to find the words to finish his thought.

I shook my head.

"It's okay, Torres. I can't imagine what you're going through, man," Adams said as he patted him on the shoulders.

"Are you guys ready to go?" We snapped our heads up, and there she stood. The woman who'd just ripped my heart and stomped on it.

"Yeah. We were just grabbing a few things," Torres replied as he adjusted his suit jacket.

"Okay. Let's go end this. We've already lost Marshall. I won't lose anyone else." Torres softened at the sound of Marshall's name, his shoulders slumping as he realized the possibilities that lay before him.

"Adams, you can ride with me. You're the only one who didn't decide to take it upon yourself to hide important case information from me."

Adams's eyes darted to me and I shrugged. What the hell was I supposed to say? She was right. I had royally fucked up and there wasn't anything I could say to make it any better.

"Torres was just following along with what I said. He and Scott had nothing to do with it."

"I know," Avery said as she and Adams walked out of the precinct. Torres and I followed behind, the guilt, pain and loss hanging around us both.

We piled into the police car and made the trek to the farm. The ride was silent with just the sound of the siren piercing through the feelings of lost love, death, and sadness that had followed us from the precinct.

As we neared the farm, police cars and agents lined the road. Their sirens were off so as to not give away their presence. Dusk had fallen, and darkness masked the farm. As each minute ticked by, I knew it would be harder and harder to apprehend Jameson and Lorelei. We were unsure of how many followers they had. Would they fight back? Would I have to take the lives of people who were struggling with who they were? I hoped not. Because I would just have to add that to my list of things to bury away.

I followed the motion of an agent's wild hands as they pointed to where we could park. I pulled in behind an unmarked vehicle. Clearly, someone else from the FBI was here. As we all exited the car, the fresh air, the smell of earth touched my nostrils. It was different from the city where the constant smell of smog and pollution pulled you down.

What those wild country smells brought were memories of home. They rushed through me, like Avery on that day we'd fought in the ring. Fierce, relentless, and volatile. A ticking time bomb.

Louisiana and my childhood home brought back the emotions I had fought so hard to push aside. The loss of my parents, the loss of my childhood home, and now, the loss of Avery. I saw it all so clearly and it hurt. It was piercing, the type of pain that made you double over and hold your gut. Years of pain barreled through me, and I grabbed the hood of the car to keep myself upright. *Oh, God. Not now.*

"Are you okay?" Her voice. That voice. The voice that had caused me so much pain.

"Yeah. Just a little dizzy from the ride." I cleared my throat. I looked at Avery, my eyes traveling up her face. She was beautiful. The moonlight caressed her freckles and highlighted her red hair. All the parts of her that called to me. I stopped and looked into her eyes. They were soft, more so than her hardened exterior. With her arms folded at her chest, she pursed her lips closely together; they formed a thin line. But what she felt wasn't any of those things. In her eyes, I saw that she cared. Pieces of her still cared.

"Avery." The deep vibrato of the voice brought us out of our moment. Avery whipped around, and her hair cascaded down out of her neatly tied bun.

"Dad? What are you doing here?" She changed in that moment. Shifting awkwardly between her legs, she straightened out her buttoned-up shirt and quickly retied her hair.

"I had to come. I heard that this case was an absolute disaster." He eyed me with bits of hatred, mixed with what I was sure was disgust. "You dropped the ball, Grant. You got wrapped up in something else." Avery glanced back at me quickly. "Or wrapped around someone else."

She placed her hand on her father's forearm and tried to get him to move away, but I'd be damned if he was going to waltz onto this crime scene and scold his grown daughter for something that was not her fault. I went to blaze forward, and Adams's firm grip on my arm stopped me.

"Don't do it, man." I turned around and faced him, my eyes firing with anger. I spun around to face Avery again, but she and her father were gone.

Chapter Thirty-Six

AVERY

"I don't have time for this." I pulled my father aside, out of the reach of Evan and Adams. I knew my dad, and he wouldn't keep his mouth shut, especially when he felt strongly about something.

"You think I do?" His fierce green eyes bored into me. The familiar fear mixed with resentment swirled within me. I had let him down. I'd only ever wanted to make him see me. To see me as worthy. "It's quite embarrassing when you hear about your daughter from the other agents. Talking about how she's fraternizing with a local detective."

The hair on my arms stood on end at his tone. My disappointment was quickly replaced with annoyance. My father was an asshole, and he was so clearly trying to insinuate that Evan was a lesser man because he was only a local cop.

"I thought I taught you better than that."

The laugh that spurred from my throat was anything but happy. I glared at my father as he firmly placed his arms across his chest. Something he had taught me. And it dawned on me. My own father had taught me how to be an asshole.

I remembered one of the few times my father took me to the park.

"Look at me, Daddy!" I waved as I hung upside down from the monkey bars. He barely smiled as he talked on the phone. I frowned. Maybe if I swung with one leg, he'd notice me!

One leg and no hands sent me falling to the ground, hard.

"Owww!" I writhed on the ground in pain. I watched through the tears as my dad hung up the phone and slowly walked over to me and knelt beside me.

"Is anything broken?"

I stared at him wide-eyed. I was nine. Not privy to the art of broken bones. I shrugged.

"If you can shrug, nothing's broken. Get up." I winced as I put weight on my leg to stand. My dad stood over me and didn't lend me a hand. I glanced around as people watched, a few mothers shaking their heads in disgust.

"My ankle." I limped as I followed behind my dad.

"Life hurts, Avery. You need to push all the feelings aside and focus on the task at hand." I stopped when he turned around and looked at me. It was the first time he'd looked me in the eyes in a long time. Usually, he walked by me without a second glance, but now, when he should have held me and checked me over for injuries, I was being scolded. The sad thing was, all I could think about was what I had done wrong.

"Do you know what the task at hand is?" I shook my

head, wiping my eyes with my shirt.

"To be the best. To never let anyone know your weakness. That's how you'll succeed because they'll have nothing to use against you."

I nodded and squared off my shoulders. He gave me a small smile with those actions. I guessed it showed him that I took his words to heart, because I did. I always did. I'd do anything to get my father to notice me, to love me. That day my father taught me to be disconnected. A hard worker who took no shit, but refused love and friendship because anyone I was close to was a weakness.

That memory caused such clarity I was furious. Furious with myself for believing what he told me and never doing anything beyond training, working, and molding myself into an agent. Some people would think that I was ambitious, but at what cost? Madison, Marshall, and Garcia were my first real friends. I was beginning to realize that weaknesses made you stronger when you faced them head-on. My friends, even Evan, they were the first attempt at that, and I wouldn't give any of them up and I most certainly wouldn't let my father talk badly about a man who helped me to realize these things.

"Taught me? What have you taught me, Director Grant?" My father's formal name rolled off my tongue with as much malicious intent as I could muster. "You taught me nothing of any use. I am a closed-off bitch who is too afraid to love because of you." I moved closer to my father, pushing his chest with my finger. "You've been too busy to care about me since the day I was born. I've tried so hard to be like you. Leaving my dolls aside and trying to fight crime and mirror your image, and what did you do? You left Mom and me alone, only saving your words for when you'd tell me how I could be better. How I wasn't good enough." I took a deep breath.

"Well, Dad, you got your wish. I let someone in. I fell in love. And it hurt even worse than falling off that jungle gym when I was nine and you making me walk all the way home on my sprained ankle. So screw you and your lessons that I believed! All I wanted was to be loved. Some attention, a hug, a kiss goodnight." I threw up my arms. "But look at me now, graduated top of my FBI class, but I have nothing to show for my success except this job." I chuckled. "That even you control, Dad. Or should I say, Director Grant." I backed away. I looked into my father's eyes. The man who had never once showed me any affection. I blamed him for a lot of things. It wasn't fair, really, because I was an adult, and I could choose what I wanted. Who I wanted. Who I wanted to be. Who I wanted to love. But I didn't. I still saw myself as that little girl, wanting her father to love her.

"I won't embarrass you again, Father. But like you taught me, love in this field is just a nuisance. So, he won't be a problem anymore. *I* won't be a problem anymore." My father didn't try to comfort me. He just looked around as I raised my voice, making sure no one could hear what I was saying.

"I'm just like you, Dad. Aren't you proud?" As tears streamed down my face, I turned on my heels and walked away. I heard nothing. He didn't call after me. He let me walk away.

"Grant!" Torres ran toward me, and I swiped away the

tears. I knew my face was probably bright red and showed that I had been crying, but I also knew no one would dare mention it.

"Everyone's here. We are heading in now." I was handed a two-way that I firmly secured in my pants.

"Scott and Madison?" I asked as I checked my weapon to make sure it had plenty of ammo.

"They're still too far behind for us to wait. We have to go in now." Before I could reply, a blood-curdling scream shattered that little bit of hope that was floating within us— the hope that told us Garcia and Marshall were really safe, and we'd just had faulty information.

"Shit, that sounded like Garcia." Torres spun around and ran toward the scream.

"Let's go," Evan's voice called after me as he and Adams ran after Torres. My legs pumped underneath me as I ran to save my friend. I had to save one of the few people I had let into my life and into my heart. I whispered silent words to myself, sending them off to whoever was listening. *Please, just let her be okay.*

Agents and police dogs roamed the vast acres of land before us. Large and daunting, it felt nearly impossible that we would get to her in time. I let my legs carry me, but I lost sight of Torres, Adams, and Evan in front of me. Instead, I came to a field of corn, the stalks tall and blocking my way. Forcing my way through, they hit me in the face as I slowed my pace. And then I heard it: voices, chants. With each step I took, they were getting closer.

As I neared the end of the cornfield, I hid myself behind

the nearest stalks. My breathing was staggered and uneven from the run. Fear pounded at my chest. I wasn't fearful for myself, but for Garcia. For what I was about to see. Glancing around the cornstalks, I held onto my gasp.

Garcia was bound, her hands tied behind her back, her feet in front of her. Her jet-black hair was matted and clung to her tearstained face. Blood stained her bare skin. She was naked to the world, to everyone chanting to the darkened skies above. Exposed and alone.

I thought briefly about what I could do to stop this. Using my two-way would bring attention to myself. While I was a good fighter, I couldn't fight the mass of people before me. From what I could see there were at least ten, not including Lorelei and Jameson.

Taking in the surroundings again, I saw a huge hole in the ground, dug and ready for something. *Someone*, I thought to myself as I shuddered.

"We are gathered here to offer the last sacrifice to Lucifer!" Lorelei's voice carried over the blazing fire. "Bring me the cup!" Jameson hung his head as he walked over to Lorelei with a cup.

"We give this sacrifice the blood of all of our sacrifices. To make her strong. To make her perfect for our god." Lorelei smiled as she pried open Garcia's mouth. Garcia fought, moving wildly and trying to clamp her mouth shut. I smiled to myself. *Fight, Garcia. Don't give up.*

"Help me!" Lorelei screamed to Jameson.

He looked around at the blazing fire at his followers, and I saw his entire body stiffen at the sight before him. It was something out of a horror film: the people's eyes reflecting the fire, Lorelei's smile that seemed so out of place for the occasion. He looked how I felt. Scared.

"Lorelei, enough. This is crazy." Jameson took the cup from Lorelei.

"Shut up, Jameson. You promised me that we would finish this!" He sighed, and his shoulders slumped in defeat. Lorelei smiled when she was finally able to get Garcia's mouth open. Jameson let the contents of the cup flow into Garcia's mouth. And after she was forced to drink it, Lorelei kicked her in the back, sending Garcia plummeting into the grave below. They were going to bury her alive. I had to do something. Pushing aside my own safety, I reached for my two-way.

"Evan!" I whispered into the device.

"Avery? Where are you?"

"Just at the end of cornfields. Send backup. They are going to bury her alive," I whispered frantically.

My whispers were in vain. I looked up, and there she was. Lorelei. Standing right in front of me. I smiled at her. She was so different than I'd imagined. Her long blonde hair cascaded around her body. She looked so innocent. But with the unfolding scene, and from the scene I'd watched on the Down Under Pub surveillance videos, this woman was anything but innocent.

I quickly glanced back to make sure Garcia was okay. Jameson stood in front of the fire and the fresh grave. Sadness flickered across his face as Garcia's moans filled the air.

Lorelei didn't once take her eyes off me as she screamed, "Bury her!"

"Don't worry, Garcia. Help is coming." I projected my voice as loud as I could, so Garcia could hear me.

All I heard in return were Garcia's screams. They had been loud at first, but as the followers grabbed shovels and began filling the hole with dirt, those sounds had lessened. Jameson stood there, watching as his followers covered Garcia in dirt. He held a shovel in his shaking hand. I knew then that I had to make my move.

I ran toward Lorelei, catching her off guard as she smiled at the scene before her. We fell to the ground with a loud thud, and I took my fists and I beat into her pretty little face. She held her arms up in defense, but it didn't matter. I found her exposed weaknesses. I found the places she couldn't protect.

A loud crack ran through my ears, and my skull cracked under the pressure of steel. My eyes fought to stay open, but the pain took me, and I fell beside the bleeding body of the woman who had killed my friend.

Chapter Thirty-Seven

Evan

"Avery, don't do anything stupid! I'll be right there!" The muffled sounds coming from the two-way set my heart rate quickening. Either she was trying to stop them all on her own, or they had found her. Neither situation was good. I released my weapon from its holster and brought it closely to my side. I had a feeling I'd be needing it.

"Torres," I screamed across the clearing. "Get everyone into those cornstalks. Avery is in there and spotted Garcia! They're fucking burying her alive." I turned to Adams. "Come with me."

"I'll always have your back, man. Let's fucking do this!" He had his gun drawn and the look in his eyes told me he was ready. He lived for this stuff. For the thrill. I used to, but I just hoped that nothing would happen to Avery or Garcia. Our footfalls were heavy, and the sound of our shoes crunching against the dirt-covered earth speared through the frantic sounds of agents running through the fields. But it didn't matter. My heart was the only sound I heard.

As we neared the edge of the field, the smell of fire invaded my senses, and the bright orange flames were visible from over the stalks of corn. I knew we were almost there. Adrenaline pumped through my veins as my legs surged me forward.

Whispers and frantic chants quickly replaced the sounds of our feet against the earth. I stopped ahead of everyone and made the hand motion for everyone to fan out in efforts to cover the perimeter.

Looking in front of me, I saw something that would be forever embedded in my mind. It wasn't bloody. There weren't bodies lining the ground, but there were people. At least ten people stood chanting, helping bury an innocent woman. The blind faith they gave Lorelei and Jameson was astonishing. No questions asked. No remorse or feelings of sadness. Their faces didn't show concern, and they didn't second-guess their actions. Instead, they smiled. I watched as one woman gathered the earth on her shovel and covered a woman. I couldn't see Garcia, and her screams were getting fainter. Fuck! She was the one being buried alive. We had to make a move, or she'd die.

I motioned to Torres who made sure the rest of the agents knew that it was time. My eyes searched frantically for Avery. Then, I saw her, crumpled on the ground at the feet of Lorelei, who looked a little worse for wear. *Good job, Avery,* I thought with pride. She definitely didn't go down without a fight. I caught her chest moving with deep heaves and said a silent prayer, thanking God she was alive. I grabbed my gun and positioned it in front me, quickly making my way into the mass of people. I pulled the heavy metal gun in front of me as I yelled, "Let me see your hands!" Adams flanked my back, his gun positioned on someone else.

No one listened as my gun pointed directly at Jameson. "I said, let me see your hands!"

A slow smile crept across Lorelei's bloodied face as she laughed beside him. Jameson seemed scared as he slowly raised his hands in defeat. Lorelei smacked his hands down, a scowl replacing the smile that had just been on her face.

My mind reeled with thoughts of what Lorelei was doing. In the short time I'd worked with Madison, I had learned a bit about human personality, and it seemed Lorelei was in charge. It also seemed that Lorelei wanted to complete this mission more than anything else.

"You're too late. By the time you unbury her, she'll be dead!" Lorelei laughed as Torres's eyes pleaded with me. Chants continued from the others. I was only able to make out pieces of their words, but they were saying something about accepting them into *his* world with this sacrifice.

I motioned for Torres and Adams to head over to the grave, but as they did so, the followers lined themselves around it, blocking our path.

"Tell them to stand down, Jameson. It's over," I demanded. "I know you don't want this anymore." I took a deep breath and watched Jameson's face scowl with confusion. Lorelei looked between us and frowned. I needed to talk to Jameson. To get him to think.

"Jameson, I know your father was a cruel man. But

this isn't the way. Violence, hate, murder, it isn't going to fix your childhood." I took a breath. "These people trust you. They all still have a chance to redeem themselves. You have a chance to redeem yourself. Just tell them to back away, and no one else has to die." I tried to plead with him while Lorelei continued laughing, and I moved closer. I eyed Avery at her feet. I heard a faint moan and thought I caught a flicker of her eyes moving.

With my gun drawn and all the agents surrounding the area, it would be easy to take them all down, but the preservation of life kept ringing in my head. These people were messed up in the head. They didn't know what they were doing. No. Killing these unarmed people was not the way. I also knew I had to do something or Garcia would die. If she wasn't dead already. I tried to listen, to get any sense that she was still alive, but her once-muffled cries had stopped.

"Take him down!" I heard Avery yell as she sprang up from her position on the ground.

Her hands were tied in front of her, but that didn't stop her from elbowing Lorelei in the face. I watched Avery bring the ropes to her mouth and untie them. Blood gushed from Lorelei's already bleeding nose and loud screams echoed around us. Agents rushed forward, their guns drawn and ready to use if need be. Everywhere I looked people ran and screamed. Although it was chaotic, Jameson's voice pierced through the madness.

"Don't fight them! I have misled you in my own beliefs. My own beliefs that taking the lives of the innocent is the way." I went over to him and I holstered my gun as I moved behind him. He wasn't going to fight me. Not anymore. Maybe what I had said did impact him somehow.

"Lucifer is not a god. He exists in each of us. He is our inner battle. Our inner struggle with ourselves. We have all lost our path, but we can find redemption."

"You coward. You fucking coward!" Lorelei screeched as she lay on the ground.

"She's dead. I did it. I'm so sorry," Jameson cried as I cuffed him. I watched as police and anyone who had a spare hand dug into the grave. Dirt flew and covered the outside of the makeshift grave. Garcia was buried deep and I tried desperately to remember how much time had passed. It couldn't have been too long. She had to be okay.

"I see her!" Adams yelled. Avery let go of the Lorelei who she'd just cuffed and handed her to another agent.

"Special Agent Harper, she's—"

"Just fucking take her to the squad car!" she yelled at him as she ran over to Garcia, pushing Adams out of the way. I held my breath, looking at the scene unfold in front me. Clumps of dirt were flung into the air as Avery scrambled to the ground, trying to pull her free. Seconds, that felt like minutes, ticked by as she dug with her bare hands, not letting anyone else get close. Then, she was free, and Avery pulled Garcia's body from the earth. Garcia was limp and dirt lined every inch of her body.

"She's not breathing," Lorelei gasped as she was being dragged away. I glanced back as a smile flitted across the psychotic woman's face. I heard the voice of Avery's father close in. *How convenient.* He was able to sit back and watch as we did all the heavy lifting, but he heads in just in time to take credit.

EMTs and paramedics rushed onto the scene with Director Grant. They took Garcia out of Avery's arms, but Avery held onto Garcia's hand till the last minute. And then Avery was left—empty, alone—kneeling in the dirt that covered her. Her right eye was swollen almost completely shut, and for the first time since I'd met her, she looked fragile. Adams patted her back as he stood, walking toward the people who were cuffed, and began hauling some away.

Jameson was taken away from me and brought to the waiting squad cars. Torres knelt down beside Avery and whispered something into her ear. She hugged him, and as her face turned to meet mine, I could have sworn I saw tears glistening. Standing, Torres ran to the gurney that carried Garcia away. I felt like I had to do something, say something in that moment.

I walked over and knelt beside her, reaching my hand out to hers. It landed on her knee. She stood, pushing me to the ground.

"Don't fucking touch me. I can't stand it. I can't stand to see your face, feel your touch. It's just a reminder of what we did. How I let Garcia and Marshall down." Her voice was loud and people were turning to see what was going on.

"I just wanted to comfort you. This has to be—"

"Hard? Yes. It's hard but I don't need your comfort. I need Marshall not to be dead."

"If you are both done making a spectacle of yourselves, I'd like to speak with my daughter. Alone, please." Director

Grant puffed out his chest and inserted himself directly in our space. I wouldn't let him talk to me like that. Not this time.

"No, you can't—"

Torres rushed back toward us. "She's going to be okay." Avery grabbed him and he picked her up and swung her around. She laughed, happiness filling her. As I watched her let the tears flow freely, I knew this was the Avery I had met just the night before. Carefree. Full of life, happiness, and hope.

"Avery, get a hold of yourself." Director Grant pulled her out of Torres's arms. "This isn't how the daughter of the Director of the FBI is supposed to act. Or an FBI agent for that matter." He spoke in hushed tones, but it didn't matter. I heard what he'd said, and the smile that had peeled away from Avery's face gave indication to the fact that she did not appreciate his words. I'd only seen the man with her tonight, but with just those few times, all I'd seen was judgment and scrutiny. There didn't seem to be any love radiating off him. No proud parent showing off his daughter who had made a place for herself in a field dominated by men. Instead, he only showed her off when it was convenient for him.

It made me mourn for Avery, and for the loss of her mother, who, in just the one time she'd spoken about her, seemed to have given her all the love her father had failed to. Yet, her mother had left her all alone, with a loveless father, and I'd be damned if I stood back and let him speak to her like that.

"Sir, you can't speak to her like that." My voice was a low growl as I placed my hand at the small of Avery's back.

"Excuse me? Who do you think you're speaking to? I am the—"

"The Director of the FBI. Yes, we all know." I wedged myself between him and Avery. All eyes were on us. I didn't care.

Let them all watch.

"It doesn't matter if you're the goddamn President of the United States. This woman here is an excellent agent. She graduated first in her class at the academy."

"You don't have to spit out my daughter's credentials. I know she's the best. How do you think she got that way?" A small smile crept on his face.

"Seriously?" Avery's shocked voice interrupted the tirade I'd wanted to continue. She pushed past me, now face-to-face with her father.

"You think you had anything to do with my success in life? Sure, I watched you when I was younger running off and playing cops. But the only reason I did any of it, trading my dolls for GI Joes and playing cops and robbers instead of dress up was to get your attention. And Mom, well, Mom drugged herself into oblivion to get attention from you. But you were too blind to see what you had in front of you. Two women who loved the hell out of you." She took a deep breath, and I reached out for her hand once again. It felt cool in mine, and she gave me a quick squeeze. "I thought that by doing all this, looking the part, being the part, and never disappointing you, I thought I'd be worthy of your attention. But I realize now, that no matter what I do, it will never be good enough for you. I will never be good enough for you."

"Avery—" Her father's voice was interrupted by the sounds of gunshots in the distance.

I released Avery's hand from mine, grabbed my weapon and ran toward the sounds. Avery was on my heels, her weapon drawn as well.

"We needed another sacrifice. I had to finish it, and he was a coward anyway." Lorelei stood before her husband, a crumpled heap on the ground. A single gunshot wound wept from his head. All I saw were his eyes. More than the blood pooling at his head like thick syrup, his eyes drew me in. They had that same pleading look like they'd had earlier. He had wanted my help. He had pleaded with me to end it all, but he was dead.

Next to him, an agent writhed in pain, holding his leg. Blood seeped from between his fingers, staining them red. The paramedics were already on scene, but there was nothing they could do for Jameson. Avery went over to Lorelei who didn't protest at all. She gave herself to Avery willingly.

"Who the hell cuffed her in front?" Director Grant ran up behind us, out of breath and annoyed.

"Shit," I murmured. Avery had cuffed her in front.

"It was me, sir," I said.

Avery's wild eyes met mine, her red lips parted, ready to interject, but I shook my head slowly.

"Your boss will hear about this, Detective Bradley. Two agents down and Jameson dead because of your carelessness." He took out his phone and walked away, ready to make whatever call to get my ass in trouble. He was happy. I could tell by the extra pep in his step. Ever since he'd found out

I was interested in his daughter, he'd thought I wasn't good enough, and *this*, this was just the icing on the cake.

"What the hell, Evan? Why did you say that?" Avery asked as she placed Lorelei into the back of the police car.

"Because, I'd do anything to protect you, Avery, even from your own father. He doesn't realize what a great person you are. All that verbal abuse. You deserve better."

"Well. Your protection isn't needed. I can take care of myself. I always have." She let her shoulders fall, the weight of her words forcing them back down.

"You shouldn't have had to take care of yourself for so long, especially as a child. That's just wrong." I shook my head.

"It is wrong. But it's all I've known. It's how I survive. I only rely on myself." She opened the car door, turning her back to me. "Then that way I don't get let down." She slammed the door, revving the engine and driving away.

All the guilt I had tried to push aside, to focus on bringing Marshall and Garcia back, yeah, that wasn't possible anymore. Marshall was dead, Garcia expected to survive but with mental scars so deep, I couldn't fathom how she would overcome them. I couldn't help but feel that there was nothing for me anymore.

The job in Shreveport was looking better and better.

Chapter Thirty-Eight

AVERY

As Lorelei and I drove in silence to the precinct, I was lost in thought. My mind buzzed, unable to settle down. Lorelei had given her all to Jameson. She had lost herself in what he wanted, his goals, his mission in life. She had become him at the loss of herself. She became psychotic and obsessed, unable to be rational or logical.

I'd watched my mother go down that same path. I'd watched her love my father more than herself, losing any personal identity that had once existed. That much love was dangerous. Lorelei reminded me a lot of my mother. She had become so infatuated with Jameson and his mission that, in order to make his dreams come true, she'd taken his life. She'd taken his life so his dreams could be fulfilled even though he'd wanted the madness to end. She was just too damaged to see it.

Watching Evan defend me against my father should have stirred some emotions within me that made me want to throw myself at his feet and be at his mercy, but I was tired of trying to be someone I wasn't. I was tired of trying to make a man happy. I had lived in my father's shadow my whole life. I had struggled to make him happy, to make him want to be around me, to make him want to be a father. I was afraid that I would end up like my mother. Attached to a man who didn't see me for who I was.

I pulled up to the precinct and put the car in park, realizing I'd gotten there by sheer memory and without thought. I sighed, placing my head against the back of the seat.

"For what it's worth, he cares about you. He looks at you like Jameson always looked at me." I glanced back at Lorelei, who sat shackled in the backseat of the police car. She smiled to herself as she looked out the window.

She was delusional.

She'd just killed the man who loved her. She didn't know what she was talking about.

"That's what I'm afraid of," I mumbled. An officer came to the car and took Lorelei, but as I exited the vehicle, her loud voice caught my attention.

"Love is overcoming fear, but fear makes you strong. It makes you want to be a better person. It makes you want to change. It gives you courage, strength," Lorelei called after me.

"Keep it moving," the officer said as he pushed Lorelei ahead of him. Fear, for me, was nonexistent. It meant weakness. And I was anything but weak.

Chapter Thirty-Nine

GARCIA

The beeping of the hospital equipment was annoying. For two days it had kept me awake. In that time, Torres hadn't left my side. Avery, Madison, and Scott came daily, but Torres was plastered on the chair next to me, and he looked horrible. His face was covered in the start of a beard. His normally tailored suit had been replaced with a wrinkled T-shirt and baggy jeans, both of which looked like they hadn't been washed in days. I went to sit up, and he rushed over to adjust my pillows.

"I can do it, Torres," I said as I swatted his hands away.

"I know. I just want to help. I just...." He sighed. It was a sigh that held much more than frustration. It held loss. It held regret. And that sigh was all for Marshall. I had been here before, watching those I cared about mourn over someone who they'd loved. Someone *we'd* loved. And once again, I had lost a sister.

"I miss her, too. A lot." Tears stung at my eyes, and I had to stop myself so I could take a deep breath.

Torres slumped back into the chair, fidgeting with his hair.

"I'm sorry. I promised Avery I wouldn't say anything about Marshall, but I can't. I feel so messed up over it. How am I supposed to move on?" Torres asked, his eyes pleading with me to give him the answer.

I smiled at him and reached out for his hand. He placed his in mine, and I squeezed.

"She loved you, you know?" I let out a small laugh. "Although she didn't want anyone to know about you two dating, she talked about you all the time. Even when we were kidnapped. She was more worried that you wouldn't know how she felt than the fact that we were going to die."

Torres looked away. "Stop. I can't—" He shook his head at my words.

"Please. I need to say this. She made me promise." Torres looked at me, and his face was strong and steadfast.

"She told me she loved you so much that it scared her to the point that she questioned everything. Her job, wanting a marriage and kids. She wanted all of that with you, and she was going to tell you… before she died." Torres looked at me, a single tear falling down his cheek. He wiped it away and straightened out his shoulders, becoming brave again.

Sometimes, that was all you needed; words to heal the parts of you that were shattered. I had fallen. Not just from my family, but from my faith. I'd grown up a devout Catholic, and the church had always been there for me. But there was something about losing those close to you that made it harder to remain steadfast in your belief. There was something about losing loved ones that made us humans lose faith. But this case... watching Lorelei unravel and worship something that was filled-to-the-brim with hate... this case had made me miss so much. My parents. My mentor, Karen. Although I had gained so much, the memories that had surfaced were painful. The past couple of weeks had ripped open the wounds I thought had finally scarred over from losing Tallie and Lola.

"Thank you, Garcia, for sharing that with me. I loved her, too. So much."

"She knew, Torres. She knew." I sat up and swung my legs over the bed, my head spinning slightly. Being buried alive was a challenge to heal from. It had been two days, and I still felt dizzy every time I stood. It was getting better, but I couldn't wait to go home. *Home*. My head spun again with thoughts of my family.

"I'm going to take a shower." Torres helped me to the bathroom and headed out for the evening. It was clear he'd received the closure he'd needed. What I'd shared helped him on his way to moving on. Me, I wasn't so sure anymore. As I let the water pour down my body, I hoped it would cleanse away the memories. I wanted to stay. I wanted so badly to stay with Avery and Madison and build my life here, but once again, I had lost someone. The itch I always felt when faced with pain and loss returned. I wanted to run away from it all, just like I had all those years ago.

I toweled off and climbed back into the hospital bed, waiting for the doctor to tell me if I could be discharged. I picked up the phone and dialed my father's number. I needed to speak with the man who had always been there for me, even when I'd turned my back on him. On *them*.

"Papa?" I said and then cleared my throat. "Papa, I'm coming home." I barely managed to get the words out as the tears lodged in my throat.

"Mi Hija," I heard my mother screech in the background.

"We've missed you. God is so good," he whispered into the phone. "We'll be waiting."

"I'm so broken, Papa. So, so broken," I cried. I let the tears for my sisters, for Marshall stream down my face. My father offered soothing words, which comforted parts of me I had buried and forgotten.

When the doctor discharged me, I packed my clothes, e-mailed my resignation to my boss, and booked on the first flight to San Diego. To my family. To my home. To the only place I felt could heal me. I sent Avery and Madison a text because I couldn't face them, not yet.

Me: I'm sorry for not saying good-bye in person. You all have become like my sisters, the sisters I lost all those years ago. I never told you about Tallie and Lola, and how I lost them. You both were so much like them. Beautiful and full of life. Losing Marshall made it all come back. All the shit I'd tried to bury. I'm going back to where it all started. To my home. But what you've both taught me is no matter how hard you try to forget, you just can't without conquering that fear, head-on. I love you both. Please don't forget that.

Chapter Forty

Six Months Later

"Avery! The baby's coming!" I held my cell phone close to my ear as I lay in my bed in my studio apartment.

The past six months had gone by quickly. Madison and Scott had transferred to the FBI office in Connecticut to be by Scott's mother, and I missed her terribly, but we talked all the time and we'd visited each other at least once a month since she'd left.

Garcia had gone back home. No one had heard from her in months, other than the good-bye message she had sent us. I could only imagine what she'd experienced being kidnapped, being sacrificed and surviving. Sometimes, the pain of surviving was too much and you had to break free. Start fresh. Madison and I weren't mad at her. Sad, of course, that she was gone, but Madison and I knew what loss could do to a person, and we all had to heal in our own way, in our own time.

Me, well, I wasn't doing anything other than working. Evan had left shortly after the case ended. I avoided him at all costs when we had to testify in court. I normally would face everything head on. The reality was, I was afraid of losing my resolve and giving in to the pull I still felt toward him. I hadn't fully forgiven him for what happened, but I realized that it wasn't just his fault; it was mine too. I had been forced to see a counselor since. It seemed the bureau had a policy about so many deaths in a short period and were concerned about my mental state.

I must admit though, it had been refreshing talking to someone. I owned up to the parts of what happened that fell on me. Talked over my issues with someone who didn't judge or have an agenda at the end of each session. He just listened and helped me shift through all the shit that had happened in my life.

I hadn't heard from Evan since that night. He hadn't tried calling me to convince me to come to my senses. I'd expected the silence, but it still stung. It hurt just as much as the day I'd looked into my mother's dead eyes and realized I would never see her again. James, my counselor, said I wanted him to call. That I hoped he would come back and want me again. I denied that of course, but I missed him. Fuck, if I didn't miss that man. James mentioned how it made sense that I would fall so hard, so fast. He claimed I had a lot of love to give, but I just didn't know how. That "know how" part, I certainly agreed with.

As I looked at myself in the mirror, gathering my things to visit my new niece or nephew, I realized my eyes looked just like my mother's had on that day. Dead. Void of any feeling. That was what was inside me. An endless abyss of nothingness.

Scott had tried mentioning Evan to me on occasion, as they still kept in touch, but the death glares I'd given him had shut him up pretty quickly. Sure, I had been talking shit out, but it didn't make any of this any easier. I remained afraid I would become my mother and love so much that it would kill me.

The entire nine-hour drive was filled with these thoughts. The back and forth and replaying of what could have been. I still missed Marshall, my mother, Evan. All the people who came and were ripped away from me traveled with me, letting me know that maybe I wasn't so alone.

When I pulled into Middlesex hospital, I suddenly remembered all the bad shit that had happened here. It was where Scott had been brought after Walsh had stabbed him, where so many bad memories plagued me. Finally, the place held something good. The birth of a new life. A new beginning. I tried to focus on the positivity.

I rushed to the maternity ward. I tried to barrel through the door, barely able to contain my excitement. I shifted between my feet as I waited to be buzzed in. It only took a few minutes but I couldn't help but wring my hands together over and over again.

As I stepped into the room and saw my best friend holding her new baby with the man she had always loved, I lost it. I started bawling. Everything surrounded me. The good. The bad. The fucking terrible. Madison and Scott let me cry, the silent tears breaking the knot that had been permanently stuck in my chest for the past six months. Who was I kidding? That knot had been there for the past twenty-one years. Like a rock crushing my heart.

"Want to meet your new nephew?" Madison asked, holding a blue bundle in her arms. Scott stood and squeezed me on the shoulders before placing a kiss to his new baby's head and to Madison's cheek.

"I'll be back, ladies," he said as he winked at me and left the room.

"Give him to me." I reached out to him and just then, he opened his eyes. They were blue, just like Scott's. That was where the similarities between him and his father ended. His ears were like Madison's, and he had a full head of curly brown hair.

"Oh, Madison. He's perfect." I kissed his forehead while counting all his fingers and toes.

"So, remember when I asked if you would be the godmother?" I looked up at Madison, tears glistening in her eyes.

"Me?" I was shocked. I was also a bit concerned for my friend's mental sanity at the fact that she wanted me to be responsible in any remote part for this precious gift.

"Yes, you." Madison adjusted herself in the bed so she sat upright. "You're my sister, Avery. I love you so much, and I would be honored if my son turned out to be half the person you are."

I brushed tears away from my eyes.

"The person I am? I have a life of fighting crime. That's

all I am."

"Avery, that's no one's fault but your own. You push everyone away, even people who truly care about you." Madison sighed. The baby squirmed in my arms, stretching and yawning before snuggling back to sleep. "You deserve just as much happiness as anyone. You're scared, and that's okay. Sometimes you have to leap, Avery. Just say 'screw it all,' close your eyes, and jump." I thought about what she was saying. It was true. I was afraid of who would be on the receiving end if I jumped.

"What if no one's there to catch me?" I handed her back the baby, and Madison laughed softly. It was crazy really. I never needed anyone. It was just me, myself and I.

"Someone will always be there. I'll always be there. Scott will always be there." Madison kissed the baby's cheek. "But more importantly, Evan will be there to catch you, Avery. He asks about you sometimes. He knows he screwed up but you have to forgive. We only have one life to live. We have to live it to its fullest." Madison lay her head back on the bed, looking tired and worn-out. I leaned forward and squeezed her hand.

"How'd you get so smart when it comes to love?" I asked jokingly.

"I had some pretty amazing people in my life who loved me despite all the shit I had been through. It made me realize what love is worth. It is worth it all, Avery. All of it."

The door creaked open and in popped Scott, holding three coffees.

"Here you go." He handed me a cup and placed the

other two on the table next to Madison's bed.

"Let me take Liam, so you can relax, baby." He reached out for him.

"What did you call him?" My heart stopped.

"Liam. We named him Liam."

Tears streamed down my face again as I stared at Scott. It clicked then for me. The people who had loved Madison were not just her mom, and me, Garcia, Marshall, and Scott, but Liam too. We had all shaped her into the woman in front of me now. Strong, happy, and loved. My father. My mother. They had all made me who I was today, and I was damn proud of the woman I had become.

Madison's voice warmed me as she sang to him "Sweet Dreams" by the Dixie Chicks. She hadn't sung since her father had taken that from her. But Madison had healed. She had overcome her past, and she was able to live without fear or doubt. She was able to open her heart, live her life, and accept that all the things that had happened to her, good and bad, had made her the wonderful woman she was today. Strong. Determined. Successful.

And most importantly, happy.

The next few days I spent organizing my life. Trying to break down years of a routine that didn't bring me nearly the amount of happiness I had hoped. While I loved my job, looking into my nephew's eyes, I had seen something I hadn't seen since I was a child. Hope. Maybe there was someone watching over us. Guiding us on these paths of life to a higher purpose. He or she was there giving us all that we needed in an effort to make us see what we were truly capable of. And I, Avery Grant, was capable and deserving of love, and I'd be damned if I didn't go after it.

I'd left all my boxes from my studio apartment in storage. I'd finally moved out of the Extended Stay and got my own place, if you could even call it that. The studio apartment was smaller than my dorm room in college. Not exactly a homey environment. But it didn't matter because I was never there. I worked whenever I could. Working 24/7 no longer did it for me. I wanted more.

So I packed up my life and decided to take that leap of faith, as Madison kept calling it. Evan was that leap. And my faith? Well, my faith rattled around in my chest beating for the only man who showed what life beyond work, beyond structure and chaos could be.

I was sweating like a goddamn pig as I boarded the plane, knowing that the next few days would be hell. I didn't know what I was going into or what Evan would say to me. Would he forgive me? Had I lost him forever? Or, oh, my god, what if he were seeing someone else? But like Madison had said, I was all in. I just hoped I came out on top.

When the plane landed, the first stop was to the real estate office. Shannon had all the paperwork ready for me to purchase Evan's childhood home. A house I knew had meant so much to him and Mia. He had tried to keep the house over the past two years since his parents died but this year, Mia's tuition and just surviving, it had fallen into the bank's hands. I figured all the money I had should be put to good use. And what better use than to invest in putting down roots somewhere and showing Evan that starting a life with him mattered to me, too.

I laughed as I clicked the keys on the rental car. It was a Chevy and reminded me of the night Madison had cracked on Evan and me for our infatuation with cars.

As I pulled up to my new home, I stared at it in awe. The pictures didn't do it justice. The house was beautiful. Built in the late 1800s, the structure and integrity of the original home was still there. It looked a little run-down, due to lack of maintenance since it had gone into foreclosure, but it still held that old southern charm.

Pillars held up the structure and a vast amount of land stretched out for acres before me. An old widow's peak adorned the top of the house, and I smiled to myself as I pictured Evan mowing the lawn while I rested there, watching him. The inside of the house was even more beautiful than the outside. I felt the memories, the love and the happiness left behind. It lingered like the smell of freshly cut grass. That kind of love just didn't want to go away, and I didn't want it to, either. I knew instantly why Evan had loved the house. It felt so right and perfect. It felt like a home.

I dragged in the few bags of stuff I had brought with me, and I started working, trying my best to make this place shine. I spent days scrubbing, washing, folding, and moving furniture. It was a good distraction because I couldn't go to Evan, not yet. But each step I took to making the house what it had once been, each day took away bits of fear that had found me. I wasn't used to letting go. That and feeling was something I had been taught made you weak, less of a person, a coward. But what I had learned over the last months showed me that having to let go and feel was a part of each of us. Emotions taught us to jump. To take a leap of faith. And when we were successful, even with that fear that followed us, it was that much sweeter.

I was ready.

What did one wear when trying to profess her love for an ex-boyfriend? I shuffled through all my bags of clothes, but each button-up shirt and pair of slacks seemed dull in comparison to how I felt. The pounding of my heart settled in my ears, and I was convinced someone had taken up residence and was playing the drums in there. I was sweating and contemplating taking a third shower. I hadn't quite adapted to the Louisiana heat.

I had asked Shannon, the real estate agent, to get Evan to come by under the ruse that the new owner of the house had found a box of items that belonged to his parents. I glanced at my phone. Fifteen minutes and he'd arrive, and I looked like I had just scrubbed the toilets. Which I had, but I was trying to make an impression to show him that I'd made a mistake. That I'd let my past dictate my future, and that I'd given him up, when I should have held him closer.

"Right this way, Mr. Bradley. Have a seat." I heard Shannon's voice.

"Fuck," I swore as I looked at myself in the mirror. Freshly cleaned toilet look it is. I sighed as I opened the bedroom door and descended the stairs. Each step creaked, making me more and more nervous. I was used to being composed and collected, but I didn't know what I was going to say. I hadn't quite thought that far ahead. I just wanted to get him here in front of me, and I hoped that would be enough for me to realize what I wanted to say.

"Whoever's living here now has decent enough taste," Evan said with a grunt. I smiled to myself as I rounded the corner to the living room. It was my favorite room. With high ceilings and windows surrounding it, and the refreshing sunlight, it made me feel at peace. I was glad Shannon had brought him in here.

I cleared my throat. "Thank you, Shannon. I think I can take it from here."

Shannon nodded as Evan turned around. His eyes scrunched in confusion. I glanced down at myself, at my oversized shorts and ripped T-shirt, stained with god knew what. But I was here, standing in front of the man I loved, and I just hoped he would listen.

"Avery…." Evan's voice sounded bewildered, which was exactly how I felt. He looked so handsome. He had let his usual five o'clock shadow grow out a bit, and a small beard covered his face. I thought about what it would feel like between my legs, and I had to bite the side of my lip as my eyes traveled the length of him. He wore a gray suit that matched his eyes. It was perfectly tailored and fit his body like a glove. Much like how I remembered my body fitting his.

"I'm here," I said, unable to form any other words.

"I see that. Why are you here, Avery?" His words were hostile and accusatory. I gulped, willing myself to find the words I wanted to say. I closed my eyes, and I did something I hadn't done since I was a child. I prayed. *Please, just give me the words.*

"I forgive you, Evan." I opened my eyes just as I said the words. He tilted his head to the side, studying my face. He looked even more confused than when I'd entered the room.

"All of the shit that happened, it tortured me. Brought up bad memories that I'd rather have forgotten." I sighed. "And you lying to me about Marshall and Garcia, it just reminded me so much of my father going about his life and making choices for himself with no concern for me. I thought that was your reasoning behind it."

"Avery, that isn't why I did it. It was to protect you," Evan said, touching the scruff on his face.

"I know that now. It just took me time." I released a small laugh and lifted up my arms in defeat. "I have no idea what I'm doing. All I know is that when you are with me, I feel different. I feel like I can do anything. Like I can be anything I want to be." I focused on the floor in front of me. "When I'm not with you, it's like I can't breathe. There's been this rock on my chest since my mother died, and when you came into my life, it lifted. I felt like, for the first time, I could breathe again. Then you left, and I felt like I was fucking suffocating in my own body." I breathed in, and all I smelled was him. His cologne. His breath. His clean, masculine scent. He intoxicated me. I saw him move, and then I felt his hand on my chin as he lifted my face to his. His gray eyes hooded, appearing more seductive than ever before.

"You gave me no choice, Avery. You made it clear that nothing more would happen between us. There was no point in me staying there." Our faces were inches apart, his breath brushing against my lips.

"I know. I was just so afraid. I didn't know what to do. I thought I was protecting you from all the stuff that had happened to me and protecting myself. Sometimes, I'm going to make stupid mistakes, but I want to learn how to love. How you deserved to be loved." I looked him directly in the eyes as I said these last words. "And I want you to teach me." He studied me, his eyes wandering over my face. I didn't look away.

"I'm not a very good teacher," Evan said as he released my face from his hands. The tug on my heart made me feel like I was going to pass out. I had lost him. I had waited too long and been too wrapped up in my own stupidity. As a result, I had lost the only man I had ever loved.

"But we can learn together. We can teach each other," he added.

Crumble. Fall. Crash.

What-the-fuck-ever.

Those walls I had put up. They were gone. That rock that had firmly planted itself on my chest for the past twenty-one years, I had thrown it.

I was ready for love.

I jumped into his arms, and he barely caught me as we fell to the ground, laughing. Everything I'd struggled with over the past months seemed to fade away in Evan's arms. A rightness settled in my chest, a sense of belonging, a sense of love. I didn't try to push it away or rationalize it. I let it stay. No, I wanted it to stay, forever.

"So, this house… is it yours?" Evan held me close to

him as we lay on the living room floor.

"It's ours. I want a home with you. A life beyond the FBI and the precinct."

"But your job," Evan commented as he sat up, eyeing me with curiosity.

"My job will be here and starting in a few weeks. Rumor had it they needed a new narcotics detective at your precinct. Figured I'd give back. Help keep drugs off the street. Help some little girl not become motherless." A tear fell slowly down my cheek. Evan brushed it away and a smile took over his handsome face.

Almost as if it were in slow motion, he leaned forward. It was like one of those corny old movies Madison watched, but when his lips hit mine, and our tongues battled it out like they were fighting for their lives, I made myself a mental note to maybe, just maybe, give one of Madison's movies a try.

Epilogue

One Year Later

Little Liam teetered down the aisle toward Scott, who waited nervously at the other end of the church. The sounds of "awws" and clicking cameras followed the rambunctious one-year-old, who'd just learned how to walk. It meant there were just as many falls as there were steps. But it didn't matter; he was adorable. His little suit and blue bow tie matched the sky-blue color of his eyes. His curly brown hair ran wild on his head. My heart was fuller than it had ever been.

I had settled into our new house in Louisiana. Evan was it for me. It wasn't always easy. My insecurities and bullheadedness made things a challenge, but Evan was true to his word and loved me, all of me, the good and the bad. I loved my new job. I really felt that I was making a difference in the world. Not that I wasn't with the FBI, but keeping drugs off the street was a choice that I had made. The job that I had chosen. I had more time to spend with Evan, instead of running around from case to case. We talked about marriage but were content in how things were between us. But secretly, if he asked me to marry him, I would say yes. I was petrified, but I wanted it all.

As I glanced around the church, my gaze landed on the people in our lives who loved Madison and me, who believed in us. Sunflowers lined the pews. The room was magical, filled with light and the sun. Madison chose this church because of its floor-to-ceiling windows, which captured the sunlight shining in on their special day.

Just as the sound of Pachelbel's "Cannon" sounded, everyone's focus shifted to the end of the aisle. Liam sat on Lorraine's lap, clapping happily as he watched his mother walk down the aisle and toward the man she had loved her entire life. Mia, Evan's sister, sat next to Lorraine and had become a permanent fixture in mine and Evan's life. She still lived in California but she was like a sister to me and had grown on Madison too. Uncle Tom walked Madison down the aisle, his eyes looking like they would spill tears at any point. Dr. Wilson sat at the front of the pews and as Uncle Tom passed by her, he winked. She blushed and I couldn't help but smile. Dr. Wilson wouldn't admit that they were an item but she called him her "man friend." I laughed every time she said it. As I looked around the church, it wasn't filled with people. But those who were there were something that I struggled with not having for a long time, family. I had family.

I stood next to Madison feeling the weight of loss. Marshall was gone. It hurt to think about her every day. But I cherished the time I spent with her. She taught me a lot about life. Garcia chose to stay away and moved to California to heal and start fresh, but she came back for this day, to celebrate our friend. She reached out and grabbed my hand and squeezed as tears welled in her eyes.

I glanced at Evan as he winked at me and I got weak in the knees. I was turning into a mushy mess being with this man. Messes could be filled with chaos and unease but sometimes in the mess, we found the beauty, the art of differences and change. We had to shift through it to get to the other side and that other side, it was worth it, so fucking worth it. If someone would have told me a year ago that I would be watching my best friend marry the man of her dreams as Torres, Adams, and Evan, stood in a place of honor next to the groom, I would have laughed in their face, and I probably would have punched them for being stupid. But there I stood, believing in something I'd never believed in before. Love and happy ever afters.

THE END

Acknowledgements

Jasmine, I want to thank you for reading everything that I write and being such a huge support. Every time I have an ounce of doubt, you reel me back in. So thank you for believing in everything I write and becoming such a great friend.

Mark, at Visual Changes Salon, you are amazing! Thank you for opening your doors to me as a local author and helping me get my name out there. You're such a kind soul.

All the ladies at Hot Tree Publishing, I couldn't have asked for a better group to guide me through another book. Here's to many more.

And lastly, to all my readers, thank you for giving a newbie author like me a shot. Without you all loving my crazy mind and embracing the stories I have to tell, I wouldn't be where I am today. Love you all!

About the Author

You can find Gen curled up reading paranormal romance and romantic thrillers, or frantically typing her stories on her laptop.

Psychology is her trade by day, teaching and molding the minds of college students. Her interest in psychology can be seen in her books, each including many psychological undertones. Although she loves teaching, her passion, her true love, lays in the stories that roam around her in head. Yes, they all come from her mind—the good, the bad, and the totally insane.

She lives in Massachusetts—no not Boston—with her husband, daughter, and American Eskimo dog. With each story she shares, she hopes her love for writing and storytelling seeps through, encompassing the reader and leaving them wanting more.

Follow Gen:

Facebook: www.facebook.com/genryanauthor

Website: www.genryanbooks.com/

Twitter: twitter.com/genryan15

About the Publisher

Hot Tree Publishing opened its doors in 2015 with an aspiration to bring quality fiction to the world of readers. With the initial focus on romance and a wide spread of romance sub-genres, we envision opening up to alternative genres in the near future.

Firmly seated in the industry as a leading editing provider to independent authors and small publishing houses, Hot Tree Publishing is the sister company to Hot Tree Editing, founded in 2012. Having established in-house editing and promotions, plus having a well-respected market presence, Hot Tree Publishing endeavors to be a leader in bringing quality stories to the world of readers.

Interested in discovering more amazing reads brought to you by Hot Tree Publishing or perhaps you're interested in submitting a manuscript and joining the HTPubs family? Either way, head over to the website for information:

http://www.hottreepublishing.com

CPSIA information can be obtained at www.ICGtesting.com
Printed in the USA
BVOW03s2035080916

461347BV00001B/1/P